FINDING LILACS

CYNTHIA BIRK

First paperback edition August 2022

Book design by Picnic Basket Press
Cover photography by Picnic Basket Press

ISBN 979-8-9867388-0-2 (paperback)

Published by Picnic Basket Press
picnicbasketpress.com

For all the Emmas out there.
Stay strong. Be brave.
You've got this.

FINDING LILACS

lilac (*n.*)
First known use 1625.
A widely cultivated European shrub of the olive family
that has cordate ovate leaves and large panicles of
fragrant pinkish-purple or white flowers.

~

Lilacs symbolize:
Spring and renewal
Confidence
Wisdom
Lost love
First love

Definition: Merriam-Webster.com

Symbolism: FTD.com

~ 1 ~

"Mom, I got a raise!" Emma blurted into her phone. A gusty spring squall pushed her along as she strode toward the office parking lot.

"What, honey? I can't hear you. There's a lot of wind noise," her mother responded, pressing the phone harder to her ear. "Did you say you ate a raisin? You're not allergic, are you?"

Emma laughed, "No, silly! A *raise*, I got a raise!" shouting as she ducked behind the corner of a building to shield herself from the blustery weather while she spoke. "And I got a promotion too!"

"Oh honey, that's wonderful!" Her mother's voice overflowed with delight.

"I'm now the Customer Service Manager, and I'll oversee the junior team members in my department," Emma explained. "The extra money in my check will help toward paying off the last chunk of my school loan on time."

"You earned that promotion so quickly. That's a significant accomplishment. You always make us very proud, Emma," her mother gushed. "This calls for a celebration. What's that restaurant you always enjoy? Mario's, right? Let's meet there for dinner tonight. Does 7PM sound OK? I'll make the reservation for four people. You can bring Chip if you want."

"Aw, thanks, Mom! That's super sweet. Mario's sounds great! We'll see you there at 7." Emma ended the call as she surveyed the sky. Ominous gray clouds were starting to billow overhead, but if she hurried, she might be able to make it to her car before the rain started.

In the excitement her brisk steps became a run. She tumbled into the front seat as large drops plopped on the windshield. Catching her breath, she held up her phone and issued a command to the automated assistant, "Call Chip."

She glanced in the rearview mirror to assess the damage the wind and rain caused to her hair and makeup. Pretty blue eyes peered back at her from beneath a neat fringe of long dark lashes. However, the soft waves in her light brown hair were wind whipped into a chaotic mess. She made a comical face at her reflection, then reached for a stretchy hair tie stashed in the cupholder.

Chip answered on the second ring. "What's up?" There was a din in the background. It sounded like he was in a crowded room, a bar perhaps?

"Hey, you," she said. "Guess who just got a promotion?" Her voice was effervescent as she shared her news.

"That's awesome! Congrats, babe!" then Chip added smugly, "See, I told you we were gonna be a power couple."

Emma rolled her eyes. She was proud of the level of success she had already achieved this early in her career, but the whole social status element was definitely more Chip's desire than hers. "My parents are taking me out to dinner tonight at Mario's to celebrate, and they want you to come. Can you pick me up at 6:30? This is so great – you'll finally get to meet them!"

There was a slight pause. "Uh, yeah. I should be done here by then. Hey girl, I gotta run. Great job on that promotion." With an abrupt click, the call ended.

Emma stashed the phone in her purse and absorbed the glorious moment. Things were falling nicely into place in her life. All those years of following the rules and exceeding people's expectations were finally starting to pay off with a visible return on her investments of time and effort. She was on a roll, marking off dozens of items on those checklists in her mind.

In her career, she was fast tracking up the corporate ladder. Her new boyfriend seemed like a near perfect match to a description of her dream man: smart (top of his class), successful (a lawyer), and handsome too (like a movie star).

Whenever she was with Chip, she talked nonstop about her parents and they in turn heard a constant string of stories about him. Having them all meet would be a huge step forward, and she was thrilled her mother had suggested it.

The upcoming summer months were going to be so much fun. Her calendar was filled with "save the dates" for friends' bridal showers and weddings. Maybe next summer, no – the following one (she didn't want to rush Chip), it would be her turn.

Her heart was bursting with happiness. Everything she hoped to have at this point in her life was falling neatly into place. Thinking about it made her mouth curve into an easy, joyful smile.

What Emma didn't know was that in just over two hours, her whole life would be turned completely upside down.

$$\sim 2 \sim$$

Emma loved dining at Mario's. With its dark wood paneled walls and classic red and white checked tablecloths, the restaurant hit the tone of unpretentious retro elegance she enjoyed. Chip politely stood aside and let her slide into the large corner booth. It was neatly prepared with a small vase of white flowers and a card that read, "Congratulations, Emma!"

"This is my favorite table. It's the best spot in the whole place," she proclaimed as she settled in. A small spotlight illuminated an autographed photo of Sophia Loren on a nearby wall. It was arranged so the actress's seductive gaze was directed at whoever sat in that corner booth. Notes of a familiar Frank Sinatra song glided through the oregano and garlic scented atmosphere. Tonight, amid the inhospitable weather, she appreciated the cozy, candle-lit ambiance.

Her parents hadn't arrived yet, so she and Chip each ordered a glass of wine. He started aggressively working on the contents of the breadbasket.

"Didn't you eat lunch?" Emma asked.

"Well, yeah, but that was a long time ago. The happy hour thing after work kinda made me hungry," Chip defended himself as he reached for another slice of bread.

Emma fidgeted with her phone, checked the time, then frowned. It was already 7:08 PM. "I can't believe we got here before my parents," she said.

In contrast to her emotional high a few hours ago, everything about this evening was starting to feel a bit off-kilter. Her parents were always on time or even a few minutes early. This much of a delay was out of character for them.

"Traffic, the storm. It made me late too," mumbled Chip between mouthfuls of sesame semolina. He was more interested in the breadbasket than in the whereabouts of her parents.

Emma swept a few crumbs off the tablecloth and wondered if he had a valid point. All over the metro area, traffic was tied up due to the nasty weather. That wasn't her only concern though. When Chip reached her apartment to pick her up, she texted her mother to let her know they were finally on their way to the restaurant, and her mother didn't respond. That was odd. Her mother always promptly replied to her texts.

Each passing minute made her more uncomfortable. "I can't believe they still aren't here yet. Something's not right."

The waiter brought their wine selections. Chip took a big gulp of his. "Your dad's picking up the tab, yeah? Maybe we should get a bottle."

Emma left her glass of pinot grigio sitting next to her empty bread plate, untouched. She lifted her phone from the table and selected her mother's cell number from the recent calls list. She waited a moment for the call to connect and then frowned, staring at the screen. "That's weird, it went right to voice mail."

"Chill, Emma. Take a drink." Chip nodded toward her wine glass. "Maybe she's on a call. She's allowed to talk to other people on her phone besides you. Or maybe she had one of those 'senior moments' and forgot to charge it."

Emma wasn't crazy about the tone of his voice, and her mother wasn't prone to being forgetful, but perhaps he might be right. Why was she being so paranoid?

"So, did you get a raise with that promotion? That'd be awesome. You'll be supporting me!" Chip guffawed in amusement at the idea. He caught his reflection in a gilt framed mirror across the room and ran his hands over his hair, smoothing it down.

"Did he just wink at himself?" Emma thought. This callous, pompous display was a different side of him she'd never seen before. Maybe he was nervous about meeting her parents and was overcompensating? If he kept this up, things wouldn't go well, especially with her father.

Her phone vibrated where it lay face down next to her plate. "See?" said Chip, pointing at the phone with a breadstick. "Nothing to worry about."

"Finally!" Emma sighed with relief as she grabbed it off the table and looked at the screen. She furrowed her brow. "Oh, it's my grandmother. She probably wants to congratulate me on the promotion."

Emma was mildly disappointed it wasn't an update on her parent's location status but talking to her grandmother for a few moments might take her mind off Chip's obnoxious behavior and the whereabouts of her mother and father.

"Hi, Grandy," she answered in a pleasant tone.

"Emma, darling, where are you?" Her grandmother's voice was laced with concern.

"I'm at Mario's with Chip, waiting for my parents. They're late because of the weather or traffic or something, I guess," she said, trying to sound nonchalant and bubbly. "I got a promotion and a raise today, did my mom tell you?"

"Emma, honey, there's been an accident. You need to get to the hospital immediately."

~ 3 ~

The next seven days of Emma's life were a disjointed blur. She remembered little between that horrible phone call and the following Friday. There was a frantic trip to the hospital, the words "too late" and "both" and "gone," a river of tears and an abyss of disbelief. Every day she prayed she would wake up from a bad dream, hoping perhaps it was a hallucination induced by subconscious worries about her new work responsibilities. But to her dismay this nightmare didn't end, and its crushing anxiety filled both her hazy waking hours and the long, dark nights.

Lost in an emotional fog, Emma felt useless. Conversations about what had happened or what needed to be done left her weepy, uncertain, and confused. Her grandmother somehow pushed past the burden of her own grief to efficiently manage the grim logistics of the funeral, "the arrangements" she called them. With her chic cropped cap of white-blonde hair and trim little black dress, Grandy looked like a model in a funeral home brochure, sorrowful but still poised and elegant as she graciously received the continuous parade of somber friends, relatives, and colleagues.

"Where does she find the strength to do all of that?" Emma wondered as she disappeared to take refuge in the solitude of the funeral home's tastefully decorated restroom or in the lounge downstairs, any quiet place that was away from the overwhelming epicenter of grief.

A growing variety of food kept appearing on the lounge countertop, a buffet of soup-based casseroles, boxes of doughnuts, raw vegetable trays, and creamy pasta salads, delivered by neighbors and members of her parents' church. Emma opened the lids and peered inside the containers, but she had no appetite. There was enough food for an army, and she pondered who was supposed to be eating all of it. Her previously bright and sunny wardrobe became black and navy blue and gray, with pockets for tissues.

Time was a blur, with one shapeless hour merging into the next. Her clarity returned on a day filled with long and tearful goodbyes, a week after the instant when everything changed. Everyone went back to their homes and resumed their old normals, and Emma realized there was no such thing for her anymore. Her old normal was gone. Erased. Permanently.

An odd feeling swept over her as she stood in the middle of her kitchen. It felt something like homesickness, but how could that be? This was her apartment, the address where she lived for more than a year. That meant she was "home," wasn't she? An integral part of how she defined the concept had been stripped away. The piece of home that was more than a structure or a set of numbers and a street name had dissolved. The world was a different place now and she was adrift. Unanchored. Disconnected.

That evening she sat alone in her silent living room, perched upright in an uncomfortable chair as if still ready to greet last-minute mourners. She was surrounded by wilting floral arrangements, leftover displays from the funeral home for which there was no room in her tiny apartment. Well-intentioned people had insisted she take them home with her, and she obediently complied.

The flowers were still colorful but something about them was starting to give off a decaying smell. The unwelcome aroma was a continuous reminder of the sadness of the past week. She reached out for a glass of water on an end table and took a drink. It tasted stale. She swallowed it but frowned and studied the emblem on the tumbler and the evaporation lines. It was a glass of water poured the previous Friday. Back when she was in such a festive mood while waiting for Chip to arrive, back when she had parents, back when she had a normal.

Chip. She could use some company right now, a dose of emotional support, and a good hug. He'd been there that awful night at the restaurant, and he supported her at the hospital as the unthinkable truth unfolded, but since then she had not seen him. He sent her a text saying he'd been asked to work long hours on an important legal case, and they barely spoke to each other all week.

Emma located her phone and selected his number. He answered on the fourth ring, just before the call was sent to voicemail.

"Hey," he said abruptly when he answered.

"Hey," Emma echoed softly. "I… I know you're super busy and I'm sorry to bother you, but do you think you can come over? I'm not sure I can handle being alone tonight." There was no response.

"Chip?" She asked. "Are you there?"

"Yeah, I'm here." He paused. "Um, listen, Emma, I'm glad you called. It feels like you've changed lately. You're different. You've been acting kind of needy."

Emma's head spun. What was he saying? Needy? Was he criticizing her about asking for support at a time like this?

She thought she heard a female voice in the background. Chip's voice became muffled as if he unsuccessfully tried to cover the phone's mic, "Give me a sec, I'm on a call," followed by something that sounded like a woman's giggle.

His voice came back on the line. It was clear again. There was no mistaking what he said.

"So, yeah, uh, this isn't working for me anymore. Good luck, Emma."

And then he hung up.

~ 4 ~

For the next several months, Emma tried to keep herself extra busy so she wouldn't notice the gaping holes in her life. On the Monday after the funeral, she started her new role at work, or at least tried to go through the motions of it. She believed throwing herself into the challenging responsibilities of being a manager would provide a welcome distraction from the emptiness in her personal life.

Her coworkers reacted to her loss in one of two ways. Half of them behaved as if the earthshakingly tragic accident had never happened. They avoided the issue entirely. Emma preferred this. It was less complicated and easier to deal with in a public setting. When the more inquisitive colleagues stopped by her desk, visibly sad faced and offering statements of condolence, she felt obligated to answer their probing questions.

She tried to speak openly to them about the accident, appreciative of their concern, and she told herself it might help her process the sudden series of events. But then these coworkers kept pushing deeper and she ended up fielding one too many questions. Without warning, the initial, manageable trickle of feelings led to a bursting of the emotional dam, which left Emma with a tear-stained face and a sprint down the hallway to take refuge in the restroom until she could get the crying under control.

It was never clear how far into the exchange she would get before the tears would start. She would wade into a conversation, feeling stable, monitoring the depth of her emotional ocean. But then without warning the bottom dropped away beneath her, and she would be submerged, unable to find footing.

Following a few early episodes like this, she concluded she was not yet strong enough for this type of conversation at work. She resolved to remain stoic, emotions hidden behind the tiny brick wall she hastily constructed around her heart to protect herself and preserve her professional image. But then the inquiring coworkers seemed oddly disappointed about her composure and her refusals to discuss personal details.

Emma was puzzled. "What's that about? Do they want me to lose control and have a big messy daily breakdown in the middle of the office? Are they sincere in their interest for my wellbeing, or are they just looking for drama?

"I should talk to my friends about the accident, instead of coworkers, but most of them seem uncomfortable discussing serious issues. It feels like no one else I know has ever been through anything similar. And I don't want to scare them away."

A week after her return to the office, she looked up from her desk and spied Maggie, the local Human Resources representative, prowling in her catlike way through the department cubicles. It was well known throughout the company that she only ventured forth from her fortress-like office when there was a problem requiring direct intervention. Now her impressive mass of copper-colored curls appeared to be headed in Emma's direction.

"Red Alert. Danger," came the usual instant message someone cascaded throughout the computer network whenever Maggie was on the move.

Emma panicked. Were there complaints about the earlier weepy spells? "I haven't cried here in a few days," she thought defensively. "At least not in public. Or maybe people are saying I'm being too cold, too detached?"

She took deep breaths and shoved her emotions behind the brick wall. "No tears. There must be NO tears," she commanded herself.

Gathering up a few scattered papers on her desk, she made a display of tucking them into a random folder to create the illusion of being organized and productive.

"Maybe if I look normal and busy, she'll keep walking and won't stop. Or maybe I'm not even the reason she's on this floor of the building today," she told herself. Those thoughts evaporated when Maggie's saunter came to a full stop next to her desk.

"Oh, hi, what's up?" Emma asked, feigning surprise. She set the stuffed folder aside while her guest helped herself to a seat in the visitor's chair. Maggie arranged herself as if she was posing for a photo opportunity, crossing her legs, tossing her hair, and resting a forearm on the edge of the desk.

"Emma," she began, her lowered voice oozing with uncharacteristic compassion. "I'm so sorry for your loss."

"Thank you," replied Emma. She folded her hands, placing them on her desktop, attempting to appear calm and casual. If she limited her words, she'd be OK.

Behind her controlled façade, her mind still raced, "I will not cry. I will *not* cry. Think of something emotionally neutral like Paris or the consumer price index or a big yellow dump truck. Keep my mouth shut. Maybe say I'm busy with something important and can't talk right now. Or change the subject if I have to. I'll bet she's going to ask questions. Oh no, here it comes!"

Maggie tilted her head a bit to the side and leaned in. "How *are* you, Emma?" Her green eyes narrowed with intensity as she asked the exact question Emma had hoped to avoid.

"I'm fine," Emma said. Short and sweet. No elaboration. Steady tone of voice. She calmly gazed back at Maggie with a neutral expression and blinked several times, attempting to convey an air of normalcy and composure.

There was an awkward pause, a stalemate of several seconds as each woman silently jockeyed for control of the conversation. It was a wordless, passive-aggressive game of "You go first. No, please, I insist, *you* first."

Finally, Maggie raised an eyebrow, pursed her lips, and used one red manicured fingertip to push something across the desk toward Emma. Without any further discussion, she stood up, and walked away.

Emma drew a sudden gasp of air. Had she been holding her breath the whole time during this awkward exchange? She looked down at the thing Maggie had pushed toward her. It was a business card.

"Confidential Grief Counseling
Drop-in sessions available"

There was the familiar welling up of tears in her eyes and by the time she reached the restroom, there were damp streaks on both sides of her face.

Emma didn't make any social media announcements about the breakup with Chip. She updated her relationship status on various apps, and made it private, for her eyes only. It was simply one more topic she didn't feel like discussing.

The first major social event she attended a few weeks after the funeral was a bridal shower for her friend Samantha. "I'll be a good listener, a good party guest," Emma vowed, looking forward to a bit of socializing but hoping to avoid any emotional outbursts of her own. "No talk about the accident. No discussions about Chip or the breakup. Just be pleasant. Ask them about what they've got going on. Smile and nod. A lot."

The shower was held in a banquet room at a local restaurant. After balancing her carefully wrapped present on the mountain of other gifts for the happy couple, she looked around and spotted several of her friends. They were gathered in a small group near one of the tables that displayed a tempting array of appetizers and snacks.

"Emma!" the women said in enthusiastic unison as she approached.

Cassidy, a close friend from college, hugged her warmly and surveyed her outfit, "Cute dress, Ems!" Then, thinking it was a safe topic, she continued, "How's Chip? Are you bringing him to the wedding?"

Chip had been the center of attention at one of their after-work parties a few weeks before the accident. Now everyone's eyes were on Emma to see if she was bringing her intriguing new beau to the wedding. Her smile faded, and she answered in a lowered voice, "No, we broke up."

Concerned and curious, the group of women all took one step forward, clustering around their friend and sending out a shocked breathy chorus of "No!" and "Oh my gosh!" and "What happened?"

"He was a jerk. I'd rather not talk about it."

The awkward silence that followed was deafening.

Emma attempted to fill the air space, "It's OK, I'm better off without him."

"Wow, sorry."

"Totally his loss, Emma."

"For sure."

The friends all nodded in agreement. And just as they all had in unison taken a step toward her a few seconds before, now they all took an even larger step backward, distancing themselves from her unfortunate situation, as if by standing farther away they could avoid catching her bad luck.

There was another uncomfortable pause. One of the women finally spoke up, "So, um, hey, I'm going to get more chardonnay, anyone else want one?" and the group (minus Emma) made a chattery beeline to the bar table and did not come back, finding more cheerful company elsewhere, grateful to be separated from the gloom in the room.

"I am officially a total party pooper. I suck all the fun out of a conversation, don't I? I'm a literal minefield of forbidden discussion topics," Emma observed as she dropped cubes of meat and cheese onto a small plate like tiny bombs and made quiet explosion noises as they landed.

"Are you back to normal after the funeral yet? Boom!"

"How's work going? Pow!"

"How are things with Chip? Oomph!"

If she ate slowly, focusing on stabbing each morsel with a frilled toothpick, she could make herself look busy without bothering anyone. She sat quietly off to the side while the shower gifts were opened. Afterward, she politely hugged the bride-to-be and then left without speaking to anyone else.

The first weekend in June, she attended Samantha's wedding. Dateless. It was the first of the many ceremonies she would be invited to that summer. "A few months ago, I looked forward to going to all of these events with Chip. This was supposed to be my summer of fun. But now, as the grieving dumpee, it's awkward. And hard," she thought.

However, she was still genuinely happy for her friend. Samantha's fiancé was much nicer than Chip ever was. She put on the new dress she bought for the event, guarded her emotions, and made a valiant attempt to be pleasant.

She did fine, until after dinner. The bride and groom were finishing the first dance and the DJ announced, "Let's have all the couples out there join our newlyweds here on the dance floor for the next song!"

There was a small flurry of activity as people set their drinks down, pushed their chairs away from the tables, and headed hand-in-hand in the direction of the dance floor. Emma remained seated and smiled at her friends as they began to sway to the smooth jazz oozing from the speakers.

There was a noticeable shift in the room's atmosphere. It seemed lopsided. Emma became aware of a feeling of emptiness now surrounding her. She first tentatively looked to each side, and then turned fully around to scan behind her. She was the only guest left sitting at a table.

"Am I really the only dateless person here?" she thought in disbelief. Everyone else in the room was on the dance floor. Her chest tightened. She couldn't breathe. Why did it feel like there was a spotlight on her, highlighting her single state, her aloneness? She was reminded of the feeling that night after the funeral when she was in her apartment and Chip tactlessly dumped her over the phone. Outcast. Abandoned. Unwanted.

"This should not be a big deal," she thought, attempting to shake off the negativity and be rational. Still, tears welled up in her eyes. "Ugh. Not again. I am NOT going to cry here," she thought in desperation as she grabbed her purse and bolted for the door. Where was that restroom?

Spying a sign indicating a ladies' lounge, she dashed down a small hallway at a surprising pace considering the height of her heels. Thankfully, the open area where the sinks were was empty as she burst through the door, sobbing. "I just didn't want to feel alone again tonight," she whispered.

She laid her purse down on the bathroom counter and placed her hands on the cool marble surface. Leaning on her straightened arms, she blew out a deep breath. Emma looked up and saw her tear-streaked reflection.

When she glanced at herself in a mirror before leaving her apartment earlier in the day, she thought she looked nice, even pretty. She always considered herself to be intelligent, hardworking, and successful.

"But now look at me," she thought, shaking her head. "I keep ending up as a mess. Am I always going to be alone? No one wants to be around the sadness, and it seems like I can't make it go away. It feels like it's never going to end. Is this how my life is going to be now, with everyone all paired off and I'm left out?" This dreary thought renewed the flow of tears from her eyes.

It was time to get back to the ballroom. If she was gone longer people would ask awkward questions about where she had been. Pacing back and forth on the bathroom tile, she considered her options.

"I can say, 'I needed to use the restroom,' or 'I stepped out for some fresh air.' I don't need to go into detail," she rehearsed and coached herself.

Emma turned on the water faucet, letting a stream of cold water run over her forearms and hands until she regained emotional control. Next, she worked through a small mountain of tissues pulled one by one from the box on the bathroom counter, first dabbing at her tears, then removing smudges of makeup from her cheeks.

"Maybe they won't notice how long I've been gone or that I've been crying," she said to her reflection in the mirror, trying to sound optimistic, but still feeling skeptical. "Maybe the lights in the ballroom will be so low they won't be able to tell my mascara's messed up, my eyes are puffy, and my nose is all red."

She placed her hands on her hips in a power pose and made a final attempt to convince herself.

"OK, I can do this."

Emma cautiously emerged from the restroom and looked both ways to see if there were oncoming persons to dodge before reaching the more forgiving dim lights of the ballroom. There was a small exit sign glowing like a beacon at the far end of the corridor, the opposite way from the reception. An escape route.

She instantly assessed this new development and turned in that direction. Instead of rejoining the others, she made a beeline down the hallway, and passed through the exit door into the chilled night air. Using her key fob to activate the lights and give a quick beep of the horn, she located her car in the massive parking lot.

Emma drove back to her apartment where she would still be alone, but at least there was no crowd of couples there to which she would compare herself.

~ 5 ~

Decline. Decline. Emma RSVP'd with regrets to the next set of bridal shower and wedding invitations that appeared in her mailbox. She sent gifts and well wishes but did not attend, imagining her friends being more than slightly relieved they wouldn't have to navigate her emotional minefield and deal with any more awkward Sad Emma moments. The remainder of the invitations she received that summer were also handled in the same way. "Too soon," she rationalized. Groups of friends and coworkers posted selfies from Happy Hours and Girls Nights Out on social media, and Emma began to realize she wasn't being invited to join in.

She wasn't angry and couldn't blame them. "I'm not exactly fun to be around anymore."

She clicked on their posts adding a "Like" or a "Love" or a "Haha," and sometimes composed short witty comments. She still struggled with balancing her feelings of grief against experiencing happiness. The sudden death of her parents still felt raw, how could she be out there, laughing it up at a cocktail hour?

"I should organize my own cozy get-together," Emma decided. "With trusted friends, small and intimate, not overwhelming." She was fearful though something would trigger her emotions, and her little event would end up being a dud, an embarrassment. Another negative mark on her social scorecard. Under the weight of this concern, the carefully crafted invitation sat in her "drafts" file collecting electronic dust and was never sent.

Anxiety about potential weepy breakdowns blocked her from making the first move, others stopped reaching out, and the gap she left in her circle of friends seemed to close up without her. She still felt lonely, somewhat depressed, but also more authentic and truer to her own feelings when she stopped forcing herself to act as if things were normal. If she attempted to put on a façade of socially acceptable happiness, it left her feeling like a fraud, like she was betraying the grief that was tattooed on her soul.

For the first few months after the accident, Emma made an extra effort to stay in touch with Grandy. Emma admired and adored the woman, her only remaining grandparent, but the relationship was always somewhat formal, like they held each other at arm's length.

"With Grandy being so much older and having such an independent, strong-willed nature, there is no way she can relate to my perspective," Emma considered, placing her on a pedestal.

Afraid of appearing weak or needy, she downplayed her internal emotional struggle whenever they spoke to each other. As a result, she wished her grandmother a cheerful "bon voyage" when Grandy left on a long-planned excursion to hike glaciers in Iceland.

Whenever things were quiet at work or if she was home without music, a movie, or another form of distraction, she mentally replayed the sequence of events that led to the accident over and over. Her brain stored a mental list of "what ifs" surrounding the fateful day when she lost her parents. That day hinged on a handful of simple decisions, and because of those choices her once bright future took a dismal turn.

What if the promotion had been awarded to someone else?

What if she had waited until the next day to tell her mother about it?

What if her mother had suggested a different restaurant?

What if the weather had been clear instead of raining, or if her parents had left five minutes earlier or 30 seconds later?

What if, what if, what if?

That day began as such a good day, one of her best. She had been so happy. Now, whenever she encountered anything like happiness, she was quick to push it away. "Don't tempt fate. Show the world you have nothing of which to be envious, and maybe what little you have left won't be taken away too."

There was no denying her disintegrating emotional situation. She needed help. She made an appointment with the grief counselor from the business card HR Maggie had slid across her desk. Emma attended several sessions, but the guidance offered to her was like water poured on a hot surface. It evaporated before it could sink in.

The counselor told her, "Time will lessen the burden of pain, and eventually you will be happy again." She knew there was wisdom in this advice, but she still struggled to accept it. Yes, the passage of time would help, but each day crept forward with such aching slowness it seemed like she made no visible progress. She tried to read the booklets the counselor gave her, but her eyes skimmed over the words on the page, and nothing wanted to stick.

Perhaps healing would happen, and she could enjoy happiness again on some distant day, but for now she decided it was inaccessibly out of her grasp. The world was moving on without her, so she got out of its way, came straight home after work every evening instead of going out, and attempted to preserve the remnants of her once vibrant social life by relying on apps and online resources. Then, the headaches started.

Emma sat wearing a flimsy gown on the paper-covered table in the examination room, her feet dangling awkwardly off the side of it while the doctor spoke to her. After a thorough examination uncovered large knots of tension in her neck and shoulders but thankfully no other major issues, her physician said the headaches were most likely from too much screen time, complicated by work stress. Emma nodded dutifully and obediently agreed with the suggestion she should cut back on both, but as soon as she left the doctor's examination room, she pulled out her phone to check in with her office. In the parking lot she sat in her car and scrolled through her app feeds.

"The doctor doesn't understand," she protested. "I need my screens right now because all I have left in my life is work and my online social media presence. If I reduce my screen time as much as they want me to, I will basically disappear from the world."

Without implementing the recommended change in her routine, the headaches continued. She found another doctor for a second opinion. This time in describing her ailments and symptoms, she glossed over the amount of time she spent on social media. She hoped there could be a solution that didn't involve taking away her electronics. And something not requiring her to be heavily medicated because she worried about all those side effects she saw on TV commercials.

Perhaps there was a holistic solution. Vitamins? Meditation? Yoga?

She wanted this doctor to guide her, to offer a good recommendation so she didn't waste even more time flailing around making ineffective choices from randomly selected websites.

The second doctor asked a few basic questions concerning her stress level. He inquired about her life events from earlier in the year and what sort of impact they still had on her emotions and daily activities. After listening to the details of the accident and how it affected her, the doctor's flippant proclamation was that her grief reaction was "excessive."

Emma repeated the word, drawing out each syllable, as if it was new to her. "Ex-cess-ive?"

It was an odd appraisal of her condition, as if there was some sort of socially approved range of behaviors for reacting to such a massive and sudden loss.

Cry this much if you lose one parent, and this much for two, but not one tear more, and only when you're in this specific place, and don't make anyone else feel uncomfortable, ever. Otherwise, you've broken the rules. Your grief shall be deemed inappropriate. Excessive. Bad mourner, bad!

"Yeah, that's not a normal response," the doctor added with a bit of a laugh.

A laugh? Emma frowned. This interaction was going downhill, and fast. Was he amused with her struggle? Something about him reminded her of Chip right before their breakup.

His insensitivity made her feel ill. It eroded her trust like a belt sander on old paint. Shouldn't doctors have a better bedside manner? Where was his empathy for her situation? To this doctor, she was a series of data inputs in a cold, clinical diagnostic formula.

"Not a normal response," he said. Was there even such a thing as a "normal" way to grieve for what she had been through? Weren't the circumstances of the accident the extraordinary thing, and weren't her reactions appropriate for that?

"I know I need help, that's why I'm here," she thought in frustration, "but where's his compassion? Does he have to be such a jerk about it?" Her annoyance hit a tipping point, and she confronted him.

"Look, I've been through a lot. I came here because I'm trying to find ways to cope with an enormously difficult situation, not be judged or shamed about it." She looked the doctor squarely in the eye and asked, "You said my grief was 'excessive.' Can you even imagine what it feels like to suddenly lose both of your parents?"

He gave an odd smirk and clicked the end of his ballpoint pen. He shifted his gaze downward as he reached for his prescription pad and began to scribble on it. "No, my parents still live in Connecticut."

Without waiting for him to finish writing, she stood up from the chair and walked out of his office, grateful this time she was still fully clothed and not wearing one of those paper gowns.

She was fuming when she got into her car and slammed the door.

"Well, maybe that wasn't the smartest way to handle his attitude, but at least I didn't cry."

Emma was perilously close to running out of options for help. It wasn't smart to keep rejecting the offered solutions but everything they proposed always seemed to be a bit off, like it was sized for someone else. She wanted to find balance, but to do that she needed some form of a support system. Her social infrastructure no longer existed. She wanted to reach out for someone, something to lean on, but there was nothing there. Chip bolted on her as soon as things got tough. Emma's friends now acted uneasy around her. Most of them hadn't ever experienced anything remotely like Emma's loss. They were unable to comprehend the depth of what she was going through, and they changed conversation topics whenever anything got serious.

Grandy appeared to be constantly on the road, always traveling to someplace new, Santa Fe or Key West or Machu Picchu, and the rest of her other relatives lived out of state, spread out across the country like a random scatter plot of data. One doctor wanted to remove her only remaining connection to the last remnants of her social life, and the other one laughed at her for the way she expressed her grief. Perhaps there was a kernel of truth in his assessment, but could she place her trust in him after he ridiculed her? No.

At the office, her emotional toggle switch was still stuck in the "off" position. She was a robot, simply going through the motions of life day after day. There was no passion, no spark, no fuel to push her forward anymore. She was exhausted, and there was nothing left in her tank in the evening or on weekends to even think about how to start rebuilding her life.

And so, one day in December, everything ground to a halt. As the strains of Elvis singing "Blue Christmas" flowed on repeat through her ear buds, Emma stared blankly at the rotating winter scenes on the screen saver of her oversized computer monitor. Call after call went unanswered and ended up in voicemail until it became full. Her email inbox reached its capacity limit.

Instead of going to the end of year office holiday party at a local bar with the rest of her team, she composed an apologetic but professional resignation letter to her boss, cc'ing HR Maggie.

"As of the close of business today, I am resigning from my position. Unfortunately, it's taking longer than I anticipated to get back to my full operating capacity after my parents' accident earlier this year. I still need some time to figure out a few things, and it's not fair to you, my colleagues, or the company for me to continue at my currently limited level of performance. I apologize for any inconvenience I may have caused over the past several months."

Emma printed two hard copies of the email after she hit send, placing one on her boss's chair and folding up the other to take with her.

While gathering the few personal possessions she kept on her desk, she took a moment to study her favorite old family vacation photo. She gently placed it face down on the top of the small stack of items in a cardboard box she found in the mailroom. Donning her wool coat and leather driving gloves against the cold temperatures outside, she carried the box down the hallway to the elevator, through the lobby and out to the sidewalk that led to her car.

Not long before, Emma made another, happier journey down this exact same sidewalk. This was where she had been for her last phone conversation with her mother. She was so hopeful that day, excited and optimistic. Unbelievably, that was less than a year ago, and now everything was different. Her parents were gone. Her friends were distant. And she just put the brakes on a once promising career. Was happiness erased from her life forever too? Numbly, she set the box inside the trunk and closed the lid with a thump.

Not wanting to be confronted by cheerful holiday music, she muted the radio, and in silence, drove back to her apartment.

Cloaked in the darkness that falls so early in December, she skipped dinner, crawled into bed, and cried herself to sleep.

~ 6 ~

A garish ray of June sunshine squeezed through a gap in the bedroom window blinds and made it clear to Emma: she slept far past her 7AM target wake up time. Again. Since leaving her job almost six months ago, she spent most of her time alone at her apartment, venturing out for trips to the grocery store, occasional fast-food runs, and once to get her hair professionally trimmed. Sometimes her bleak mood lifted a little, and during those stretches she attempted to resurrect a makeshift version of a daily routine, with limited success.

She squinted in annoyance at the harsh beam of light poking into her space then groggily rolled over and bid good morning to the closest relationship in her life – her cell phone. "How did I sleep through my alarm again? You were supposed to wake me up!" she grumbled aloud in frustration at the device.

Unplugging it from the charger, she sat up, and adjusted the alarm volume settings before checking her social media apps, entering a few likes and comments. After stretching a bit, she slid out of bed. She tried to ignore the haggard image reflected by her bathroom mirror, but she had to admit, it was starting to bother her. She didn't look like "Emma" anymore. Perhaps caffeine would help.

Her bare feet padded down the hallway into the kitchen where she began her daily coffee ritual. As it brewed, she pulled out a chair and slumped over her phone where it lay on the kitchen table, checking the headlines on her bookmarked news websites.

She glanced through an emailed copy of a museum newsletter and paused at the image of Cezanne's painting of the Young Italian Woman at a Table. "It's like looking in a mirror," she said sarcastically. Both she and the woman in the painting had an elbow on a table and their head resting on the palm of their hand. The original portrait was missing the coffeemaker and the cell phone. Emma's raggedy sleep t-shirt was definitely more modern than the puffy sleeved garment in the Cezanne, but there was still a resemblance, an amusing and ironic visual rhyme. "Some days I do feel more like a Picasso though," she said, rolling her eyes and forcing her lips into an asymmetric expression.

The coffeemaker gave an angry sputter as she searched for an update on the day's weather. "Sunny this morning with a slight chance of showers later," the forecast said, but it didn't matter because she probably wouldn't venture outside anyway. She noticed her usual headache was still only a mild one and considered that a small victory. It could, in fact, be the highlight of her day.

She filled her favorite travel coffee mug (which never travelled anymore unless you counted the journey from kitchen to living room) and she carried it carefully across to the corner where her spin bike stood. She wedged the mug precariously into the water bottle holder, slid her feet into an old pair of laceless sneakers, and climbed onto the bike.

"Exercise is good for me, exercise is good for me, exercise is good for me," she mumbled.

She pedaled slowly and brought up the latest episode of a true crime drama from the podcast library on her phone. She felt a sense of uneasiness when she became attracted to that genre of podcast, thinking it was out of character for herself and worrying the details of the crimes would give her nightmares. Still, it was a growing habit for her over the past several months.

She always enjoyed a good mystery. Her grandmother's personal library displayed a whole shelf of vintage Nancy Drew books that Emma worked her way through as a child. Tales of suspense were fine, but she hated violence. It baffled her that she was drawn to these tragic podcast stories over and over.

One day, though, she realized it wasn't the crimes that she connected with. The violence still disturbed her. What kept her coming back to these stories was the sadness experienced by the survivors. Like Emma, their lives were interrupted, their loved ones were gone, and their hopes, dreams and plans for the future were in disarray. Even though the circumstances surrounding their losses were different (the death of Emma's parents was through an accident, not a crime), she sometimes believed she had more in common with these total strangers on a podcast than with many of her friends who failed to understand her.

She imagined that, like her, the crime survivors were emotional outsiders from society, and from a distance she empathized with them. These people understood deep sadness. It kept her from feeling alone. The survivor's friends might not understand loss and pain, but Emma did. They could be there for each other.

The podcast's intro and catchy theme music faded away as the narrator began laying out the details of the episode. His familiar, gravelly voice unrolled the latest developments in the tale of a small-town tragedy. Emma's legs pumped on the pedals of the bike. Her heart rate increased as her body began the gradual process of waking up. She took another sip of hot coffee, squeezed the travel mug back into the holder, and then closed her eyes as she escaped her own isolated world of sadness and momentarily transported herself into someone else's story.

A loud knock on the door startled her so much that in her groggy, minimally caffeinated state she almost fell off the bike seat. "Who is that?" she thought, as a deep frown spread over her face. Her pedaling slowed and she touched the pause button on the podcast to listen for noise from the hallway.

Her heart and mind both raced. She never had visitors. Did she forget an appointment? Was someone supposed to be coming over? She considered sliding quietly off the bike and tiptoeing to the door to look through the peep hole, but then she looked down at what she was wearing.

"I'm not dressed to open the door anyway. Why bother even checking?" Then she concluded, "It's probably someone selling something I don't want or some survey I don't feel like answering. I'm going to sit here until they leave."

The knocking repeated, this time more insistent and followed by a familiar strong, clear voice, "Emma, dear. It's Grandy. Open up."

$$\sim 7 \sim$$

Jolted into action, Emma leapt off the spin bike.

"Hang on, Grandy!" she called. "I'm coming! Give me a sec!"

It was much closer to lunchtime than breakfast, so she was more than slightly mortified at her disheveled "I just woke up" appearance. She spotted a hoodie haphazardly tossed on the end of the couch and threw it on over her makeshift pajamas. There was no time to fix her hair. She performed a quick breath check and took a glance through the peep hole to ensure there were no others in the hallway. After inhaling deeply and pasting on an awkward smile, she unlocked the door and swung it open with a cheerful, "Hi, Grandy!"

Emma's smartly dressed grandmother stood in the hallway on the other side of the open door. They threw their arms around each other in a warm embrace. Panicked and puzzled, Emma asked sheepishly, "Did I know you were coming?"

Grandy laughed, "No dear, this is somewhat of a surprise visit. May I come in?"

Embarrassed by her lapse in hospitality and unkempt appearance, Emma stood aside. Grandy marched in, hauling an attractive wheeled suitcase that looked like a mini steamer trunk. She left the bag at the end of the sofa and began moving about the room. "Is it OK if I open the curtains, Emma? Let in a little daylight?" Without waiting for a reply, Grandy walked over to the set of windows in the living room and drew the fabric coverings aside. "Maybe I'll let in some fresh air too." She slid open a window. "It's beautiful out there today."

Sunshine illuminated the space and Emma's stomach lurched. "When was the last time I dusted? Or vacuumed?" she thought in horror. The living room was relatively tidy, but over the past few months she had begun to let several housekeeping details slide. At least the kitchen was clean, so she directed Grandy's attention in that direction.

"Would you like a cup of coffee? I just made a fresh pot of it. Or maybe some tea? I have that too."

Grandy chose coffee, black, and took a seat on the sofa. Emma poured the coffee into a pastel polka dot mug and handed it to her grandmother before settling down next to her.

"It's lovely to see you, Emma," Grandy said, taking a sip. "Oh, that's good coffee, thank you." She set the mug on a coaster.

Emma reached out to squeeze her grandmother's hand. "It's wonderful to see you too, Grandy. I've let myself become a little… isolated lately."

"I know, dear, that's why I'm here."

Emma cancelled the last two times they had made dinner plans. Embarrassed by her inability to move forward with her life, she dreaded fielding questions about it and avoided visits or long discussions. She tried to give her grandmother the impression she was fine, just "busy", but during their periodic phone calls, Grandy sensed something was off.

"I'm sorry about the apartment, it's a bit of a mess," Emma apologized.

"Oh, it's fine, dear. Nothing I haven't seen in my own place now and then," Grandy graciously countered. "I didn't give you a heads up I was coming because I knew you would try to talk me out of it. And I wasn't going to change my mind this time, so here I am!"

Emma knew her grandmother was right. As much as she adored Grandy and needed the company, she probably would have declined the suggestion if she had known about it in advance. Her grandmother was lively and strong. Lately Emma felt deeply inadequate in her presence. She envied Grandy's fortitude, her resilience, and she worried Grandy would see her as flawed because she was not the same way.

"So, get me caught up, Emma. Tell me what's going on with you."

Emma looked down at her wrinkled, pajama-clad lap, then up at Grandy in her impeccably styled ensemble. With a grimace she confessed sheepishly, "Not a lot?"

Grandy affectionately laid her hand on Emma's shoulder and waited with an expectant expression for her to continue. Emma was stuck. She couldn't fool Grandy. And right now, her grandmother was offering compassion not judgement. Emma went on.

"I just feel broken. I couldn't focus on work. I kept crying. All the time! It's so embarrassing. And my friends don't get it. I don't think most of them have ever lost anyone close to them, like a family member, let alone two! It feels like they want me to act all normal and be happy, like nothing ever happened!"

Her emotions welled up to that tipping point where she could no longer hold them back, and the familiar streams of tears spilled down her face.

Grandy put her arm around Emma's shoulders and hugged her close, "Oh honey, I know," she said. "I know."

Emma continued, "And if I do allow myself to be happy about something, I end up feeling so incredibly *guilty*, because if my parents just died how can I let myself be happy? Does it mean I don't care about them anymore?"

Grandy kissed the top of Emma's head. "Oh, Emma. You can still miss your parents and be happy too. There's no rule saying you can't do both."

Emma nodded, initially understanding the intent of the message, but then shook her head adding, "I can't figure out how to do it though. I'm so… *conflicted* inside."

Grandy squeezed her granddaughter's hand gently until Emma eventually pulled it away to wipe tears from her face. "I'm honestly so tired of crying, Grandy. I'm just sick of it. I hate living like this. I know it's wrong, but I don't know how to change it. I tried to get some help to deal with it, but none of the solutions anyone provided seemed to be right for me. I know I need to get back to work. I don't want to keep using up the money from my parents' will. That's supposed to be for my future if I ever get married or have a house someday, but right now, I can't even imagine it." She shook her head in frustration. "I'm stuck in this dark hole."

"Oh, honey, please don't be so hard on yourself," Grandy consoled. "You've been through a lot. Taking a few months to sort things out after something like this is a totally reasonable thing to do. But if you're ready for a change, and it sounds like you are, it might be time for you to take a few steps forward. In a new direction."

Grandy touched Emma's hand again and said "I have something for you to try. Do you think you're up to it?"

Emma wiped her tears with the hoodie cuff of her free hand and nodded.

"Do you remember those vacations we all took together when you were a little girl? You, me, and your parents, when we went up north?"

"Up to Mackinac Island?" Emma asked.

"Yes. That's right. Do you have happy memories of being there?"

Emma nodded. "Out of all the places we went those trips were my favorite." She smiled at a momentary pleasant recollection of the historic northern Michigan island known for its horse drawn carriages, bicycles, and fudge shops.

Her grandmother continued, "Do you remember that little game we used to play in early summer, when we took the bike rides around the island?"

Emma thought for a moment, "Finding lilacs?"

Grandy nodded. "That's the one." She reached around the edge of the sofa and tugged the small suitcase forward. "That's what I want you to do for a few days. Find yourself some lilacs."

Emma looked at the suitcase. "Are we going to Mackinac Island?"

Grandy raised her eyebrows. "Not me, dear, just you."

"Oh," Emma said, a little puzzled. "Why aren't you coming?"

"This needs to be your journey, Emma. I want you to spend a few days there." Grandy swung her arm in a semi-circle around her. "Get out of this stuffy apartment. You've had too much solitude. Too much solemnity. Be somewhere lively and beautiful. Meet some new people. Talk to them. Search for the happy memories of your parents on the island, like we used to look for the lilacs, and maybe make some new happy memories of your own too. I'll help you get started, but I think, no – I know if I went with you, you'd just follow my lead. I'm nudging you out of the nest here, Emma. You need to learn by doing. You need to learn how to work the magic on your own."

Grandy pushed the suitcase closer to her granddaughter. "This is for you. Most of what you need for the trip is in here."

"That's for me?" Emma asked pointing at the stylish wheeled bag. "I thought this was because you were staying here overnight."

"No, I'm not staying long, just visiting for a few hours, getting you set up for your little adventure. I'm on my way to visit some friends at their lake house. My own overnight bag is still in my car," Grandy clarified. "This adorable suitcase is yours. And I put a few new things for the trip inside. We'll have to sort through it this afternoon and add a few pieces of your own, but between the two of us, we'll have the bases covered."

"Thank you," Emma said but her voice still sounded a bit hesitant.

Her head was spinning, trying to wrap her mind around Grandy's plan. When she first saw the suitcase, she thought her grandmother would be staying with her for a visit. Now Emma realized she herself was going to be the traveler.

She loved vacations, especially Mackinac Island, but going by herself? She had never considered that. Could she do that? Especially now, in her current frame of mind?

A cloud of concern billowed up. Her initial excitement about the trip was starting to be overshadowed by wariness. She had never solo travelled before. The idea of the long drive alone made her anxious. "Here I go again," she thought, as the lid of her escape hatch began to close and trap her in isolation once more.

"Grandy, I don't know if I can drive that far. I've been having panic attacks when I get behind the wheel lately," she confessed. "On the highway, since, you know…" her voice trailed off.

For the past several months an intense, choking fear gripped her any time she drove in bad weather or heavy traffic, anything resembling the conditions on the evening of her parents' accident. And to complicate the situation, the longer she went without driving, the worse the fear became the next time she sat in her car.

"We'll make a plan," her grandmother said reassuringly. "We'll look at a map and figure out how to get there. And we'll pick some good places for you to stop along the way. It will break the drive up into small sections. You won't feel like it's such a long trip. That's how I travel all the time!" she said with a nonchalant wave.

Grandy sprang up from the couch. "Now, my darling granddaughter, what do you have to eat, or should we go out for lunch?"

~ 8 ~

After assessing the contents of the refrigerator, Grandy prepared a simple elegant brunch of two cheese omelets, accompanied by toast with strawberry jam and glasses of orange juice while Emma took a shower and freshened up. Later, they did the dishes together before Grandy opened the suitcase and showed Emma the items she purchased for her trip.

There were two cute casual outfits (one with a skort, one with capris), as well as a fun hot pink polka dot sundress. "Oh my gosh, I love this!" Emma said as she held it up. There was a silky, cream colored scarfy-shawl thing, with fringe. This item elicited an involuntary frown from Emma. She couldn't picture how she would wear it. Grandy usually had impeccable taste, but this piece looked a bit old fashioned, almost "grannyish" to Emma.

"In case it gets chilly if you're sitting outside in the evening," Grandy stated.

"Oh, that's nice," Emma responded politely. She quickly refolded the odd item, setting it on the pile of other clothes. It wasn't worth making a fuss; it was thin and wouldn't take up much space.

In a side pocket of the suitcase, there was a small square box. Emma opened it and withdrew a necklace made from a few dried and pressed individual lilac blossoms preserved in a crystal-clear pendant on a delicate chain.

"Grandy, it's gorgeous," Emma said. She held it up. It captured the light from a beam of sunlight coming through the window.

"This way, you can have your lilacs close to your heart whenever you want."

"I'm putting it on right now!" Emma exclaimed and fastened the clasp behind her neck.

They went through her closet, selecting the remaining garments and a few accessories Grandy advised she should include to round out her trip wardrobe. The final item she removed from the suitcase was a stylish and functional black leather backpack with brightly colored embroidered flowers on it.

"Today feels like Christmas, my birthday, and the first day of school, all in one," Emma laughed.

She lifted the backpack. By its weight, she could tell it wasn't empty. "Wow, there's more inside too!" She unzipped it and withdrew a spiral-bound sketchbook, along with a set of pencils and a sharpener. "It's been years since I've drawn anything," she said with a small grimace. "I'm totally out of practice."

"Well, just have fun with it then. I'm sure you'll find many things on the island that will make good subjects. There's something important in the inside pocket too, don't miss it."

Emma searched inside the bag again and located a zippered compartment. She opened it and pulled out a credit card. "That will cover all of your trip expenses," explained Grandy.

Emma shot her grandmother a wide-eyed look. "Oh, this is too much!"

"Nonsense, I want to make sure you have an enjoyable trip." Grandy pointed into the backpack's opening, indicating Emma wasn't done discovering the contents. "There should be one more thing in there, at the bottom."

Emma reached deep into the main compartment and removed the final parcel from the backpack. It was a small document folder with a Velcro clasp. She opened it and found a series of sealed business size envelopes. On the face of each was written the instructions for when it was to be opened.

1. Open In The Morning Before You Leave
2. Open At The Ferry Dock
3. Open After Check In
4. Open At Breakfast, Day 2
5. Open At Breakfast, Day 3

"What are these?" Emma asked.

"A few notes of encouragement along the way. No peeking now, open each one only when it says to."

Emma smiled. She always enjoyed her grandmother's sense of playfulness. A thought occurred to her, "You never mentioned where I will be staying. Do I have a reservation somewhere?"

In years past when she vacationed with her parents, they stayed in little local motels, cute vintage motor courts with a heated pool, always on the mainland, visiting the island as a day trip. Grandy reached over and tapped an envelope, the one to be opened the next morning.

"That one has all the details," and then she added a wink. Emma had a suspicion of what her grandmother might have arranged but she was too afraid to get her hopes up. She would have a hard time not sneaking a peek at the first envelope before morning.

For the remainder of the afternoon, Emma and Grandy put the suitcase and backpack aside and set to work on cleaning her apartment. "I always like to come home to a clean space," Grandy said. They dusted and vacuumed, did laundry, and washed windows. Emma picked out an upbeat housecleaning playlist, and they both danced and sang as they organized, scrubbed, and polished. A Rolling Stones song came on and Emma looked at Grandy with her tousled platinum pixie-cut hair, belting out the lyrics while grasping a broom handle as if it were a microphone stand and wondered if there was some chapter in her grandmother's past where she had secretly been a rock star.

By dinnertime they were both pleasantly exhausted. Rather than mess up the kitchen again, they opted for takeout and came home with a container of sweet and saucy bourbon chicken bites, a small bucket of savory pork fried rice, and a California roll with wasabi so pungent it made them both squeal with delight.

Before Grandy left that evening, they sat down at the kitchen table and planned out the route Emma would take for the long drive north. It was going to take several hours to get to Mackinaw City, where she would leave her car in the ferry parking lot. "I'm starting to feel anxious again," Emma said. "I've never driven that far by myself."

"The secret is to focus on one section of the trip at a time," advised Grandy. "Are you comfortable with driving one hour?"

"Yes, I think so," Emma said tentatively. "If traffic's not too heavy."

"Then look at it this way. Start out with a one-hour drive. The first thirty minutes will go quickly, and at that point you'll already be halfway done with that leg. After an hour, stop and get a coffee. Collect yourself." She made a centering, yoga-like gesture and continued in a nonchalant manner. "Then do it all over again, and the next time maybe get yourself a sandwich or stop at some interesting little touristy place. Buy a fun souvenir to celebrate your progress. Or get an ice cream. After that, you're practically there!"

Grandy's tone of voice was casual and confident, and her eyes flashed a spirited twinkle when she mentioned the words "ice cream."

Emma was beginning to believe her, to think it was possible she could pull this off. But then, she cocked her head to the side and gave her grandmother a skeptical look. "It seems like a lot to go through, just to drive somewhere. How embarrassing." She shook her head in frustration. "I used to just jump into a car and go whenever I wanted to get somewhere, and now I have to play all of these ridiculous head games with myself."

Grandy grasped both of Emma's shoulders and looked her square in the eyes. "The anxiety will get better, dear. I promise. But it's not going to simply disappear one day on its own. You need to push through it. If you don't face it, it will take over and hold you prisoner. There's nothing ridiculous about this. You make it go away by dealing with it, one challenge at a time. Don't worry about how long this drive will take. It's not a race. No one's judging you. Make the journey enjoyable."

Grandy leaned forward toward Emma. "The main thing is, you're getting back out there. And the destination is worth it."

"I wish I had your sense of adventure, Grandy," Emma said wistfully.

Her grandmother took on a serious expression and posed a question. "Emma, how do you think I got this way?" There was a moment of silence as the two women stared at each other.

"I guess maybe you have a more outgoing nature than I do," Emma suggested.

"I'm sure you don't realize how that statement couldn't be further from the truth." Her grandmother's gentle voice had become serious, almost harsh. Grandy raised a hand and placed it on her own heart, and it landed there with a passionate thump. "I've earned this, Emma. This spirit. I've worked hard for it. I've had to fight for it."

Her voice softened again.

"Years ago, when your grandfather died, I went through a similar thing to what you are going through right now. It was like I lost my whole world. I had to deal with depression and anxiety and panic attacks too. And since your parents' accident, that door flung wide open for me again. So, yes, I *do* know what it's like. I know how hard it is. And every single day, I know what I need to do, what I *must* do, to move beyond that place. And I feel terrible because now I see how I've dropped the ball with you the last few months. I was blind to how alone you were and how much you were struggling."

"I… I'm sorry," Emma said, embarrassed. She bit her lip and guiltily averted her gaze. "I tried to hide it, and I wasn't thinking about what you were going through either. I never knew…" Her voice trailed off.

"It's OK, honey," Grandy said gently. "We never talked about it before. You have nothing to apologize for. I know it's not a pleasant topic to discuss. But I'm telling you about it now because you need to understand the way I am today is the way I have *chosen* to be. I make the conscious decision, every single day, to not let the sadness and loss be what defines me. I choose to honor the people I have lost, my husband, and now my daughter and son-in-law, I choose to honor them in a positive way. I still feel their absences, but I make sure I fill that hole with what I loved about them, what was unique about them, what made them special to me. And I remember what they said they loved about me, and I put it back out into the world as *hard* as I can, so wherever they are they can *feel* it."

The moment became a turning point. Emma's perception of her grandmother took on a new dimension. This incredible woman wasn't always this way – she had chosen her path and was intentionally growing into it, day after day, through one decision after another. That's what Emma wanted to do in her own life. She was filled with a new admiration for Grandy and with a blossoming sense of hope for her future.

Taking a deep breath, Emma let it out. "So that's what I'll do then. I'll find the good memories, the lilacs." She reached up and touched the pendant hanging around her neck.

"Yes, that's it," Grandy said encouragingly. "You'll still have times of sadness, and you'll still feel the loss. This process is not quick, nor is it a straight line. But make it a point to intentionally seek happy memories of your parents. And put the best parts of yourself out there, boldly, every day. You might not think it's even possible to have those good experiences right now that will turn into happy memories in your future, but I promise if you put yourself out there, it will happen."

Emma always loved her grandmother, but this conversation was turning out to be transformational, letting her see the older woman in a fresh, new light.

"I always assumed your spirit, your..." she chose the next word carefully, "your *exuberance* was something you were born with. I never considered it was something that could be cultivated or developed, something I could learn."

"I suppose a few people have the good fortune to be born that way, but for me, I have to work at it. It's a daily thing, like vitamins or exercise. Now that I've *seen* the results from it, I wouldn't have it any other way." Grandy reflected for a moment. "I do wish I had started younger though, perhaps it would have helped your mother to be a bit more lighthearted. I should have done more to show her how to handle the challenges in life, not shelter her from them. But I guess it's always easier to see what we could have done in hindsight. We're never sure what the future will bring."

Emma sighed. "I always assumed there would be time to ease into finding my own way. But in an instant, I was on my own. I didn't have much experience dealing with adversity. When this big catastrophe came along, it totally shut me down."

"That can happen sometimes," Grandy acknowledged, "but now you're getting back up again. That's one of the important points about dealing with problems. You fall, but then you get up, and move on. Of course you'll make mistakes, honey. You'll even get a little dirty at times. But usually that's when you realize you've just learned something good. You need to brush yourself off and keep trying."

Emma nodded.

Grandy continued. "We've got to keep the momentum going now. Let's get together again in, hmm, two weeks from today? We can meet for dinner. Put it on your calendar, no backing out this time!" she added, the last part of the proposal sounding slightly like a warning.

"Got it," Emma confirmed, entering the appointment into her phone's calendar. "And I promise, no cancellations!"

"Don't give up entirely on the idea of seeing a counselor or therapist either. When you get back, we'll see how you feel, and if you still want to, we can find one who's a better fit for you," Grandy advised. "Just because the first one doesn't work out doesn't mean the next won't be wonderful. They have different personalities, different styles of dealing with patients. Or perhaps a bereavement group is more along the lines of what you're looking for."

"A bereavement group?" Emma inquired.

"Yes, a support group. For people who have gone through similar experiences losing someone they love. I joined one for a few sessions when your grandfather passed away." She sighed. "That's another thing I wish I'd been more open about sharing with you and your mother." Grandy's voice displayed a note of frustration. "I guess times were different back then. People didn't talk about needing help, as if they were ashamed of it. But it's only human to need some assistance or encouragement during the difficult parts of life, isn't it? It helped me to be around others who went through a loss like I did. I didn't feel so alone."

It dawned on Emma – that connection with others who had similar experiences was what she wanted. It was exactly what she was trying to do by listening to those crime podcasts. Her friends didn't understand how she was processing her grief, but perhaps she could find a small group of others close to her age with shared experiences.

She thought about her own bouts of depression she wrestled with over the past year and shuddered to think her beloved Grandy was also tormented by similar dark moods. Instead of seeing herself as being alone and misunderstood, now Emma identified several ways her grandmother was a bit of a kindred spirit. She never imagined they would have this much in common.

Grandy's insights were an inspiration, a beacon through the fog illuminating a new path forward. If her grandmother could take these steps to create a strategy to manage her grief during her own difficult times, then perhaps she had the strength to do it too. In her mind, Emma envisioned the unfolding plan. She could take this trip up north to begin the process and continue to work on it afterward by following these suggestions, with Grandy providing understanding and encouragement. Could she do this? Maybe it really was possible!

When it was time for her grandmother to leave, Emma walked her out to her car. "Grandy," she said, "I love you so much. Thank you for all of this. You are absolutely the best."

"And so are you, honey, so are you." They hugged each other tightly.

Grandy settled into her car and lowered her window. "Keep me posted on your trip tomorrow. No texting and driving, just send me a quick update when you stop if you feel like it. And no peeking on those envelopes tonight!" With a wave she whooshed out of the parking lot.

Still buzzing from her unexpected whirlwind of a day, Emma floated back into her apartment. After all the scrubbing and reorganizing she and Grandy had done that afternoon, it looked and smelled pleasant and clean. More importantly, it felt different. The rooms now possessed a positive energy, an essence of optimism, and it aligned with Emma's desire for a fresh start. Their actions elevated her into being ready for a new beginning, and now she had a plan to get there.

She found the "1. Open In The Morning Before You Leave" envelope in the backpack and propped it up on her travel mug, which once again, would travel farther than the short distance between the kitchen counter and her spin bike.

$$\sim 9 \sim$$

In spite of the anxiety that crept in when she thought about her fears of accidents, erratic drivers, and being alone on the highway far from home, Emma fell asleep shortly after tumbling into bed.

She awoke early, before the rising sun cleared the horizon, excited to start her adventure. The first thing she did, even before her coffee ritual, was race down the hallway like a giddy child on a holiday morning and open the envelope which revealed her accommodations for the next two nights.

"Please, please, please," she whispered silently, tearing off the sealed flap. She withdrew a folded sheet of paper and read the instructions in Grandy's beautiful flowing script:

Good Morning, Emma!
I'm so proud of you for agreeing to take this little adventure. Have a pleasant trip north and enjoy the journey! When you check in for the ferry, let them know you'll be staying at Grand Hotel, and they will handle the luggage transfer for you. Now, go! Find your lilacs!

Much love,
Grandy

Emma threw her hands into the air in a gesture of victory, shouted "Yes!" and did a joyous little dance of celebration. She had fervently hoped it would be Grand Hotel!

For more than a century, the elegant historic landmark (officially without the "The" in front of its name) has stood on a northern Michigan island bluff, welcoming seasonal travelers during the warmer months of the year. On previous trips to the island, her parents often talked about staying there, always mentioning it would be "someday," but for some reason unknown to Emma, they never did. Now, for their daughter, her "someday" had arrived.

Emma liked how this trip was a blend of creating new experiences and uncovering old memories. It was balanced. She would find growth in one and comfort in the other.

Scrambling about the kitchen, she hummed an upbeat tune while hastily toasting a bagel and brewing a small pot of coffee. It had been a long time since she was this energized about starting her day. On this morning there was no slumping over the phone to scroll through bland social media posts. She made one quick check of the island weather forecast – 74 degrees and sunny!

By 8AM, she had eaten, showered, dressed, and double-checked her packing list. Emma stood at the door for a moment, travel mug of coffee in hand, trying to think if there was anything she had forgotten to pack in her bag.

"But then if I truly forgot about something, why do I think I would remember it now?"

She reassured herself she had the credit card from Grandy and could buy any necessities that were overlooked once she got to the island. Then, she glanced over her shoulder and appreciated the living room was still tidy from the previous day's cleaning blitz. She grabbed her new suitcase and backpack and headed out the door.

Before they picked up their takeout meal the night before, Grandy wisely suggested they should fill the gas tank and check the oil level and tire pressure on Emma's car. Initially Emma had been slightly annoyed at the detour before dinner, but today she was glad they hadn't procrastinated. The actions only required a few minutes and now there was nothing to interrupt the momentum of her morning. The car was ready to go, and it gave her confidence for the day's expedition.

She hoisted her new suitcase into the trunk, then tossed the flower-accented backpack onto the passenger seat. Settling in behind the steering wheel, she heaved a sigh.

"OK, here we go. Let's do this!"

Pulling out her phone, she brought up the first destination of the trip on the navigation app, a fast-food restaurant she and Grandy identified as being about an hour away. Then she selected "Route" and "Go." Her stomach gave an involuntary spasm as the chosen roadway on the screen turned from the standard blue to bright red, based on real time traffic volume.

"Rush hour, ugh."

Since the night of her parents' accident, she avoided being in heavy traffic as much as possible. Ugly visions of driving on a chaotic highway raced in, filling Emma with dread. Checking the clock, she considered delaying her departure, but then boldly squashed the idea. She wiped her sweaty palms on the thighs of her jeans as she felt the rapid thumping of her heart. Fanning her hands in the air, she created a breeze against her face.

"I'm not going to let this control me," she resolved. "The whole drive won't be bad, maybe just a bit at the beginning, right?"

She fastened her seat belt, took a deep breath, and turned the key. The engine roared to life, and she guided her car out of the apartment complex parking lot. The confidence boosting affirmations of, "I've got this. I can do this. I've got this. I can do this," ran through her head in a continuous stream like an emotional stock market ticker.

She easily maneuvered through her local streets and prepared to merge onto the highway. For a moment, the short drive down the entrance ramp was familiar, like her old daily commute. But then the "I've got this," mantra spontaneously morphed into a surprisingly colorful string of exclamations as she saw multiple lanes of traffic travelling at an unreasonable speed. A nauseating wave of anxiety washed over her. Her heart pounded even faster, and she gripped the steering wheel tightly.

"No, no, no, no, no! Oh my goodness, what am I doing?" she asked herself.

She forced a new ticker tape message to run urgently through her head, "I'm fine, I'm fine, I'm fine." Taking deep breaths, she signaled to merge and squeezed her car into the tight stream of vehicles.

She allowed a buffer of space between her car and the one in front of her. Inevitably, another vehicle would pop into the gap and remove the cushion of stopping distance she intentionally built, but then she would ease off again and make new space, which would immediately be claimed by another vehicle. After a few minutes of this frustrating exercise and prompted by a sharp horn honk from the truck behind her when yet another car squeezed in front of her, she considered taking the next off ramp.

"Maybe I should get out of this madness and take a side road for a bit? It's a long drive, I don't want to wear out my nerves in the first few miles."

It sounded like a good option. If she was going to do that, she needed to be in the right lane. She put her blinker on and politely waited for a space to appear, but the aggressive commuter traffic would not let her in.

"Come on, let me over!" she grumbled. "I have my blinker on!"

The exit grew closer, and she attempted a move to the right and tried to squeeze in a small opening between two vehicles. The giant SUV to the rear of the space responded by speeding up to close the gap and emitted a loud blast of its horn. It startled Emma, and she swerved back into the center of her original lane. This made the pickup truck driver behind her lean angrily on the horn again in response. He already had his sights set on the spot Emma planned to vacate. Had drivers become ruder, more aggressive in the past few months?

She held her lane, stuck there as traffic flowed past the off-ramp she hoped to take. "Bye, exit!" She said sarcastically. "That's OK. I didn't need you anyway. I can adapt. I'll make another strategy. I'll get in the right lane now and take the next one, ha!"

Traffic in the right lane was less hostile since she passed that last exit. The gaps between the cars were larger and this time, she successfully shifted one lane to the right. Emma's confidence surged higher.

"See, that was easy, totally nailed it. I'm back in the groove now."

Three miles later, she realized the exit she wanted had recently been moved to the left side of the roadway, on the opposite side of where she was.

"What the heck! When did they do that?" she asked herself, her voice rising as she added, "Who puts an exit on the left?"

There was no way she could safely get to the opposite side of the packed highway in time to make the exit. She stayed securely in her lane and started looking for a sign indicating where the next off-ramp was.

When the sign came into view it was covered with a temporary orange 'Exit closed for ramp construction' label. 'Use alternate route.'

"Oh that's perfect," she said. "I *am* trying to use an alternate route!" she shouted at the sign. The absurdity of the situation finally bubbled up. She emitted a comical squawk and then laughed out loud.

"I used to do this drive every day on my way to work. Yes, they made some crazy changes to the exits, but I am perfectly capable of doing this! I own this highway!"

She adjusted herself in her seat, sitting up taller, and devised a new strategy. "I can make it to the end of this song, and then decide if I want to exit," she proclaimed, singing her updated plans in tune with the melody. Her hands were becoming sore from a white knuckled grip on the steering wheel. She carefully released the grip of one hand and flexed her fingers, open shut, open shut. Then she grasped the wheel again with that hand and released the other, open shut, open shut.

She attempted to talk her way through the tension.

"Breathe. Sing. Leave space between the car in front of me. I can do this."

It seemed like she was battling the traffic for a substantial amount of time. Emma congratulated herself on the progress she was making, but then she checked the clock on the dashboard.

"What? I've been on this highway for only seventeen minutes? You have got to be kidding me! This drive is going to take forever!" Her motivation plummeted.

"Nobody else gets this stressed out when they drive. It's totally not fair. They just get behind the wheel and go," she ranted.

She cast a sideways glance over at the next lane. The driver there was intently looking at her, frowning. She felt a wisp of self-consciousness.

"Oh great, now I'm the crazy person talking to herself in the car," but then, she decided anyone who saw her would assume she was having a conversation on speakerphone.

"Yes, yes, that's it! I'm on a conference call," she asserted. "I'm multi-tasking. Commuting and deal making. I'm a real go-getter." She made a few gestures as if she was emphasizing a conversational point and looked over at the neighboring vehicle again to see if he was buying her act, but the driver had pulled ahead.

"Whatever," Emma mumbled. "So I talk to myself when I drive. Deal with it," directing the statement at both herself and the other motorists around her.

Old habits of self-doubt started to bubble up. "I don't know if I can take hours of this. Maybe it's not worth it. Maybe I should just turn around and go home." And then she thought about the whole Grand Hotel experience. And the lilacs. And Grandy telling her she would have to fight through challenges in life to get where she wanted to be. In frustration, she made a growling sound in her throat. She took a deep breath and started a new litany of positive affirmations.

"I want to do this."

"I am getting past this crisis and living my life."

"I'm young, I'm strong, I'm brave."

"I'm capable. I can do this."

"I am crushing this like a total rock star."

One exit passed, and the song ended. Then another exit went by, and another song, and traffic began thinning out. She figured out where she was, and like Grandy said the night before, she was already more than halfway to her first stop.

A muddled mix of emotions took over when she finally pulled into the first available parking space at her initial destination and turned off the car's engine. Collapsing forward over the steering wheel, she rested her head on the 12 o'clock position and wrapped her arms around 9 and 3. She had made it, safely. The distance covered so far was about 75 miles. It was the farthest she had driven in a year. The traffic was intense and exhausting to deal with, but she reached this first stop without an incident. She was proud of herself for taking this step to conquer her fear, even if her whole body was trembling a bit. After giving herself a few minutes to calm down, she went inside to use the restroom and reward herself with a snack.

"Maybe a cinnamon roll," she thought as she surveyed the menu, "or an order of hash browns. Or both."

She reached for her phone and sent Grandy a text.

"Made it to my first stop!

THANK YOU for Grand Hotel!!!

Yahoooo!"

And then a string of heart emojis.

Energized by a dose of carbs and caffeine, she was revived when she got behind the wheel again. Despite a tiny sugar rush, her hands were steady, and her mind was clear. The next stop on her itinerary was a forest themed restaurant she used to visit with her parents. When she reached it, she would be about halfway to Mackinaw City, the final mainland destination before catching the ferry to the island.

Emma predicted she should be done with most of the difficult driving now. There would be fewer cars on the highway because she was out of the more densely populated area of the state, and thankfully rush hour was merely a memory.

"I'm glad I'm not trying this first solo trip on a Friday night or a Saturday morning," she thought, considering how chaotic the summer weekend traffic usually was. On peak weekends, it was typical to see a long bumper-to-bumper line of traffic for most of the northbound journey.

"I mean, I guess I could probably do it, but I'm glad I don't have to." Emma acknowledged, "Score another point for Grandy's planning wisdom."

She made good time on the next leg of the journey. There was a large bridge arching high over a river. She remembered how, in contrast to her father's calm demeanor, her mother used to stare straight ahead with one hand clamped firmly on the passenger side armrest and the other tightly gripping the edge of her seat.

Her father would point toward the water and say, "Do you see the freighter out there in the river, Ems?"

His wife chastised him, "Joseph, please!" using the long form of his name she reserved for the rare occasions when she was upset. "Keep both of your hands on the wheel and watch where you are going!"

Emma was glad she didn't have her mother's fear of heights. It did make her a bit tense when she thought about how high the bridge was, but in the light traffic the span was manageable even if she still found herself gripping the steering wheel more tightly than was probably necessary. She even bravely ventured a quick glance to the side to check if any freighters could be seen in the distance. No ships were visible in the river or the bay below, but high above there was a large bird soaring. Was that a flash of white as it made its lazy circle on a thermal? Could it be a bald eagle?

Crossing that large bridge was like achieving a huge milestone toward being "Up North." Once beyond it, larger stretches of farmland began to appear, replacing the earlier patchwork of industry and suburbia. Emma began to relax a bit. She was starting to enjoy the drive. This was what being behind the wheel used to feel like for her. Normal. Comfortable. There was an openness here, with unobstructed blue sky above and miles of flat-as-a-pancake fields all around. It was the exact opposite of the cocooned environment where she spent the last six months. A person could breathe here.

She approached another key landmark on the trip – the split where a northbound driver needed to make a critical choice. Would her itinerary be the slower coastal route up the "sunrise side" of the state, along the shore of Lake Huron, or the more direct northward track along the main highway, straight up the middle of the state's mitten shape? Her family took numerous trips along the scenic east coast of Michigan, sometimes on the way to Mackinac or as a slower paced dawdly way to prolong vacation a bit longer on the way home. Her parents preferred that route, and there was a string of their favorite stops along the way – a bakery here or an ice cream spot there, a diner for fish and chips with a lake shore view, followed by a place to go "beaching" on warm summer sand, or photos with a giant statue of Paul Bunyan in another small town. There were sure to be lilacs there, but Emma stayed focused on her target destination. Her newfound sense of confidence was still fragile, and too much deviation from the plan might be more than she could take. She chose the shorter, direct path on the interstate, which to her meant less time on the road.

"If the island part of the trip goes OK, maybe I can try the coastal route on the drive home."

After the highway split, the scenery made a dramatic change. As if a switch was flipped, she went from farmland to forest, with thick stands of pines hugging the roadsides. "I'm definitely up north now," she said.

A yellow "deer crossing" sign on the side of the highway inspired Emma to mentally repeat the safety slogan her father taught her.

"Don't veer for deer."

He made sure his daughter knew swerving to avoid an animal often resulted in a car hitting another vehicle or a tree. She shuddered and hoped she never was put in that awful situation, but knowing she was entering an area with a higher population of wildlife that could dart out into the road made her anxiety start to spike again.

A delivery truck started to follow her a bit too closely after the place where the highway split. Pressing harder on her gas pedal, she went faster for a few miles, trying to build up some space between the two vehicles but the truck accelerated too. She checked her speedometer. Her eyebrows raised at the surprisingly large number on the screen.

"Um, no. I'm not going to get a speeding ticket because of this jerk."

She eased off to a pace five miles per hour below the speed limit, hoping the lead-footed delivery driver would find it too slow, and it would entice him into going around her. That strategy had no effect on the truck either. It continued to follow her like a shadow.

"Dude, just pass me," she said aloud, but the driver seemed content to be tailgating her. She considered making a gesture indicating she wanted him to go around her, but decided against it, concerned any movements would be interpreted aggressively and could trigger road rage.

"Should I exit?" she wondered, "or try to ignore him? But I don't want him to keep following me. What if I change lanes quickly and then slow way down and let him go past me like I saw in that spy movie?"

She was annoyed this driver was dragging a cloud over her otherwise pleasant drive. "Think happy thoughts," she advised herself and forced her mind to ponder more appealing things, like lunch.

There was a red glow of brake lights ahead. Her distraction with the delivery truck driver and attempts to focus on her upcoming food options had shifted her attention away from the road in front of her. Now she only had a split second to react. She pushed hard on the brake pedal to slow her car, feeling the pulsation as the ABS kicked in. The delivery truck behind her squealed its tires as the driver aggressively jammed on his brakes. At the sound, Emma's body involuntarily tensed up.

"He can't stop!" she thought in horror, and she waited for the sickening crunch of metal and the terrifying jolt of an impact.

~ 10 ~

Her own car came to a stop a mere inch from the SUV in front of her. The slightest contact from behind surely would have pushed her into its back bumper. When she heard the squealing tires, she kept her foot firmly planted on the brake and screwed her eyes shut, wishing, hoping, and praying the tailgating beast would somehow be able to stop. But even after she opened her eyes to the image of the delivery truck's bug-studded chrome grille motionless in her mirror, and her brain registered there hadn't been any contact, she still didn't believe she had escaped, unscathed.

How could such a large vehicle have stopped in time?

"That thing is so close to my car. I can't believe it didn't crash into me!"

Her heart thudded in her chest. She uttered a quick "Thank you, Jesus" prayer of gratitude for this small miracle and wiped her sweaty palms on her jeans.

She sat up as tall as she could, trying to see the road ahead.

"What's happening up there?"

There was a queasy feeling in the pit of her stomach, and she found it hard to breathe.

"Do people my age have heart attacks?" she wondered as she rubbed her chest.

All the cars around her were at a standstill now. Emma's face grew warm, so she redirected the air conditioning vents to blow directly on her face and reached for her travel mug to finish off the last gulps of cold coffee. She closed her eyes momentarily, a long blink, and took a deep breath, fighting to keep the panic under control.

"Can't lose it here. I still need to be able to drive."

After about a minute, cars started slowly inching forward again at a snail's pace. The delivery truck changed lanes and passed her.

"Good riddance."

The string of vehicles crept along. Emma could finally see some of what was going on. Cars were merging away from the left lane to go around an accident. The shrill whine of a police car siren filled the air and flashing lights appeared in her side mirror as the cruiser approached from behind.

"This is what it would have been like at my parent's accident scene, except it would have been dark and raining."

She struggled to push the horrible image out of her mind.

"I'm safe right now, nothing bad has happened to me," she recited, trying to override her fears.

The cars crawled forward and although she knew she shouldn't, she snuck a quick sideways glance to see what happened.

Her view was obstructed but she could tell there were two cars involved, and at least one left scrape marks on the guardrail. It looked like people were out of the cars and walking around or leaning on the dented barrier. Remembering the sign warning of deer, she wondered if that was the reason for the crash. Perhaps an animal darted across the highway and the cars swerved.

As Emma inched her own vehicle forward, an ambulance arrived, and then a second police car. Finally, she was past the scene and gradually accelerated back to normal highway speed.

"This was not my parents' accident," she reminded herself. "It was just minor. Everyone seemed fine." But still her body shook, and she fought back a strong compulsion to cry. A big, green sign displayed the next set of upcoming exits. She felt a surge of relief that the first one on the list was the exit she wanted.

Her car pulled smoothly into the parking space at the restaurant, and she reached for her phone. A few seconds earlier while driving down the exit ramp, she made the decision to call Grandy and tell her she wasn't going to finish the trip. This emotional roller coaster was too intense - she couldn't do this. Between the incident with the delivery truck and seeing the accident scene, she was at her limit.

Emma was exhausted and despite her best efforts to hold them back, tears were again puddling in her eyes. Her willpower was worn out from trying to convince herself this challenge was worth it. Her arms ached from gripping the steering wheel tightly and her neck hurt from tension.

Instead of finding her phone in its usual spot, her hand landed on the note from Grandy she had opened earlier that morning. She pushed the tears away and reread the message.

"I'm so proud of you..." Grandy's words said.

Emma dropped the paper into her lap and buried her face in her hands. "Just look at me. She wouldn't be proud of me now!" She stopped trying to hold back the tears and instead gave in to the surge of feelings.

Drivers were ruder and more aggressive than she remembered from her old daily commute. The obstacle course of road construction intensified the stress. Passing the accident scene brought many of her fears and traumatic memories to the surface. Everything she held back while she was on the road now gushed out in a sloppy torrent. She cried cathartically for a few seconds then took a deep breath and waited for the next wave of tears but, puzzlingly, it didn't come.

Based on the intensity of what she felt when she first parked, she thought she was in for a prolonged weepy episode but instead, something else happened. From deep inside, she sensed a calmer, stronger version of herself pushing back. She heard whispers of confidence and positivity. "On the other hand, she thought valiantly, "I *did* handle this situation, the traffic, the construction, the accident. It was messy, but I did it." Those positive affirmations were beginning to make a small difference. She was a complicated tangle of emotions, but she had also just dealt with some of her biggest fears. Grandy would indeed be proud of her.

"I'm even proud of myself!" Emma thought. "And that's probably even more important. I've taken a big wobbly step forward. I'm doing it!"

It sparked a memory of when her father taught her to ride her bicycle before one of their long-ago Mackinac Island vacations. He informed little Emma they would be taking her "big girl bike" for the trip, but he would have to remove the training wheels.

Emma was apprehensive. "But Daddy, I *need* my training wheels!" she insisted.

He corrected her gently. "No, Sweetheart, you've totally mastered those. You're ready for the big time now."

Her blue eyes looked up at him in disbelief. "I am?"

"You are!" he answered confidently.

Emma was still not convinced when her father tossed the disconnected training wheels on the grass next to the sidewalk.

"You won't be needing those anymore," he said.

She hesitantly climbed onto the glittery padded bicycle seat and her father reassured her. "Don't worry, I've got you."

They did several passes up and down the sidewalk with her father close by her side. Emma was thrilled the clattery noise of the training wheels was gone. Maybe she really could ride a big girl bike, the way her mommy did! This was kind of fun, as long as she didn't fall. She checked to confirm her dad's strong hand was still supporting the bicycle.

He laughed. "Stop looking backward! Pay attention to where you're going, Ems. Just keep pedaling."

Emma remembered being deep in concentration, intensely focused on the narrow concrete rectangles of sidewalk laid out in front of her. She rode for a long, smooth stretch until she snuck another peek to the side and discovered her father was no longer there. He had released his grasp. She pedaled a few more feet, but then the scary thoughts rushed in.

"When did he let go? I might fall!" She wobbled, overcorrected, let out a wavery "whaaaaa!" and tipped over, tumbling into the grass.

Her father raced down the sidewalk to pick her up. She looked back at him with fear in her face, about to cry, feeling betrayed he had let go of her until she saw his proud smile and heard him cheer, "You did it, Emma! You did it! That was *awesome!*"

A glimpse of his beaming face was all she needed. She brushed herself off and said, "I'm gonna do it again!"

"That's my brave girl, Ems!" he said.

He picked her bike up and inspected it for damage while she brushed off the bits of grass that clung to her arms and legs and climbed aboard a second time. She made another attempt, going back in the direction toward where her mother stood applauding at the end of their driveway. She repeated the sequence: riding the bicycle a bit farther, then falling, but getting up again too.

"That's how this recovery process will be - trying and falling and getting up, over and over. I miss you both so much! But I know, in my heart, you want me to do this, and you're cheering me on, just like you did with the bicycle."

She paused, realizing, "I just found a happy memory… I'm not even on the island yet but I think that's a lilac!"

Her eyes scanned over Grandy's note again. "I'm already halfway to my destination anyway. If I turn around now, I'll still have travelled the same number of miles today, but I'll end up slumped on my couch feeling frustrated and defeated instead of claiming victory tonight at Grand Hotel. Grandy knew what she was doing when she booked a room for me there. That's a heck of a motivating carrot to dangle in front of me. Mackinac Island, here I come!"

She checked her reflection in the visor mirror to see if her eyes were still red then climbed out of her car and crossed the parking lot toward the restaurant entrance. This adventure stuff was making her hungry.

$$\sim 11 \sim$$

An old friend awaited her in the building's vestibule. "Oh, the bear!" Emma cooed. "I remember this!" The restaurant was fully decorated in a forest and wildlife theme, complete with an ancient taxidermied bear in the entryway.

"It seemed… much *bigger* back then. It used to be scary when I was little," she pondered, looking it over. "Used to be," she repeated, "but not so much anymore."

The bear's large teeth and sharp claws once appeared intimidating to her. She remembered clinging to the doorway and refusing to walk past it. Her mother had to carry her into the restaurant while her father blocked the bear from view, reassuring her the creature couldn't hurt her or follow them to their table. Now, Emma giggled at the thought. It was evidence of a conquered fear. Although driving in traffic was distressing today, she hoped someday she would once again think it wasn't so bad, like the bear.

She walked up to the furry old creature and patted it on the head. "Hello, Mr. Bear." She posed alongside of it and snapped a selfie. It would make a great progress update to send to Grandy.

The hostess greeted her with a warm smile, "How many in your party today?"

Emma blushed, "Um, one?"

She pictured a scene where the restaurant staff and other patrons all turned and mocked her, sneering and pointing. "Look at her. No family. No friends. Who eats alone? What a loser!"

But instead, the hostess simply reached for a menu, "Would you prefer a table or a booth?"

Emma picked a booth. A solo diner along the perimeter would attract less attention than a person sitting alone in the middle of the room, wouldn't they? The two made their way through the maze of tables to a cozy section along the wall decorated with old camping memorabilia. No one glanced up from their meals or phones as they passed by, except a nice-looking grandfatherly type who smiled at her. She tossed her purse into the booth and slid in behind it. Removing the forest green paper band holding the rolled bundle of napkin and silverware, she checked off another first from her life experience catalog.

"Eat alone in a sit-down restaurant. Done. Well, almost done. As soon as there's food." She put her phone on the table and retreated into her social media accounts while she waited for the server to arrive.

After ordering her meal, she opened the web browser on her phone and did some investigation into why Mackinaw City is spelled with the "w" while the island is spelled "Mackinac" with a "c", even though they are pronounced the same. She learned the original name of the area came from an Ojibwa word, and each group of settlers in the area took liberties with their version of the spelling. Hence, the island, the bridge, and the straits are all spelled "Mackinac" with a "c" while the US Coast Guard cutter, the mainland city, and type of water-resistant cloth are all spelled with the "w".

Periodically she checked to see if she missed seeing anyone making the "Loser L" with hand on forehead. "There has to be an immature 12-year-old in here somewhere." Repeatedly scanning the room and finding none, she ventured to think, "Nope. Not even one. Then, why have I always dreaded eating alone? And even if there was someone mocking me, who cares! They're the one with a maturity problem, not me, right?"

After successfully polishing off a cheeseburger (with a side of sour pickles), fries, and cola, Emma's energy was renewed as she checked her phone's GPS app for her next destination. Traffic was definitely lighter now. Nothing on the remainder of the drive would even come close to the rush hour madness she encountered earlier in the southern part of the state. She was confident the next segment of the journey would pass quickly, in spite of random unwelcome concerns about accidents, construction zones, and carelessly wandering wildlife that still burrowed into her thoughts.

Now though, as she drove down the open highway, she found herself wondering about the opposite situation. At times there were no cars, either ahead of her or behind. This was the most remote area she had ever been in by herself. There were eerie open marshy spaces with dead trees poking out of ponds of standing water. Then, the landscape changed, and she went through areas where the road was lined with dense stands of pine forest. No shopping malls. No gas stations. No fast-food restaurants. She glanced down at her phone. One meager bar of cell signal strength displayed briefly on the screen before it disappeared, and the "No Signal" message popped up.

"What if I get a flat tire or my car breaks down? How will I get help?"

A motley assortment of disturbing possibilities ran through her mind. All those hours spent listening to true crime podcasts were taking a toll. They populated her mind with a hundred and one ways a perfectly good day could go horribly wrong. Each time the pavement texture changed, she listened. "What's that noise? Is my engine sounding funny? Do I have a tire going flat?" Once again, her muscles tensed up. It became harder to breathe and her heart pounded. "Aw, crap. Here I go again," she thought. "It's always going to be something, isn't it?" and she reached over, turned the radio up and sang as loudly as she could to drown out the negativity.

When Emma reached the exit for her next planned stop, her stomach was still full from lunch so she kept driving. However, five miles farther down the road, she noticed a sign indicating "Scenic Lookout Area Ahead" and grew curious.

"That could be interesting. I'll check it out. After all, Grandy did suggest I enjoy the journey." She didn't feel like venturing far off the main road. After what her anxiety already put her through earlier in the drive, getting legitimately lost without a solid cell phone signal was not something in which she was interested. "This one is right by the highway though. It should be fine. I wonder if I can see the Mackinac Bridge from here or am I still too far away?"

The arrow indicating the lookout exit sign appeared in the distance. When it grew close enough, she activated her blinker and moved her car into the little lane that branched off from the highway, laughing to herself as she compared the extreme ease of it to the difficulty she had trying to exit during rush hour earlier that morning.

A narrow walking trail led from the parking lot, then meandered through a small, wooded area, and finally up a good-sized hill to an overlook platform. Emma was a tiny bit winded as she gazed out at the landscape and caught her breath.

"Note to self: work on cardio," she spoke into her phone.

A lush green forest surrounded her, interrupted in the distance to the west by the silver sliver of a narrow inland lake, and beyond that the green continued again, this time in darker hues. The far horizon was wavy, not a dramatic silhouette of large, jagged mountains like she had seen in Colorado but not pancake flat either. Instead, the terrain profile indicated the picturesque hills that drew people to the northwest portion of the state.

It was a postcard perfect panorama, except for the minor annoyance of traffic noise rising from the highway below as it stretched out north and south from the base of the viewing platform, providing a constant reminder of the busy modern world. Passenger cars shuttled people to destinations of work or play while semi-trailers dutifully hauled their loads to meet a demanding schedule. Nature vs civilization, leisure vs work, all combined in one compact view.

She rested her arms on the rustic but sturdy railing and imagined who was cruising by in the cars below: families, groups of friends, couples, perhaps a few single people too. Did they know about the view from up here? Did they care? Or were they in a hurry to get where they were going? Were they so focused on their goals they bypassed the good stuff along the way? How many people said, "Someday I'll stop at that lookout, but not today"? Maybe, like she had been for the past few months, some were in a haze of stress, grief, or anxiety.

"I almost skipped this," she admitted. "This view, or even this whole trip could have been ditched if I made a different decision back there," Emma said as she thought about her breakdown in the restaurant parking lot. I've missed a lot in the last year."

Did her parents ever stop at this lookout? Maybe they were here on a trip without her, or perhaps before she was born, or maybe when she was so young she couldn't remember it. "They would have loved this," she proclaimed confidently. Emma peered out over the highway to the north but couldn't see the Mackinac Bridge or either of the Great Lakes yet. "This would be a great spot to catch a sunset," she noted. "I'll have to find a good spot to see one on the island." She took a few photos to capture the view and sent one to Grandy before setting out again.

The remaining distance to the ferry dock passed quickly. Her car travelled smoothly around a wide sweeping curve in the interstate and suddenly the majestic Mackinac Bridge towered high above the road ahead, connecting Mackinaw City on the lower peninsula to the city of St. Ignace in the upper. What a magnificent landmark to end her long drive!

She guided her car at a crawl through the busy tourist area leading to the ferry. While she was stopped at an intersection, a large group of unhurried vacationers wandered casually across the street in front of her car. They took their time, some even pausing in the middle of the road, right in front of her, oblivious to the waiting traffic. They reminded her of the flock of ducks that often stopped traffic as they crossed the road to and from the pond at the entrance of her apartment complex. Emma laughed and wondered if any of these people were the highly aggressive drivers she dealt with on the highway earlier.

"Funny how differently people act when they're behind the wheel of a car."

Where the road ended at the lakeshore, she passed through the festive, flag-topped ferry terminal gates, unloaded her luggage with the staff who tagged it and whisked it away, then paid for her parking at the ticket window using the credit card Grandy had given her.

The woman at the counter remarked, "It's almost departure time, but if you hurry you might be able to catch this one."

Emma glanced toward the dock area. The last few passengers were boarding the waiting ferry. For a brief second, she toyed with the idea of a quick sprint in that direction before the crew finished fastening the chain across the gangway ramp. However, a momentary vision of herself performing a slow-motion, sprawling wipe-out filled her head, and she abruptly changed her mind.

"Knowing my luck, I'd trip or something and end up spending this afternoon at the local medical clinic."

She was not in a hurry, but instead relieved that what she considered to be the most challenging part of the trip was through. She had arrived at the dock area, a place she once thought was unattainably far away, and she was ready to relax. There was a wide-open selection of places to sit. She took a seat on the end of a bench in the shaded waiting area and put the colorful luggage claim check and ferry ticket in the pocket of her backpack.

Automatically, Emma pulled out her phone and started scrolling through social media again. She hadn't posted any photos yet and would have to get caught up with that when she got to the island. "I'm pretty sure the hotel has Wi-Fi," she imagined. Her thumbs swiftly tapped out a text message to Grandy.

"I made it to Mac City! At ferry, boarding soon. Thank you again for this adventure. Love you, XOXO"

The reply came back quickly from Grandy.

"That's wonderful news! Don't forget to read the message in envelope #2, as soon as possible. XOXO"

She had forgotten about the next scheduled envelope! Emma found the little document holder in her backpack and skimmed through the stack, removing the one labeled, "2. Open At The Ferry Dock."

The message inside was much longer than the first one she read earlier that morning.

Hello Emma,

Welcome to the next part of your journey. Technology can be a useful thing (I'm sure a navigation app was helpful on the drive today!) However, our devices can also be a distraction, keeping us from being fully present in the moment and from experiencing our surroundings. I hope you will take this opportunity to disconnect from the internet while you are on the island. Take your phone with you for emergencies, but leave it turned off.

At this point, Emma frowned, and her jaw dropped open. The note continued:

Use the credit card I gave you to buy an ice cream or a few souvenirs each day and I'll know things are fine. I know you like to take pictures with your phone, but perhaps for these few days you can use the sketchbook and your artistic talent to capture some special moments instead.

Much love,
Grandy

Emma let her hands holding the note drop to her lap.

"No phone? No photos? No texting or social media? No internet? Really? What the heck, Grandy?!"

She made an unpleasant face as she refolded the note and harshly shoved it back into the envelope.

She looked around at the crowd gathering to board the next available ferry. About half had their faces directed toward phone screens. "They're not giving up *their* phones," she thought in a snarky tone. This time, her thumbs pounded the screen angrily as she composed an exasperated message to her grandmother.

"I read the note. Ugh, that's cruel.

(angry face emoji)

As you wish, phone off now.

Still love you though LOL"

She added a kiss emoji to soften the tone, hit send, and hesitated for a moment, summoning up the courage to power off the device.

Grandy was waiting for her message and immediately sent a reply filling the screen with hearts.

Emma sighed and powered off the phone. She smiled and shook her head in frustration as she dropped the device into her backpack.

Grandy had been right about every step of this trip so far. She was going to have to trust her.

~ 12 ~

Crew members swarmed over the incoming ferry, securing it at the dock. When the go-ahead was given, onboard passengers streamed off, a mix of day trippers and overnighters. Judging by the array of bags in hand it had been a good day at the Island's numerous fudge shops. After a quick sweep to ensure all island departures had exited, an enthusiastic employee announced "now boarding" over the speaker system, and the people who remained seated in the waiting area rose to their feet.

It was still sunny and pleasant out. Emma presented her ticket and made a beeline for the narrow stairway leading up to the top deck of the ferry instead of the more sheltered indoor seating area on the lower deck.

She chose an open space toward the front of the boat and sat next to the railing. There was a great view from there. Her first impulse was to take a picture of the colorful harbor area with the rows of pretty sailboats neatly tied to their moorings. She instinctively reached for her phone, but then remembered Grandy's request and grumbled.

"Darn, that would have been a great photo," she sulked. "I guess I'm supposed to experience my surroundings," still skeptical of the strategy.

It was an ideal day for an island visit. Prime seating locations on the bright and breezy deck were filling up. Spaces were claimed by couples and families and clusters of friends. Among the growing crowd, there appeared to be one other solo traveler - a scowling man who looked like he might be commuting, dressed for a business meeting. He kept checking his phone screen and glancing toward the stairs. Maybe he had a business partner somewhere, possibly running late or waiting inside on the lower deck, making a call in a quiet spot out of the wind.

Emma traveled for work several times but always with a pack of coworkers. Those trips were like road rallies with a dysfunctional family in mismatched carpool caravans. On longer excursions when her team had to fly, they invaded unsuspecting airport lounges in a flash mob of unjaded youthful exuberance, wielding the magical power of the generous corporate expense account. Her vacations were with either family or friends. She had always been surrounded by people. Insulated. Sheltered. This was the first time she was traveling alone, vacationing *by herself*.

A wave of loneliness swept over her as she enviously eyed the groups and couples. "It's one thing to be alone in your own home but I guess being solo in a crowd requires a different type of confidence."

The vessel's powerful horn emitted a jarring blast. Emma, along with several other passengers, jumped in surprise.

"OK, yep, I'm still kind of keyed up from the stress of the drive, aren't I?" she thought, amused by her reaction. The ferry motored away from the dock, precisely adjusted its course, and headed toward the island.

As the boat left the relative shelter of the harbor and increased its pace to cruising speed, the wind also picked up. She reached into her hoodie pocket for a hair-tie, securing her tresses into a makeshift bun to minimize tangles as the lake breezes blew across the deck. She turned her head and looked out over the water, gazing at the long, impressive bridge spanning the straits. A teenage girl on the opposite side of the ferry stood up and angled her body to get the bridge positioned behind her before smiling broadly and snapping a series of selfies.

"I'd probably be doing the same thing if my phone was on. And there's nothing wrong with that!" She was feeling a bit dismayed, jealous, and uncomfortable at being separated from her nearly omnipresent device.

"If I go somewhere and have zero photos of it, did the trip actually happen?"

She resumed studying the construction of the bridge. She admired the lines and angles, the arc of the suspension cables as they swooped between the towers. It would make a nice sketch, but she decided it was too difficult to draw on the bobbing ferry, with wind and spray.

"Maybe I'll try to draw it from memory later tonight, at the hotel," she mused. "After all, I'll need something to do. One thing's for sure, I won't be watching anything online or listening to podcasts."

The design of the bridge was interesting and capturing the perspective accurately would be a challenge. She made a mental note of the way the light and shadows played across the different elements and marveled at how small the cars and trucks appeared. Her thoughts wandered to the logistics of building such a massive structure, spanning nearly 5 miles across water, with all the complicated calculations done manually, in a time before computers were used for engineering.

"That's pretty incredible."

An assortment of other boats also navigated through the straits – another ferry with a hydro jet plume returning to the mainland, a few sporty sailboats cruising along, and a large freighter approaching in the distance.

A few years earlier, a friend she knew from high school participated in an organized event where he swam from the lower peninsula to the upper. She always thought that was a major accomplishment. Now, from this perspective on a boat between the two land masses and seeing the distance and the chop of the waves, his achievement took on even greater significance.

Her thoughts were interrupted when the ferry took a big wave and made a stomach-churning dip. A strong gust of wind followed and caught the passengers by surprise. There was a moment of chaos as light, unsecured items were sent airborne, including the Detroit Tigers cap on the head of a small boy in the row in front of her. It sailed across the back of his seat, landing on the deck at Emma's feet as he yelled, "Daaaaaad, my hat!"

Emma snatched it up before another gust had a chance to blow it out of her reach and send it overboard. "I've got it!" she proclaimed in triumph, and then handed it to the boy's father.

He gave her a wide-eyed look, his expression showing a mix of panic and relief. "That was close. It's his favorite. Thanks."

He took the hat from Emma and then turned to his son, "I'm going to hang on to this until we get to the island, OK buddy?" He gave the child's hair an affectionate tousle.

The man was handsome. Neatly dressed in a trim fitting t-shirt and jeans, he had curly hair like the boy, a bit golden from the sun, and messy from the wind.

With every swoop and dip of the ferry on the waves, the island grew nearer. Even from the straits, the bright white mass of Grand Hotel perched high on the island bluff was clearly visible. A short distance away and equally identifiable was the historic Fort. The two landmarks were connected by the string of buildings that made up Main Street. Offshore, the harbor's dual lighthouses came into view.

Emma continued casually spying on the little family in front of her. A ponytailed girl, perhaps a few years older than her now-hatless brother, was dressed in blue denim shorts and a shirt emblazoned with glittery yellow and white daisies. The girl pointed across the lake and called out, "Daddy, it's a Lego lighthouse!"

Emma looked where she indicated, smiled, and silently agreed. Round Island Light, with its blocky red and white shape, rose from a small rock-strewn land mass and did indeed resemble a tower constructed with the toys. Shortly afterward, the ferry passed the second lighthouse, one which gave Emma the impression of a white chimney protruding from the peaked roof of a sunken structure.

She nonchalantly glanced at the family again. The boy had disappeared below the top of the seat back but now, like a cautious little animal peeking out of its burrow, his head was rising up so he could catch a glimpse of Emma. She kept her face turned to the side, gazing outward at the lighthouse. When she peered back at him out of the corner of her eye and smiled, he dipped below the seat back again.

There was an empty space in the family's group of seats, for the children's mother, Emma presumed. She made another quick scan of the deck to see where the mother was, but not seeing anyone who seemed like she belonged with the father and children, Emma wondered if she had chosen to stay on the lower deck, out of the wind, like her own mother sometimes used to do on breezy days.

~ 13 ~

Hi. My name is Sophie. I'm eight years old and I just finished second grade with my teacher, Mrs. Gordon. She was very nice. I have a brother. His name is Liam. He is a total pain in the neck, but I love him because he's my baby brother. He's not actually a baby anymore though. He's five years old and he likes baseball. He loves to act like he's a dinosaur.

My mommy likes to take trips with her friends. She calls them "Girls Weekends." I'm a girl, but I don't get to go with them. Mommy says they do grownup stuff like drinking wine and shopping. They usually go up north to Traverse City, but one time they took the train to Chicago. When she comes back home, she brings me presents, like a t-shirt or a stuffed unicorn or a box of pink cupcakes with rainbow sprinkles.

When my mommy goes on the Girls trips, my daddy takes my brother and me somewhere too, like to the lake or to a water park or up north, but not to the same up north place that mommy goes. It would be so funny if we ran into her someday.

My mommy is very pretty and super fun. She rides bikes with us. She makes the world's best macaroni and cheese and sings the Train song "Drops of Jupiter" into the big wooden spoon like it's a microphone. Her favorite color is blue, and she loves my daddy a lot.

$$\sim 14 \sim$$

The captain maneuvered the ferry through Haldimand Bay while a crewmember ran through a series of scripted arrival and safety announcements, including a reminder for everyone to remain in place while the vessel docked. Impatient passengers on the upper deck perched in anxious readiness until the all-clear was given. Then, they swiftly jockeyed for prime positions in line to be among the first to descend the narrow stairs and spill out into the busy terminal like ants onto a picnic to rent bicycles, purchase souvenirs, and eat world famous fudge.

Emma hung back to avoid the bulk of the crowd. She glanced down at her wristwatch, relieved that the old batteries in it still worked. It was an accessory she hadn't worn in a long time, but Grandy insisted she take it to round out the collection of items they packed for the trip.

"Now that request makes sense, since I won't be using my phone to check the time."

It dawned on her that long before they started to fill the suitcase yesterday, Grandy had already decided to have Emma put her phone away as part of her master plan. Sneaky woman. What other little tricks did she have planned for her granddaughter?

The hands on the watch face showed it was approaching 3:00PM, but unlike most of the other passengers, she was not in a hurry. There would be several days for her to explore the island at a leisurely pace, not a mere handful of frantic hours.

On her childhood visits to the island, her mother was always vigilant about keeping track of the time on their day trips. "When is the next ferry? When is the last one in the evening? We don't want to miss it and be stuck here on the island!" As if that would have been such a tragedy.

Her father didn't seem to be concerned about missing the final boat back to the mainland, but when he joked they could camp inside the Fort with the spirits of the old dead soldiers if they needed a place to stay overnight, Emma found herself clinging to her mother and frequently checking her own little cartoon character watch, keeping an eye on the time to ensure her sleeping accommodations were ghost-free.

Her luggage was tagged back at the mainland terminal, identified for delivery to Grand Hotel, and would be taken directly to her room. She loved that convenience. It left her free to explore the town without needing to worry about the logistical details of transporting her suitcase.

Strolling along behind the flow of arriving passengers, she absorbed the high energy of the bustling resort community. The island terminal dispersed the crowd right into the heart of town, and she was greeted with a burst of sensory stimuli. She remembered this atmosphere! It was a pleasing commotion of light and color and motion, sounds of clip-clopping hooves and bicycle bells, and the twisted, unique aromatic blend of grilled food and sweet sugary fudge, all mingled with the unavoidable earthy smell accompanying the presence of a large population of horses.

She wandered up Main Street, with its pastel-hued store fronts, carnival striped awnings and colorful flags. Carried along by the flow of tourists, she noted a vast collection of bike rental stations, clothing shops, and souvenir stores as she meandered. People popped in and out of a small market, a bookstore, and various tempting restaurants. Grandy suggested she get a daily ice cream cone or a t-shirt with the credit card she provided. That would not be hard to do here. Instead, the challenge would be in limiting which ones to get.

She crossed the street to go back in the other direction. Not a car was in sight, but there was no shortage of traffic as a steady stream of bicycles and various horse-drawn vehicles travelled up and down Main Street.

After completing her reconnaissance loop and arriving back at the ferry terminal, Emma headed for the taxi stand and located her ride: the signature glossy brown carriage with Grand Hotel emblazoned in script on the side. She paused and admired it from a distance.

"Wow, today is the day I finally get to do this!"

When she was a little girl, her family bought tickets for an outing with the State Park carriage tour on one of their day trips to the island. Those sturdy sightseeing vehicles were roomy and adequately comfortable to fulfill their purpose of carrying loads of passengers to various scenic locations around the island but, to young Emma, they were too utilitarian. She longed to ride in one of the beautiful Grand Hotel carriages. They resembled an elegant royal coach from a fairytale or from one of the movie versions of a Jane Austen novel she and her mother sometimes watched on TV. Little Emma tugged on her mother's sleeve and asked, "Mommy, can we ride in the pretty one, please?"

"Someday, honey, but not today," was her mother's gentle reply as she steered her daughter in the direction of the tour vehicle. Emma's young heart sank a bit at her mother's words, but she decided one day, she was going to be riding in a beautiful horse-drawn carriage. And now, years later, it was finally happening. Thanks to Grandy's plan, she was going to indulge her inner Cinderella!

She consulted with the driver and climbed aboard. So far, she was the only passenger.

"This totally rocks."

In a flash, her backpack was open, and she was diligently burrowing for her phone to take a selfie before remembering it had been powered off. Throwing her head back, she rolled her eyes.

"Ugh, Grandy, you're driving me crazy here. This would have been an awesome photo."

She envisioned the super cool "#fairytaletaxi" post she would have made. Heaving a sigh, she began studying the carriage interior.

"I guess if I've wanted to be here my whole life, I should pay attention to what's around me and not be on my phone."

Well intentioned, she examined the seats, the ceiling, and the tiny safety warning plaque, but then in an excited burst of silliness, she struck a goofy and dramatic pose, because "Yes, dahhling, that's what you can doooo when you have a sweet carriage all to yourself," she noted using a comical accent.

She peered out the taxi window, seeing how the bikes zipped by on the street, followed by an impressive team of draft horses methodically plodding along with their cargo of passengers. Clearly, bicycles were the preferred transportation mode if you were in a hurry.

Emma snapped back into a somewhat more dignified posture when an older couple dressed in matching purple velour jogging outfits peered in the open carriage door, said a cheery hello, then joined her inside. They settled into their seats and the driver leaned his head into the door, inquiring, "Are you waiting for anyone else?"

Emma smiled and shook her head, and the wife of the purple couple issued their confirmation, "No, we're all set."

Satisfied his passenger list was complete for this trip, the driver secured the door, then took his seat at the front of the carriage. He called out to the horses, and they set off for the hotel. They traveled no faster than the other carriage she saw earlier.

"It's a paradox," Emma thought. "The island is so animated and energetic, but the pace of transportation is much slower than the mainland."

The horses drew them up a side street toward the dramatic tree-lined boulevard of Cadotte Avenue. The gray-haired woman looked out of the carriage window and remarked, "Oh see, Carl. Like I told you, there are still a few lilacs in bloom here."

Carl grunted, unimpressed, but Emma swung her head around to see where the woman was pointing. Lilacs! The real thing, still in bloom!

Back at home, the peak blooming time for them had passed but in the northern part of the state, the growing season lagged by several weeks. Finding these flowers was one of her few responsibilities on this trip and yet amid the excitement of her arrival she forgot to keep watch.

A group of lilac bushes grew in front of one of the island's picturesque vintage inns, its plumes of fluffy fragrant blossoms arching over its front sidewalk. She almost missed it! Even without staring at her phone screen, she was still not fully present or focused. She was lost in thoughts, distracted, not taking in her surroundings.

"I wonder what else I've missed this past year. The world is going on without me. If not for Grandy, I would still be sitting in a room with shades pulled down, consuming podcasts, and obsessing about how to find ways to stay on the radar of people who don't even care about me."

"I'm glad you pointed those lilacs out," Emma mentioned to the woman.

"They are just so beautiful, aren't they? Those lilacs right there are quite old, even older than Carl!" she added with a good-natured laugh.

Carl grunted again, but Emma thought she detected a hint of a smile softening his weathered face. The purple-clad woman asked, "Is this your first visit, dear?" sounding a bit like Grandy.

Emma replied, "I've been to the island before, but never on an overnight trip. This is the first time I've stayed at Grand Hotel."

"I think you'll enjoy it. It is, after all, *Grand*," the woman said with a smile.

~ 15 ~

The team of horses brought the carriage to a stop just past a row of fluttering American flags that extended out from the iconic Grand Hotel porch pillars. Since 1887, the hotel has served as a summer retreat for visitors to the island and still retains its legendary elegance and charm.

Emma jumped down from the taxi and looked around. She and her fellow passengers left the commotion of the downtown area behind, but a dynamic energy level was evident here too. Carriages and bicycles headed in all different directions. Smartly dressed staff members carried out their tasks while several tourists hurried past Emma. She stood in awe, admiring the scene.

Someone captured her attention and directed her through an open door into the reception area where she proceeded to the check in desk. The woman behind the counter welcomed her and with a smile confirmed her room was ready. Her luggage would be delivered there as soon as it arrived from the dock.

Emma giggled when the room key was presented. "Really? An actual key?" She couldn't recall if she ever stayed in a hotel that used metal keys, not a plastic card with a magnetic strip.

The desk attendant also politely reminded her about the Hotel's evening dress code. Emma smiled and nodded along, outwardly giving a cool, nonchalant appearance, but inside she felt a pang of panic and her mind rapidly processed the situation.

"I know I have the new pink sundress from Grandy, I can use that for tonight, but did I bring anything else that will work for tomorrow? I don't even remember what I packed. Did Grandy throw another dress in my bag without telling me? She must have known about this! Or maybe she wanted me to go shopping? She did give me the credit card. There might be a boutique here in the hotel, and I do remember seeing some stores in town. Maybe I need to check those out tomorrow?" She decided not to worry about it yet. She could figure something out later, after she settled in.

She gathered the key and her belongings, turned to her right, and headed up the stairs. A wide band of ruby colored carpet highlighted the way.

"Well, ooh la la, look at me the VIP on the red carpet," she joked.

When she reached the top of the stairway, the floor covering changed to a dramatic print. Large pops of red geranium flowers bloomed amid a trellis with green leaves on a black background. Everything around her was bursting with color.

"It's all so… so… lively! I need to up my interior design game. My apartment is a flat-out snoozer compared to this."

Following the instructions provided by the woman at the reception desk, she found herself in the parlor. The doors straight ahead led out to the long porch. To her left she could see the entrance to the dining room, demurely blocked off with a velvet rope until it was dinner time. Off to the side, stood a massive, polished turtle shell, a nod to the tribal legend about the origins of the island.   She took a right turn and leisurely made her way through the busy room, taking in the atmosphere and décor around her.

Afternoon High Tea had begun, and hotel guests were enjoying elegant refreshments while live harp music filled the air. Soft light filtered in through the large windows along the south-facing side of the long room. These were indeed true "picture windows." From each one the view of the porch, the island, and the lake beyond would have made a spectacular painting.

Furniture in the vast space was arranged in smaller, more intimate conversation groupings, just right for hosting clusters of hotel guests. Before she reached the far end of the parlor, she curiously peeked into what was labeled as the Trophy Room. It was decorated in tribute to a gorgeous award-winning Scottish Terrier and appeared to serve as a game room. A group of young teenagers played cards at a small square table at one end of the nook. One of them made a bold move during his turn and the rest offered various forms of admiration and protest.

"Hey!"

"No way!"

"Dude, what did you just do?"

Not wanting to interrupt their spirited game, she tiptoed out of the Trophy Room and upon reaching the doors at the end of the parlor, Emma entered another long hallway. "This building keeps going and going," she thought. She passed a few room numbers and then found the one matching her room key.

Each room at the hotel is decorated differently and opening the door to one for the first time reveals its own special magic. What would be behind her door?

Turning the key in the lock, she held her breath and pushed the door open to see what was inside.

$$\sim 16 \sim$$

She was greeted with a burst of sunshine and flowers.

"Goodness!" Emma said, "It's even colorful in here too!"

In contrast to the red, black, and green geranium motif used in the parlor, this room featured images of yellow roses everywhere. The walls were covered in a vibrant print of butter-colored blooms, accented by pops of lilies and fresh greenery. A white matelassé spread adorned the bed, and across the foot lay a coverlet decorated with giant yellow roses, even more substantial than the ones on the wallpaper.

Emma laid her backpack down on the dresser and continued to the far side of the room to look out the large windows. Her view stretched across the porch, then over the impeccably landscaped hotel grounds, and in the distance, she could see the lake. It was lovely. She turned around, kicked off her shoes and flopped exhausted onto the beautiful bed. She paused a moment and took it all in.

"I made it," she thought. "I did it. I really did it. I left my apartment, and nothing bad happened to me. I traveled hundreds of miles alone in my car, then on a boat, and finally in an actual horse-drawn carriage. As a solo traveler I have navigated my way to this beautiful, crazy, floral explosion of a room."

She closed her eyes and listened to the harp music drifting down the hallway from the parlor. "Is this moment real? Am I dreaming?" She opened her eyes again to check. She was still surrounded by roses and music and sunlight. It was not a hallucination; this was actually happening. She closed her eyes again.

"Thank you, Grandy," she whispered. "Thank you." With the nudge of her grandmother's encouragement, she was venturing out and beginning to prove to herself once again she could accomplish things in the world. Maybe she could still make her aspirations come true if she was brave enough to first let herself dream again.

It had been a long and sometimes challenging day, but now she began to let herself relax. She wanted to soak in the atmosphere of this moment and absorb these wonderful feelings deep into her memory.

A sharp noise awakened her.

Was that knocking?

Emma was lost in a rush of disorientation and panic.

Where was she?

Her eyes darted from the unfamiliar details on the high ceiling to the curtains and the roses on the wallpaper. Reality came into focus, and she gathered her wits.

Grand Hotel!

Her luggage!

What time was it?

How long had she been asleep?

"I'm coming!" she called out as she sprang up from the bed and met the porter at the door. After thanking him graciously, she checked the vintage-style alarm clock on the bedside table, comparing it to her wristwatch to ensure they were synchronized.

The check of the clock confirmed she had not missed dinner. Her initial wake-up confusion was cleared away. The brief period of deep relaxation followed by the adrenaline surge from the knock on the door left her feeling quite refreshed. There was still plenty of time to get ready and be presentable before the evening meal in the formal dining room.

The available preparation time was taking on increased significance as she surveyed her reflection in the bedroom mirror. The image peering back at her had a serious case of bedhead hair and was that the design from the matelassé pressed into one side of her face? What a sight she must have looked to the porter when she flung open her door!

"Hmm, I think I have another message from Grandy I'm supposed to read."

The initial excitement about arriving in her room made her forget about the next envelope. Then she had flopped on the bed and dozed off without reading it, so she searched for it now.

She found it in her backpack, "3. Open After Check In," and took a seat on one of the room chairs. Remembering the bombshell cell phone prohibition revealed in the last note, she stopped and made a small frown, wondering what the next revelation would be before she opened it. She hoped it wasn't another rule or restriction.

"Maybe she's limiting me to bread and water for this trip," she thought with a generous dose of sarcasm as she removed the folded paper.

Welcome to Mackinac Island, Emma!
I hope you enjoy your stay at Grand Hotel. I had a little surprise delivered for you. Check the closet.
Much Love,
Grandy

She bolted out of the chair and threw open the closet in the dressing area. There hung two gorgeous dinner dresses and a pair of elegant and glittery strappy sandals that would match both. "Aww, Grandy!" Emma said. Her grandmother had thought of everything!

After a long, relaxing shower, she dried and straightened her hair, then applied a light touch of makeup. She hadn't worn any in months and was amazed at how even a simple brush of mascara, a little blush and some lipstick made a difference.

Reviewing her new wardrobe options, she chose the navy blue sundress with large white gardenia print accents from the selection of two hanging in the closet. The dress was constructed with wide shoulder straps and a sweetheart neckline. It was nipped in at the waist and the skirt had a slight flare, reminding Emma of a 1950's silhouette. It fit perfectly and floated out a bit when she twirled. In addition to the lilac pendant, she added a pair of cute sparkly drop earrings to finish her ensemble. She was pleased she included those in her little bag of accessories. When she was ready to head to the dining room, she popped her key into her small satin clutch purse and opened the door.

Lost in thought about what she would find on the menu, Emma gave a small, startled gasp when she stepped into the hallway and saw someone standing there, right in front of her, coming out of a room directly opposite hers.

"Oh, excuse me," she apologized.

But then, she realized it wasn't a doorway: it was a large full-length mirror. The person she was looking at was her own reflection.

"Is that really me?"

A beautiful young woman was gazing back at her. For the first time in almost a year, she felt pretty.

~ 17 ~

Emma proceeded down the carpeted corridor toward the blurred murmurs of mingling hotel guests. The new shoes were a perfect fit. She wasn't there to try them on when Grandy purchased them, but her grandmother had some special gift for figuring these things out. It had been months since she had worn heels, so for the first few steps, she placed her feet somewhat more carefully than usual. She passed through the doorway, into the parlor, now filled with many more people than when she arrived at the hotel that afternoon.

The nightly party was in full swing. Smartly dressed hotel guests milled about, some with cocktails in hand, others seated in the small conversation clusters. The door to the porch swung open and a burst of laughter flowed in from outdoors along with a jovial group of vacationers.

From the hallway where Emma's room was located, it was a straight line to get to the dining room, but the hotel was so large it was about a football field away. With the evening dress code in effect, she took her time getting to her destination, enjoying the elegant cocktail party vibe along the way.

As she crossed the parlor, Emma gradually transitioned from walking cautiously in the sparkly sandals to secretly and subtly practicing her runway walk, silently humming the "I'm

Too Sexy/On the Catwalk" song, like she sometimes used to do for amusement in long hallways in her old office building.

She took random detours, casually weaving around several of the seating areas, over to admire artwork on the walls and other objet d'art, then looking out a window before looping back up to the main aisle again because, well, why not? People watching was one of her favorite hobbies and there was an abundance of it to be done here. She took a seat in one of the groupings of couches for a few minutes, to capture the atmosphere and enjoy the parade of other guests now clad in their evening finery.

"Having everyone dressed up for dinner makes it feel special," she observed. "It's a regular weeknight, but it feels like a holiday."

When she reached the far end of the parlor, she joined the short line of eager patrons waiting to be seated in the dining room, labeled in French as "Salle à Manger." She repeated the name in her head, in an exaggerated accent.

"Sahhhl ah Mon-Zhhayyy.

"See? I paid attention in French class" she thought as she wordlessly shared a polite smile with the family standing behind her. One side of the queue where she waited was flanked by bright red chairs. Above them hung a still-life painting of an opulent banquet table. One quick look at it and Emma's stomach growled loudly, reminding her just how long ago lunch had been. Thankfully, the line for entry notched forward like an efficient machine, and she was soon welcomed by the host at the door.

"How many in your party this evening?"

"Just one," Emma answered, attempting to sound upbeat but internally still fighting back the self-conscious feeling that was trying to bubble up.

"At least that sounded better than when I said it at lunch," she thought. The earlier meal alone had gone well, but the dining-by-yourself confidence battle was not a one-and-done thing for her. "It must be something that comes with practice." She shook off the discomfort as she was led through the busy room to a cozy two seat table.

Emma took her seat, and a member of the dining room staff swiftly cleared the place setting across from her. Somehow, that simple action made her feel unsettled. It outed her irreversibly as a solo diner.

"Table for two, rebranded as table for one. I guess now I can't tell anyone I'm waiting for someone else."

After readjusting her chair, her first instinct was to use her phone to check social media. She was glad she intentionally left the device in her room to avoid any temptation to cheat at Grandy's challenge. Still, she opened her tiny purse as if something in it needed attention. Emma stared at its minimalist contents for a moment: her room key and a tissue. She pulled out the metal key as if to examine it and then put it back in the purse.

"Well, that's good. Everything's normal in there. Glad I checked." Feeling sheepish, she closed the purse and set it aside.

There was an awkward moment where she did not know what to do with herself. Placing her hands on top of the table, she nervously drummed her fingertips, then searched for something she could fidget with, something to read. She wanted to check for email, to have the security of phone in hand, to disappear into the act of scrolling through screens, anything to avoid the awkward feeling of "everyone is staring at me and wondering why I am alone."

She scanned the room, and then felt a bit foolish. Just like at lunch, no one was staring. Why did she keep worrying about that? Was that what she thought whenever she saw a solo diner?

She questioned herself: "Am I the source of my own anxiety? Why can't people be thinking someone eating alone is empowered and independent."

Was that the image she now conveyed? She checked her posture, head up, shoulders slightly back.

"Fake it 'til you make it. Pretend like you've done this a million times," she told herself. "And remember, it doesn't matter what others think." She knew this was the right mindset, it's what Grandy would tell her. It's what Grandy would *do*. But sometimes it was still hard to put into practice.

"Maybe people don't like eating alone because they start to overthink everything!" She pressed her lips together to stifle a laugh and glanced around again. A few people had their phones out. There were some taking group shots and food photos but mostly people were engaged in conversation with each other or enjoying their meal. Emma occupied herself by watching the activity around her. Her gaze lingered a short while on each group of people. She didn't want to be caught staring.

The staff swirled through the busy space as if the large room was a stage in a choreographed culinary ballet. Water and wine glasses were filled, orders were taken, and elegantly plated meals were presented, everyone moving swiftly with precision, skill, and grace.

She ordered a glass of white wine and her waiter promptly arrived to present her with the evening's menu. Looking it over, her first thought was, "Ut oh. I might be in over my head here."

When she used to go out, she typically preferred to stick to a small collection of favorite restaurants, and she wasn't adventurous in her entrée choices. This new menu was a bit of a stretch for her. She couldn't rely on her usual backup plans of spaghetti or a hamburger. A few of the descriptions intimidated her, and she was unsure what to order, but then her server reappeared and asked if she had questions about the menu.

"Yes, I do," she said, then added jokingly, "How much time have you got?"

He set her fears at ease with appealing descriptions of each item she asked about. Once she understood what the choices were, she had a new dilemma: how to choose between the many things that all sounded delicious!

After making her selections, she took a sip of her sauvignon blanc and sat back to survey the room again. Periodically a parade of new diners would arrive, briskly following their guide in a single file as they were led to their table, while other clusters of satisfied patrons would depart at a more leisurely pace. A dapper four-piece band was stationed in a little alcove along the wall, filling the air with the pleasant notes of jazz standards.

One by one, the courses she chose were presented to her. Each one was gorgeously plated, and she again wished she had her phone to capture and share what she would be eating. "I'm a bit shocked at how often I'm wanting to text or check social media or take a picture," she admitted.

She focused on each dish as it was presented to her, absorbing all the various sensory details to tell Grandy about it later. Instead of taking its picture, she took in the colors and textures of each plate and noticed the structure of how it was arranged. Gently waving her hand over each dish, she made the aromas waft toward her nose. Each course brought forth a list of new adjectives: silky, lemony, crisp, and delicate. The first bite of each dish was seductively delicious, and she felt like she fell in love with every new plate.

"I don't think I've ever had a dining experience quite like this before," she marveled. Emma could tell this meal was waking up something asleep inside of her soul. "I've been living on frozen dinners and pizza delivery for far too long. The takeout I had with Grandy last night was fun, but this type of food and presentation style is on a completely different level. This is not something that could be delivered in a Styrofoam container or pulled from a microwave. It's not just about getting something to eat, it's an entertainment event, an artistic performance by the chef and staff."

She made a series of resolutions. "When I get home, I'm going to pick a friend I need to reconnect with and invite them out to a nice dinner at a new restaurant. And I need to start eating better and learn how to cook. Maybe I'll take a class and invest in a few time-tested cookbooks. I'll learn to master the classics instead of surviving on microwave and instant stuff."

She thoughtfully swirled the last bit of wine in the bottom of her glass. "Here's to lilacs, and here's to right now. It's time to start doing those things I've always wanted to do and have been putting off for 'someday.'"

Raising the glass to her lips, she finished off the last of the pale liquid. "'Someday' is a deceptively dangerous word. It lulls a person into complacency."

Finally, it was time for dessert. After mulling over the list of temptations, she selected Grand Hotel's signature ice cream pecan ball. The meal had drawn her into a pleasant state of satiety, a level just before "food coma."

Emma was engrossed in the rich, toasty aroma of her after-dinner coffee when something the band was playing struck a chord in her subconscious. Her attention shifted to the music which had been subtly and smoothly percolating in the background. She listened as the piano played the melody for a few more seconds and identified the jazzy little riff she had been humming along with as a cleverly rearranged version of a Pink Floyd classic rock tune. She was flooded with memories of her parents. Pink Floyd was one of her father's favorite bands. Her heart ached and tears welled up in her eyes.

"I wish my mom and dad were here with me, sharing this experience. I'm having their Someday, right now, in this moment." Despite the wave of pain and loneliness, she was sure this was a sign she was right where she was supposed to be. She closed her eyes for a few seconds and smiled, picturing what would have happened if her parents had been there with her.

Her dad would be leaning over the table and singing the lyrics at her. Her mother would have rolled her eyes and swatted his shoulder with the back of her hand, shaking her head in faux embarrassment, but then by the time they got to the refrain, she'd be singing along too. Her parents owned a great music collection, with a library of hundreds of vintage vinyl records and a carefully maintained turntable from that era on which to play them.

She opened her eyes and saw the fiftyish-looking woman at the next table regarding her quizzically, the universal expression of "Are you OK?" Emma smiled, casually wiping away a tear and trying to make it appear as if perhaps she was extracting something that had gotten into her eye.

"Eyelash," she said to the woman, who nodded in understanding. Emma thought about leaving it at that, but then leaned slightly closer to the neighboring table and pointed to the band.

"They're playing Pink Floyd," she said, trying to sound upbeat, or at least not sad. "This song reminds me of my dad."

The neighboring couple both laughed. "Pink Floyd? From this band?" They glanced over at the musicians and listened for a moment. "Well, gosh I guess it is! I knew it sounded familiar, but I couldn't quite place it. You've got a good ear," the man said, chuckling a bit.

The woman's brow furrowed inquisitively. She leaned forward and asked in a loud whisper, "Are you here alone?"

"Here it comes," Emma thought, "the emotional gauntlet." Her mood was already tweaked from the Pink Floyd memories. She needed to proceed cautiously.

Digging deep, she summoned her courage and answered without a tinge of self-pity or sadness, "Yes, the trip is a gift from my grandmother, kind of a technology detox retreat. I've never stayed here before. It's wonderful."

For a split second she thought about adding more detail surrounding her parents, but stopped short, "no oversharing with people you've just met," she thought. "Keep it together."

"Oh, technology detox, very nice, it would be a great place for that," the woman said. Emma nodded in agreement.

The woman continued, "I wasn't sure if you were vacationing or here on business."

Then her husband added, "We wondered if you got stood up at the altar or something." The woman, horrified, moved in a way that indicated she had swiftly kicked her husband's leg under the table. "Oh Steven!"

Both Emma and the man laughed lightheartedly, but his laugh turned to a scowl after the kick.

"I'm sorry," the woman said sincerely. "I do apologize for the rudeness of my husband. Please ignore him."

Emma waved her hand in a nonchalant "it's nothing" gesture, trying to channel Grandy's composure, proud of her grace in the awkward moment but also wishing the conversation topic would change. Behind her smile, she silently prayed with every fiber of her being for them not to ask any questions about her dating life.

"Don't go there, don't go there, don't go there."

The direction of the dialogue and the man's casual comment (innocently made as an attempt at humor) hit the bullseye on one of her insecurities. She knew she was hovering at the upper limit of what she could manage. For the moment she was keeping her feelings confined in a hastily knitted emotional safety net, but if the conversation pressed into more sensitive areas, she was concerned the fragile mesh would begin to unravel. Emma was frozen in place, holding her breath, dreading where the conversation would go next.

Much to her relief, the woman rapidly went on, taking the conversation in a less volatile direction. "Since this is your first visit to the hotel, I'm not sure if you know this. If you go down the long set of front steps to the flower garden and past the pool house, there is a little trail that leads down to the lake shore. It's a nice place to catch the sunset. And there's live music and dancing in the ballroom later. Maybe we'll see you there?"

Emma smiled and resumed breathing, adding, "Thank you for the suggestions. Maybe you will!"

The man rose from the table and was carefully rubbing his shin, indicating the kick from his wife was more than just a glancing blow.

Emma suspected an ice pack instead of dancing might be a more accurate forecast of his future.

~ 18 ~

Emma hadn't noticed it while seated and eating her meal, but now that she was up from her table and walking toward the exit of the dining room, the glass of wine she enjoyed with dinner was making her feel warm and fuzzy. She looked down at her feet on the brightly patterned carpet. "These sandals are super cute, but the high heels are a bit much for my after dinner exploring. If I'm heading down to check out the hotel grounds and the shoreline, I might need something different." She made the wise decision to take a short detour and stop back at her room to switch into more practical flat sandals. There would be no ankle twisting during her evening exploration!

Feeling liberated by the change in footwear, Emma scooted out the front doors, bounded effortlessly down the first set of hotel stairs, then crossed the street to the much longer staircase that descended this way and that to the garden below.

She meandered along the flower-lined path, stopping to casually admire the showy blooms as the daylight began to fade. Assortments of candy-colored blossoms filled the carefully tended beds bordering the walkway. Areas more in the shadows featured jewel box-like collections of emerald, jade, and ivory-colored hostas and other shade loving plants.

As her dining room neighbor had described, she eventually came upon the pool house. Peering in the direction of the patio area, she considered her options for the next day, "That right there is a definite possibility for how I could spend a chunk of time tomorrow," she noted confidently. "I love lounging by a good pool, and this one looks amazing."

The pathway transitioned into a grove of trees, a pocket of forest within the hotel grounds, and Emma found herself with a choice of trails. One curved back in the direction toward town and the other dropped down slightly, toward the shore. Emma chose the latter and followed it until it exited the shelter of the woods. She stood at the edge of the two-lane paved bicycle route circling the island. On the opposite side of the road from her was the rocky beach.

Clusters of people out for a pleasant evening stroll meandered along the boardwalk that extended out a short way from town. A few of the more adventurous individuals left the solid footing of the sidewalk and picked their way through the loose rocks on the beach, laughing and posing for individual photos and group shots. Emma felt a small twinge of envy as she fought off a familiar phone craving, an urge to take a selfie or post something. She fidgeted with her little clutch purse and crossed her bare arms to give her extremities something to do.

Several women she guessed to be close to her mother's age huddled near the "Is It You" tree made famous in the classic romantic film "Somewhere in Time." One of them burst out in hysterical giggles. Hearing the unusual laughter, Emma managed a weak, lonely half-smile. Two of the women near the iconic tree now comically reenacted the movie scene with exaggerated drama.

"I miss my friends and being part of a group, having inside jokes to share and laugh about. And having fun with them. Ugh, I hate being so serious. I want to be silly again."

She toyed with the idea of watching the movie the women had been acting out as she sat by the pool the next day, until she once again remembered her phone was off-limits. She rolled her eyes with a tinge of bitterness. "I guess I'll be reading a book or napping by the pool instead." She still hadn't fully come to terms with being disconnected from the internet.

It was a peaceful evening along the shore. She walked for a few more yards, then stopped and took in the view. The breeziness that added excitement to the ferry crossing in the afternoon had died down. Lake Huron was calm and above it wisps of clouds reflected the pink tones of the setting sun.

A handful of kayakers with synchronized strokes glided through the glassy bay, headed back home after a sunset tour. "That's probably fun too," Emma thought, feeling a bit jealous. "Adventures are better when you have someone to share them with though." With the side of her foot, she casually kicked an egg-sized rock that had found its way onto the walkway. It bounced off into the brush, coming to rest under a blooming rosa rugosa.

Emma took a long sweeping view of everything she could see. "So, all this activity goes on, year after year – the controlled commotion of the dining room, the hustle-bustle of the town, the bicyclists going round and round the island. It's timeless, always the same. That's why they could use this setting for the scenes in "Somewhere in Time" set a century ago. Things don't change here. For everyone else, their world is going on as it's always been, but my life has ground to a halt. And if it ever does get going again, it won't be *anything* like it used to be. Everything will be different. It's just not *fair!*"

She looked up at the stately mansions on the bluff. They were nothing like the modest bungalow in which she had grown up nor her current apartment, but the lamp lights shining warmly in their windows still spoke the language of "home," and it sparked an intense longing for her family and for the home of her past that was now gone forever.

"I don't know where I belong anymore or with whom. It seems like everyone else is here as a couple or a family or a group. And I'm here by myself. I feel so awkward, but why? I've been alone for most of the past year. Why am I not used to it yet? Why is it that seeing these people laughing and sharing experiences just totally wrecks me inside? I travelled all this way to make things better, and it's like the old sadness came right along with me."

An avalanche of negative thoughts crashed down and all the positivity she worked to build was buried. "What if my friends won't take me back again? And if they don't, what if I can't make any new friends? What if I'm not even capable of having fun anymore? Maybe I can't do this. What if I'm not ready to start again? Maybe this trip was a big mistake."

Her body responded with the old familiar tightening of her chest and tears filled her eyes, blurring her vision so she could no longer see the lovely homes on the bluff nor the sunset. She wished she could escape the island and somehow be miraculously transported back to her apartment in an instant, crawl under the covers of her familiar bed, and cry until she fell asleep.

Emma spun around to cross the road and without thinking she stepped in front of a large group of rapidly approaching cyclists. She froze in place as she looked up and saw her own image dimly reflected in the lenses of the peloton leader's mirrored sunglasses. The group of alert riders deftly split, swerved around her, and reassembled like a swarm of bees en route to a new hive. In their wake, she gasped for breath and called out in a feeble voice after them, "Sorry!"

Emma tried to not think about the catastrophe she nearly caused. The encounter amplified her emotional state, and she began to run, clumsily stumbling back up the wood chip covered path between sobs, getting small pieces of bark uncomfortably caught between her foot and her sandal. Reaching the intersection where the path split in several directions, she was temporarily disoriented. Which way led back to the hotel? She started down one path, then decided it wasn't the correct one and abruptly turned to go in the opposite direction. And that's when fate hit her squarely in the face.

At the corner of the trail stood a large lilac bush with one fluffy plume stretched out into the pathway. With tears filling her eyes, Emma didn't see it as she kept her gaze downward to keep from tripping over rocks and roots. Then, she glanced up and the lilac puff smacked her, right across her cheeks, nose, and mouth. It was gentle, but still attention-getting.

"Oh!" Emma exclaimed in an outburst of surprise. She stopped, turned around, and looked at what she had run into.

"A lilac? Seriously?" Between awkward sobs she tentatively reached out to it, feeling the softness of the flowers. Moving forward she gently lowered her face into the fragrant plume and inhaled its sweet scent. She took a step back, brushed away several tears, and surveyed the rest of the tall shrub. From that angle in the dim light, she could see there were several sprigs still in bloom. She was compelled to touch each one within her reach.

Her breathing was more controlled now. The intense surge of emotion was dissipating. Footsteps approached on the woodchips. She faced the shrubbery and played with the flowers a bit, keeping her back turned as people passed behind her on the path. "I'm sure I'm a mess," she thought. "I don't want to walk across the porch and through the crowded hotel parlor with tear-stained cheeks, red nose, and most likely smeared mascara."

After the group of people passed, she evaluated her options. Where could she go if she wasn't ready to head up to the hotel yet?

There was a pretty fountain located near the center of the wide lawn and no people were in the area. It was a good plan.

"I'll head over there to collect myself first."

$$\sim 19 \sim$$

The June sun was below the horizon now, and the northern Michigan sky pulled its summer weight blanket of darkness gently across the island. Emma crept cautiously along the edge of the garden, following the undulating border dotted by patches of light from strategically placed lanterns. The fountain was partially surrounded by a semi-circle of wooden benches. Emma took a seat, threw her head back and heaved an enormous sigh.

"I'm supposed to be finding lilacs, and one found me, wham, right in the kisser," she said, throwing a punch to the air. "That's kind of ironic. And pretty funny," she admitted. Her lips curved into a faint smile. The island itself had given her a bit of a reminder of why she was there.

The splashing sound of the fountain created a comforting curtain of white noise and its clear water danced and sparkled in carefully aimed beams of light. Emma gazed up at the elegant hotel, perched on the hill above her. Illuminated for the evening, it made a striking scene.

Grandy adored this place and now, in the moonlight, the atmosphere held an element of enchantment. For as long as Emma could remember, her grandmother had been passionate about the island. Grandy shared her fondness for it with her daughter, Ellen, Emma's mother. Now Grandy was sharing that affection for the island with her granddaughter too.

One specific photo of Grandy was always Emma's favorite. Her grandmother's name was Edith, but this photo explained why everyone, not just Emma, called her "Grandy."

In the photo, she posed in front of Grand Hotel and modeled what had become her signature look, one that seemed to symbolize several key design elements of the building. Her crisp white blazer was a classic, like the timeless style of the hotel's construction. The long mint colored silk scarf casually looped around her neck echoed the cool hues on the ceiling of the hotel's world-famous porch. Grandy's earlobes were adorned with small red crystal rosettes, similar to the familiar red geraniums lining the length of the porch, and the outfit was topped by a jaunty green fedora, her "roof." The final flourish was a vintage yellow and white Armani handbag which dangled from one elbow, a near perfect match to the cheerful hotel awnings.

Her unwavering story was that the whole ensemble had "just come together" with random elements packed in her luggage. She swore (with a wink) she hadn't intended to match her outfit to the hotel. At lunch, one of her friends called her "Grand Edith", which was shortened to "Grand E", and finally by dinner that evening and from that point forward she became known as "Grandy."

Emma studied the beautiful building and thought of her grandmother's photograph. "In a way, I feel like she's with me here right now." And in spite of the slight chill in the evening air, at that moment she felt warm and protected.

Emma stretched out her long legs, shook out a small piece of bark from one sandal, then stared at her toes and feet while thoughts about the last day and a half scrolled through her head.

"Yesterday morning when I woke up, I had no idea I would be sitting here today, on Mackinac Island." She shook her head in disbelief. This trip was unconventional, that was for sure. "If Grandy hadn't shown up at my door yesterday, I would probably be scrolling through some random social media feed, or zoned out binge-watching something mindless, or falling asleep on my couch listening to a podcast."

Then a surprising thought occurred to her. Emma reached up and laid the palm of her hand on the top of her head. She hadn't had one of those awful headaches today! There were periods of stress, but no migraine. Was it the lack of screen time or the general distraction from her usual routine that made the difference? Or was it the fresh air and being out of the same four walls? She didn't know for sure. But she was certain this was one of the few days out of the past year without one of those episodes. She hadn't even believed a pain-free day was possible anymore.

Emma listened to the burbling sound of the fountain. A distant peal of laughter emerged from the darkness on the far side of the lawn. She silently thanked Grandy for this gift, for this trip, for shaking up her world in a good way. Most of the surprises she'd had recently were bad ones. The past year was an uncomfortable blur, and she knew she needed to restart her life, but she had fallen into that very deep hole and felt powerless to get out of it. She didn't know where her life reset button was.

Worst of all were the feelings of guilt anytime she was blessed with a faint glimmer of happiness. Grandy told her it was possible to still miss her parents and be happy too. But how?

Months earlier, she talked to the grief counselor about this dilemma. He tried to help her find the balance between love and loss, but at that time she only nodded along politely as he attempted to guide her. She had not been able to put the offered advice into practice.

Now, perhaps, she was ready to try again. She could think about her parents and remember the happy times, moments they had experienced as a family on this special, timeless island. She could live out the lessons they taught her and honor them by being her true self. In the aftermath of great tragedy, life still goes on. It would only magnify the loss if she gave up on living.

She smiled thinking about hearing the Pink Floyd song played during dinner and again imagined the funny way in which her parents would have reacted. "For that moment it was like they were here with me. Maybe that's how Grandy says I can do this. I can connect happy remembrances and new experiences. That right there is a new lilac for me." She recalled her thoughts from earlier in the day about learning how to ride her bike and overcoming her fear of the bear, and then visualized a vase with several lilac plumes in it, one for each memory or new moment. She would try to collect more. She wanted a large bouquet of happy memories from this trip, both old ones and new, a big extravagant bunch of lilacs!

So far, she encountered two actual blooming lilacs shrubs on the island, the woman in the carriage pointed out one and the other literally smacked her in the face. It was a start, but she needed to find more. It troubled her she was still passively wandering through this experience, waiting for the world to present her with the flowers.

"I suppose being where the lilacs are is the first step, and now I will need to open my eyes and go look for them," she said. "I want to find the flowers and uncover the memories. I want to see the colors of the world around me. Smell the sweet fragrances, and well, OK, maybe a few not so sweet ones too if that's what it takes," she joked, humorously considering the inevitable byproduct of the island's horses.

She continued thoughtfully, "I don't want to float blindly through my time here on the island. It should be more purposeful, with intention. I know I've missed a lot of life during the past year. I'm grateful for this chance to get back on track. I can't afford to waste this opportunity. The self-pity stops right here, right now," she resolved. She looked at the beautiful fountain, at the elegant hotel, and touched the crystal lilac pendant around her neck, absorbing every detail of this special moment and locking in the promise to herself.

Another jewel of Grandy's wisdom was also gaining more clarity. If she still had access to her phone, would she be fully present in her surroundings, or would her mind have been elsewhere in cyberspace? Would she have been able to sort through her thoughts, or would every twinge of discomfort compel her to seek online distraction instead of working through her feelings?

"I will admit having a camera would be nice," she confessed. "I do have a way to deal with it, though. I will take the sketchbook with me when I venture out tomorrow."

Grandy was right about travelling solo too. Emma thought again about all the "firsts" she had accomplished that day, things she had never done by herself. She was definitely stepping out of her comfort zone.

"Knowing I can do these things is priceless. I really am learning how to work the magic myself. I've been saying I felt powerless, but maybe I have actually had the power all along. I just didn't understand how to tap into it." She floated these thoughts around in her mind, letting them take shape, enabling her to accurately remember the lesson in the future.

Next year she would love to come back here with Grandy or share this island experience with friends, but for this moment, for right now, she was eager to find out what else she could accomplish. "It's not going to always be easy, but it will pay off," she reminded herself. "In the future, when I get scared or have doubts, I need to remember this moment and draw strength from it!"

Emma took a deep breath, absorbing scents of water and flowers and cedar. Her emotions were more in balance. Her face was no longer aflame. She stood up to smooth out the skirt of her sundress. In a quick movement she licked the tip of one finger and ran it under each of her eyes to blend away any flecks of smeared mascara. There was a tiny postage stamp-sized mirror in the flap of her clutch purse, and she maneuvered herself so the light from one of the garden lanterns provided enough brightness to check her reflection. Perhaps it was not her best look, but it no longer appeared she had been crying. She was presentable enough to pass back through the busy parlor and return to her room without attracting negative attention if she didn't dawdle.

She shivered a little against the evening chill in the air as she returned to the garden path that led to the stairs and headed up, up, and up again. How many stairs were there?! By the time she conquered them all she was warm again.

"Now if I'm red in the face, it's definitely from all the cardio," she thought.

At the top of the invigorating climb, she glanced both ways to check for carriages, horses, and bicycles (one close call was enough for the evening), and then crossed the road before ascending the last set of red carpeted stairs to the hotel. She allowed herself to smile at the absurdity of getting slapped in the face by the lilac plume, and then held that comical thought and amused expression as she passed quickly through the groups of guests dotting the parlor.

Her room had been neatly prepared for evening while she was away. Emma changed into the t-shirt and drawstring bottoms she brought for pajamas and hung her dinner dress back in the closet. She brushed her teeth, then set aside the pillow chocolate as a "first thing when I wake up" treat before climbing into bed.

Emma listened to the gentle murmur of guests on the hotel porch outside her window. She couldn't hear specifics of what was being said. There were just pleasant voices close by, conversations and laughter. It was an enjoyable, comforting sound, bringing back faint old memories of when she was young, safely tucked into her bed while the grownups still socialized and enjoyed their evening entertainment in the living room. She plucked that lilac memory and added it to the others in her imaginary vase.

"I cherish this memory but I'm not that little girl anymore. Those days are gone. I'm a responsible adult and I acknowledge this trip is a turning point, a watershed experience," she considered. "A dividing line between sheltered reliance on others and thoughtful independence, between the way it once was, and the way it now will be. My parents started me off with a beautiful life, and now it's up to me to continue it. I'm at the point where it will be more painful to hang on to the past than to change."

Emma felt comforted, loved, and exhausted. Snuggling deeper under the covers, she whispered prayers of gratitude for making it safely to the island and for all the beautiful memories and new experiences she encountered that day. Grandy had indeed given her a special gift, and she was blessed with wonderful parents.

She began to think about all the different things she wanted to do the next day, and before she reached the end of the list, she drifted off to sleep.

~ 20 ~

Emma could tell it was morning by the sounds around her, even without opening her eyes. She lay in bed, listening to the musical cadence of horse hooves as they passed by the hotel. She imagined who it was. It could be a team pulling a carriage taking people into town, or perhaps a delivery wagon with cargo going somewhere farther out on the island. There was a snorty whoosh, a metallic jingle, and the clipped shout of the driver. The traffic noises were different here – no honking horns, no squeal of car tires on pavement, no revving engines.

When she opened her eyelids, she saw daylight and the sunny yellow roses on the wallpaper. She had slept deeply, the best sleep she'd had in months. Wondering what time it was, she automatically reached out to the nightstand at her right, where she kept her phone at home. There was a fleeting jolt of panic when the device wasn't where she expected it to be, but then she reminded herself with a snap of her fingers, "no phone." Instead, she propped herself up on her elbows and focused on the face of the alarm clock.

7:05am. She gave a small "oh, yay!" There was plenty of time to get ready, have breakfast, and tackle an adventure. She unwrapped the chocolate she had set aside before she crawled into bed and popped it into her mouth.

"Here's to a sweet day!"

Between the good night's sleep and an invigorating shower, she was restored and ready for a bit of discovery. "I'll do some exploring this morning," she proclaimed as she examined her clothing options. "I'll rent a bike to take a spin around the island and find some lilacs. Then after it warms up, I'll check out the awesome pool this afternoon." Thinking it might be chilly as she rode next to the water for most of the 8-mile loop, she dressed in light blue capris and a pale-yellow t-shirt then topped it with her favorite pink hoodie.

Before leaving her room, she opened the backpack and fished out the next envelope in the sequence of Grandy's letters. This one was labeled, "4. Open At Breakfast, Day 2." It felt different, a bit heavier than the previous one, like there was something additional tucked inside along with the usual note.

The first message yesterday morning revealed the hotel location. She lost her phone privileges in the second. The third announced the gift of the two beautiful dinner dresses. What would this one reveal? Another restriction? Another gift? Something different? Emma took the envelope with her as she left to go to breakfast.

The large dining room radiated a bright and cheerful atmosphere as Emma followed the energetic hostess down the aisle. "Clearly this woman has already had her morning coffee," she assessed, increasing her speed to keep up. The hostess made a sharp turn and led Emma to a small two seat table right next to the window.

"Score!" thought Emma, feeling a tiny surge of victory. She noticed these prime tables the previous evening, the ones with a view out over the hotel's porch, and now this one was hers. The coffee cup was promptly filled, and she requested a glass of orange juice. Placing Grandy's envelope on the table above her plate, she headed over to the buffet area.

Her original strategy was to try a few small tastes of things, to avoid feeling weighed down for her day of exploring, but by the time she made her way back to her seat, her plate was generously heaped with a wide assortment of offerings, including eggs, potatoes, sausage, and fruit. "I'm going to have a busy day, and I need sustenance," she justified. As she devoured each item on her plate, she gazed out the window at the waving flags on the porch and the sparkling lake in the distance. What a beautiful day to search for lilacs!

She popped the last bit of a flaky breakfast pastry into her mouth. After thoroughly wiping her fingers on her napkin, she reached for the latest envelope from Grandy. She unsealed it and withdrew a folded sheet of paper.

When she opened the note, a separate item slid out and fluttered into her lap. Emma retrieved it, leaned back in her chair, and gave it a good long look.

It was a photo of her with her parents from one of their Mackinac Island vacations. She was young, perhaps five years old and her parents stood on either side of her. Her mother's hand rested on Emma's shoulder. Behind them was a whitewashed stone wall and a metal plaque with some text just enough out of focus that she couldn't quite make out what it said. Off to the left side she could see a sign indicating it was taken at the Fort. On the folded paper that held the photo, her grandmother's familiar handwriting revealed the following instructions,

Find this spot today. Have a stranger take your photo there and ask them to email it to me.

"OK, that's weird," Emma announced out loud, immediately glancing up to see if anyone overheard her outburst. She shook her head. Grandy's free-spirited eccentricities were usually fun, but this one would be more challenging to deal with.

"Wouldn't it be easier to take a selfie? But ah yes, then I would need my phone which instead is stuffed in a drawer in my room," she considered. Emma rolled her eyes. She re-folded the sheet of paper and put it back into the envelope.

"Well, that will be a ridiculous exercise. I will deal with it later, but first I have a bike ride to conquer!" She downed the remainder of her morning coffee in one swift gulp and strolled out of the dining room to get ready for her adventures.

$$\sim 21 \sim$$

Emma ran through a mental checklist and made sure she had everything she might need for her excursion in her backpack: sunscreen, sunglasses, water bottle, granola bar, sketchbook and pencils, room key, and wallet. It felt weird leaving without her phone, but what was the point of lugging it around? Today would be old school. Low tech. She picked up an island map from the concierge desk. It showed the route she was going to take was just a big uneven circle around the island. Grand Hotel was an unmistakable landmark. There was literally no possible way to get lost.

At the hotel bike rental desk, she selected a light blue single speed cruiser with a wire frame basket in front. She tossed her backpack casually into the carrier, fastened the helmet strap under her chin, and pedaled off down the path toward the street.

She rode her spin bike often during the past year, but this was different. "It's like comparing a video chat with a face-to-face discussion."

Her balance instincts awakened. There was a breeze on her face, beams of sun in her eyes, and occasional bumps, ruts, and obstacles to be avoided. None of these were captured on her indoor workouts. And there were actual hills not resistance adjustments! She tested the brakes to get a feel of how effective they were in case she needed them. They were adequately grippy, but the rear brake gave a little squeal as the pad connected with the wheel rim.

The weight of the items in the front basket played with her center of gravity. Even though the backpack wasn't excessively heavy she could still feel how it made a difference. She wobbled a bit, but quickly became accustomed to it. Soon her attention shifted from maintaining her balance to observing the sights around her.

After initially coasting down the hill from the hotel, she now had a straight, flat ride through town. She still had to be alert. There were pedestrians to dodge, squadrons of other bikes with unpredictable wobbly and distracted tourists, an assortment of carriages, and of course the inevitable "obstacles" one encounters wherever there are horses. Fudge shops pumped seductive sugar and vanilla scented aromas out over the sidewalks, and savory wafts of breakfasty smells lingered in the air as restaurant and hotel kitchens wrapped up their early meal service.

The streets in town were beginning to fill up as ferries shuffled through the harbor, bringing eager tourists to the island and returning reluctant departing vacationers to the "real" world.

"I don't want to even think about that part yet," she thought as she eyed people entering the terminal. "So, I won't!"

Ambitious bicycle porters hustled skillfully balanced loads of luggage off to their destinations. Emma imagined trying to handle a similar load on her bike. "If one little backpack in my basket makes me wobble, I can't imagine maneuvering a whole load of full suitcases, let alone dodging tourists and horses. That's totally out of my league," she said, in awe of the porters' skill.

The whitewashed structure of historic Fort Mackinac stood vigilantly on the hillside overlooking the picturesque town. In 1780, after determining a Mackinaw City fort on the mainland was too vulnerable to attack, the British established a fort on the island. It switched back and forth from British to American control several times until 1815, when it was returned to the control of the United States for the last time.

Reaching its perimeter, Emma pulled over to the side of the road and sorted out her plan for the day. "Somewhere in the Fort complex is the spot from the photo in Grandy's envelope, but I'm not ready to get off the bike yet. I'll tackle that task after my ride. And before the pool."

For this moment, she wanted to enjoy her morning and keep her eyes open for any remaining late season lilacs still in bloom. As soon as she thought about them, she spotted several, right in front of the Fort, pink and purple and white.

"I spy lilacs," she thought and added a bunch to the imaginary vase where she was collecting them. "Did I will them into being?" she wondered. "Think about the lilacs, and perhaps they shall appear!"

She pedaled forward and read a small sign at the side of the curb. The quirky little marker announced this simple narrow road (used mostly by bikes and horses) was indeed an official state highway. Enlighted by this bit of trivia, she resumed her journey again.

Businesses and shops on her right were replaced by a neatly arranged network of docks and boat slips, and a small-scale replica of the Statue of Liberty perpetually keeping watch over the island marina. Signs along the road indicated a museum, an art café, and a butterfly house, each one sparking a little flame of interest in her. With each passing landmark, historic home, or inn, the crowd of tourists thinned out a bit more until after the sprawling Old Mission resort where the highway turned away from the town and headed around to the other, less developed portion of the island.

The rock-strewn lakeshore now lay to Emma's right and the island's limestone bluffs rose up on the opposite side. Periodically clusters of bicyclists and pedestrians pulled off onto the narrow shoulder, reviewing maps, swigging from water bottles, and snapping photos, selfies, group shots, and videos. The scenery was beautiful. As the narrow gray ribbon of road unwound ahead of her, the steep forested hillside made a green wedge cutting into the blues of azure sky above and turquoise water below. She pedaled slowly, coasted often, and breathed in the refreshing breeze off the lake. Each inhale brought a dose of serenity and beauty. With every exhale she shed a small quantity of the tension and frustration which had built up over the past year.

"I need to buy myself a new bicycle. An outdoor one. My spin bike is fine for rides when it's freezing and icy but on days like this, I should be outside. With friends. At a park."

Not far out of town, Emma spied a large group of people gathered ahead of her, partially blocking the road, and she redirected the focus of her attention from appreciating the natural beauty back to navigating a route through the crowd. Her curiosity grew. "What's going on up there?" She rode a short distance past the assembly and then pulled off on the rocky shoulder to stop and get a better glimpse of what was attracting their attention. "Oh!" she noted in surprise. "It's the Arch!"

The graceful shape of Arch Rock curved over the top of the high bluff. Was the dramatic stone formation hidden from view by the trees as she approached, or was she hypnotized by the color of the tranquil blue waters on the opposite side of the road? If not for the crowd calling attention to it, she most likely would have rolled right by and missed it on the bluff high above. She was starting to do better at noticing her surroundings but there was so much to see here.

Her hand instinctively reached into her hoodie pocket for her phone, but nope, impulse denied. "Oh, come on!" she muttered in frustration. "This is totally photo worthy."

She didn't need to stop for a break because of fatigue. However, her interest in the unusual rock formation was strong, and the area was quite pretty. She felt like taking a longer, more leisurely view of the area. "What's the rush, I've got all day." It was a small luxury to not be committed to a schedule. She found an out of the way, mostly level spot to park her bike.

She dismounted and nudged the kickstand into place. Emma removed her helmet and tossed it into the wire bike basket. Leaning over, she vigorously shook out her hair, combing it with her fingers to lessen the helmet-head effect, then grabbed her backpack and began searching to find a suitable flat, dry rock she could use as a bench.

Emma picked her way along the shore to where a large, even slab of boulder gave an excellent view of both the island's rugged coast and the rock formation. She took a seat, then unzipped her backpack, withdrew the sketchpad, and retrieved one of the pencils from the pocket where they had been stowed. Her eyes swept over the scenery.

The iconic limestone formation of Arch Rock rose nearly 150 feet above the lake and created a semi-circular frame around a portrait of blue sky, leafy trees, and seemingly tiny tourists who climbed up to the observation platform on the opposite side of the arch.

She recalled the day long ago when she took the island tour with her parents, the same day she was denied a trip in the fancy Grand Hotel carriage. Little Emma and her parents visited Arch

Rock with a group of other tourists in the large sight-seeing wagon, pulled by a team of strong and beautiful draft horses. Passengers eagerly hopped out at each stop and then the driver would remind them to be back at the designated time, adding the warning, "We will leave without you," for emphasis.

"After he said that, I was paranoid we were going to get left behind," Emma recalled, frowning. "Gosh, I worried about the oddest things as a kid, all the time, even on vacation."

She reminisced how she bravely climbed the steps to the Arch Rock observation area, holding her father's hand to feel safe. On the viewing platform, he lifted her up so she could see, and Emma remembered looking through the hole of the arch, seeing tiny kayakers in their slim, colorful boats out in the blue lake water. And now here she was on the lake side, gazing back at the tourists on the other side of the arch, like peering through some magic time portal to where she once had been long ago.

The wind made small waves lap against the weathered rocks around her and fluttered the sheets of paper as she opened the sketchbook cover. She ran her hand over the pages to smooth them down. Once she used to love to sketch and draw and paint, but that was a lifetime ago. Everything was electronic now. She was much more likely to type on a device than to pick up a pen or pencil. She couldn't remember the last time she created a drawing or even doodled on a piece of paper. "Months? Probably years," she said. She hadn't drawn anything since her parents' accident. Before that she was focused on school, then launching her post-college career and she let her hobbies languish. But now the sketchbook rested gently on her left forearm and her fingers curled around the right edge. She remembered this posture. It was natural and familiar.

Her pencil began to move easily across the page as she filled in the shapes of the bluff, the arch, and the trees. Her eyes alternated between the sketchbook and the scene in front of her. Occasionally, she would pause and swat away a bug, or use the eraser to make an adjustment on a line. Taking a bit of artistic license, she added a lilac bush off to one side of the arch, to acknowledge her earlier happy memory of their sightseeing stop here.

Emma considered breaking into the bundle of colored pencils, to add multi-hued accents, but for right now she opted to work in various shades of gray graphite from one single pencil, ranging from dark to light on the white page. She was safe from the waves where she sat, but she didn't want to be fumbling with too many different drawing tools as she perched on the boulder. Her face made a sad expression as she imagined dropping a pencil and having it fall between the rocks. Maybe it would be a good creative exercise though, pretending to lose a specific color, green or blue or yellow, and then being forced improvise, to work without it. Emma liked the idea, but if she was going to try that she wanted it to be something she chose willingly, not something she was forced into by clumsiness. The colors would stay safely stowed and be saved for a less risky location, and she made notes on the back of the sketch to add them in later.

The more she thought about it, the monochrome drawing was appropriate for the moment. She was resurrecting her outlook on life. She thought she knew where the colors would eventually go, but she wasn't feeling bold enough yet to commit to applying the hues to the page. For now, she was working on the shape of things.

When her drawing was finished, she held it up to do a side-by-side comparison with the actual arch. There were a few elements of it she struggled to get right, but it was, all-in-all, a decent likeness of the familiar landmark.

"Hey, that's pretty good," a voice behind her announced. Startled, Emma jumped a bit and turned her head. She was so focused on working on the sketch that she hadn't noticed a teenage boy wading up behind her to survey her work over her shoulder. "Did you just draw that?" he asked.

She nodded, "Um, yep, I did!" Slightly embarrassed, she snapped the sketchbook shut and clipped the pencil to the cover. "I haven't sketched anything in a long time," she said modestly, attempting to explain any shortcomings he may have seen.

"Well, it should be in one of those, like, galleries or something, 'cause it's really good," he critiqued as he turned and waded on through the shallow water, in search of colorful stones.

Emma watched him pick his way along the shore for a second. "Thanks!" she called after him, adding a pleasant "Have a good day!"

He raised his hand in a half wave of acknowledgement as he sloshed along.

"He's got a point," she considered. "I could be a decent artist or illustrator if I spent more time on it."

Stashing the sketchbook and pencil in their places in her backpack, she took a long drink from her water bottle. She rose to her feet and brushed off a bit of sand still clinging to the backs of her legs, then stretched a bit. Retracing her earlier steps along the island coast, she returned to her bike, refastened her helmet, and continued down the shoreline road.

Emma stopped occasionally to look at the quirky stone cairns stacked on the shore by obsessed tourists or at distant freighters across the lake. "I didn't remember the Great Lakes water could be this shade of turquoisy blue," she pondered. It was a color she usually associated with exotic islands in the tropics, not with her midwestern home state.

As she pedaled and coasted, she thought about lakes and water and flow – how a droplet could fall near Chicago, float north on a current blown by a breeze, travel under the bridge and head south again through connected rivers and Great Lakes out toward the Atlantic Ocean. "Flow can be an advantage," she thought, "if it takes me in the direction I want to go. Otherwise, if I don't pay attention, I could get stuck in some circular current or tossed out upon a rocky shore. I could end up far away from where I want to be." Grandy generously reached out to extract her from the eddy where she had been stuck. Now that she was moving again, she pictured herself reading the currents of her life, learning the ways in which they flowed, observing them, before choosing a new direction.

The smooth pavement rolled along beneath her wheels and periodically she checked the bluffs for any remaining lilacs still in bloom. She thought about her sketch of the Arch. It would have been nice to take a photo of the formation, but after her initial drawing exercise that morning, she was reminded how something special happened whenever she sketched an object or a scene: she felt she understood the thing better.

If she used her camera on her phone, she would click a few shots and then move on. She wouldn't linger like she did at the Arch, getting to know the light and curves and the angles of the space. Maybe she would have cropped and filtered a photo before posting it on a social media feed, but she wouldn't have paid attention to the lean of the windswept birches off to one side, the shrubby little top knot of greenery struggling to keep its place on the crest, or the shadows cast on the limestone in the morning sun. And those shadows would move during the day. If she went back to the same spot later at a different time, toward evening, perhaps she would need to draw it differently. Places had moods and they shifted with time and weather and cloud.

She captured a pleasant one for the Arch. "Grandy knew what she was doing when she told me to put my phone away."

After the halfway point on her ride around the island, the road opened into a wide intersection bordered by small buildings, bike racks and picnic tables. A boy off to one side held his right arm high like the Statue of Liberty while a creamy colored stream of vanilla ice cream dribbled down his forearm.

"Mmm, ice cream sounds yummy right now," Emma thought in anticipation. She positioned her bike in an open space in one of the large bike racks, then repeated the same helmet removal routine from several miles before and made a direct line to the building where the ice cream awaited. After consulting the menu, she threw caution to the wind and ordered a chocolate cone, grabbing extra napkins as she left the counter.

During her childhood, most of her summer shirts and blouses had faint chocolate stains preserved in the fabric from ice cream cones that melted quicker than she could eat them. Today she could have played it safe and ordered vanilla. Or requested a bowl. Instead, she decided, she was living dangerously: drips or not, today was a chocolate cone day! She rationalized that even without an unfortunate drip, she would still be changing her clothes for dinner tonight anyway. The choice of a non-staining flavor wouldn't save her any laundry.

A family collected their belongings and moved on from one of the picnic tables in the large grassy area. Emma claimed a seat there. She rotated the ice cream cone and managed the melting parts, ensuring no drips escaped as she observed a constant stream of bicyclists arriving and departing from the popular rest stop.

A mother dressed in a designer logo cycling outfit directed her two young daughters over to a large rock at the side of the picnic area. She meticulously arranged the girls in various poses on the boulder, taking a series of photos at each step of the way. The mother did not appear to be enjoying herself, and although the girls were playful when they first climbed up on the rock, they soon acted frustrated too. The sour-faced mother barked orders at the girls and posed them as if they were much older professional models. "Alyssa, get your hand on your hip! Amanda, what are you doing? Remember what I told you about your shoulders!" The girls reluctantly responded to the corrections and eventually flashed mother-approved, well-practiced smiles.

Didn't anyone do candid or casual shots anymore?

Emma considered the photos from her own childhood, slightly out of focus, unfiltered and imperfectly framed, facial expressions somewhat askew, but still precious. The eclectic collection of family photos was even more valuable to her now that she knew there would be no new ones of her parents. Every single snapshot of her mother or father, even an awkward or blurry one, was endearing. They were pure and unconstructed. Everything on social media now seemed artificially posed and intentional, an identical cookie cutter image, formula driven, according to the latest trend, all market and media ready.

"I'm guilty too, though. Been there, done that," she admitted. "For sure I would have posted at least a dozen photos by now if I had my phone with me." By taking a break from her device, she was becoming enlightened, clarifying how there were things for which technology was helpful, but also seeing the times when it was a distraction from what was truly important.

When she was very young, Emma's favorite day of the week was grocery shopping day. It was a special one-on-one event with her mother, quality time, no distractions. Little Emma would sit in the small seat of the grocery cart, facing her mother with her thin legs dangling below. She was in charge of the shopping list, with responsibilities for spotting items as they went aisle by aisle. As they progressed through the store, Emma's mother taught her short lessons in math ("Which is a better bargain: $1 for 8 ounces or $2 for 20 ounces?"), spelling ("c-e-l-e-r-y, celery!"), and geography when they got to the imported food section ("What is the capital of Thailand?") Little Emma gave a report on her day in kindergarten and her mom told her about her own workday in a way her young daughter could understand. Her mother had many important responsibilities, both in their home and at work, but grocery day was special Emma time, with few distractions, and no technology intrusions.

"Those days were the best," she recalled fondly. She thought about that in stores where harried parents on cell phones pushed shopping carts and ignored their children in tow, who in turn stared blindly at their own tablet computers instead of connecting with the parent. She was sure the kids weren't managing grocery lists. She didn't want to be judgmental, but wasn't that a loss of a good parent-child connection opportunity? And now it seemed like family trips had fallen prey to the same temptations of the technology habit.

"Are vacations good bonding time anymore or is everyone off in their own space, headphones plugged into a personal electronic device, each person doing their own thing?" she wondered. "Do families even have shared memories anymore if each individual's experience of an event is customized?"

She wasn't sure what these two girls would remember about this time with their mother. Were they having fun? Were they finding lilacs or was this just another series of poses and posts spliced into a long bike ride?

Now another child climbed onto the boulder where Alyssa and Amanda had been. "Dad!" the boy called. A few seconds later he repeated the plea for attention, "Dad, Dad, Dad!" more insistently.

Emma glanced around, concerned perhaps the little boy was lost, separated from his parents. She saw the father slouched over a phone on a picnic table. It was the same posture Emma slumped in while making coffee a few days earlier. "Perhaps he is focused on an important activity, or is burned out and taking a needed break," Emma attempted to justify in the man's defense. Was he checking the mileage on the route back to town? Informing someone where he was? Making dinner arrangements?

Or was he scrolling through a feed of mundane social media posts while his dear son pleaded for his attention?

~ 22 ~

Emma finished her ice cream cone, gave the front of her hoodie and shirt a quick once over, and spotted no chocolate stains. "Yes!" she thought and gave a mental fist pump. She took a few minutes to explore the sights in the area, checking out a large, weathered rock formation called "Friendship's Altar" and investigating the displays in the Nature Center.

With both her appetite and her curiosity satisfied, she retrieved her bike from the rack and continued her route down the coast, spotting two more light purple lilacs in bloom near homes on the bluffs. Along the way back to town, she stopped to read the signs at various displays, learning about the area's rich Native American history and some of the island's unique geologic features. Completing the full circle, she returned her bike to the rental counter and after a quick time check decided to wander across town to complete Grandy's assignment from the envelope she opened at breakfast.

She consulted the "old school" paper map and cut across town on Market Street. It ran parallel to the busy main thoroughfare where she biked earlier, but it was one block removed from where the ferry docks emptied their passengers and therefore was slightly less crowded. There were still a number of cute stores and historic buildings, but it lacked the mid-day crush of Main Street. Emma was on a mission now. She was focused on her goal and wanted few distractions until her work was complete.

Navigating her way to the Fort was the easy part. On the way there, she recognized the lilacs the purple-clad lady pointed out from the carriage. Once she arrived at the Fort though, she wasn't sure where to go. Emma didn't recall the precise location where the photo was taken. She was going to need help from someone who knew the area.

Starting at the ticket booth, she first handed the entrance fee to the agent at the counter, and then followed with the snapshot from Grandy.

"I know this picture was taken somewhere here, but I don't know exactly where inside the complex. Do you recognize this spot?"

He studied the photo for a second and chuckled. "This you?"

She gave an embarrassed nod. "Yep."

"Nice," he said with a smirk. Then his face lit up with recognition. "Oh yeah. A lot of people take pictures there. It's right at the top of the sidewalk going up to the Fort entrance. Can't miss it," and pointed over his shoulder in the general direction as he slid the photo back to her.

Emma thanked him, collected her ticket, and carefully replaced the photo in her backpack.

The sidewalk to the Fort entrance cut across the face of the bluff at a substantial angle. She began the steep climb up the hill to the top. When the walkway finally leveled out again, she stopped to catch her breath and knew she was in the right spot. She could see the metal plaque and other features matching the photograph.

Emma heaved a sigh. This was the part she dreaded. "And now folks, here's where it gets super exciting. I can't believe I'm actually going to do this," she silently narrated to an imaginary audience, rolling her eyes, and adding a sarcastic "Gee, thanks, Grandy."

"And I've definitely earned a cocktail when I get back to the pool at the hotel. A big one, with an umbrella in it."

She coached herself with one final affirmation of, "I've got this," and made a quick assessment on the assortment of people climbing up the sidewalk behind her.

Her gaze zeroed in on a matronly woman wearing a big floppy hat and large dark sunglasses who was with several similarly dressed companions. "Older, and touristy," she thought strategically. "They'll all want to take a break here at the top of the steep hill, and maybe she won't mind taking the photo while they rest."

When the woman was close enough to be in conversation range, Emma took a deep breath and blurted out one long run-on sentence in as friendly of a voice as she could muster through her nerves.

"Um, hi, I was wondering if I could bother you for a minute because I'm supposed to take a picture right here and email it to my grandmother, but I don't have my phone with me today and I was hoping you could please help me?"

The woman smiled at her, then made a mysterious gesture with her hand, and answered with a short sentence that left Emma a bit puzzled. She couldn't understand what the woman said. It sounded like it was a foreign language. Perhaps Portuguese? No, Greek. Maybe… Hungarian?

The woman and her friends all smiled and nodded, agreeing on something Emma didn't comprehend before they moved on, conversing excitedly amongst themselves.

As they left, she recognized one word as it floated up from their chatter. "Grandmother."

"I think she thought I was telling her she looked like my grandmother?" Emma withered in embarrassment.

She had been psyching herself up for this task by telling herself, "This is a simple request, and if I'm polite, of course the first person I ask will say 'yes', and then I'll be done," but that's not how it played out.

She threw her head back in exasperation and grumbled low in her throat. She was going to have to try this humiliating task again.

"Maybe I need divine intervention," she thought. "Dear God, help me!"

There was a warm, deep voice close behind her. "Excuse me, do you need a hand?"

"Wow, God, that was fast!" she thought, whirling around. She looked into a pair of bright blue eyes set in a handsome face, shaded by the brim of a faded baseball cap emblazoned with the words "Saint Ignace" across the front. A ring of sun-lightened curls peeked out from under the cap, creating a golden halo.

"God sent me a Saint?" Emma thought in amusement. But then, she had a moment of recognition. "Oh wait, is it you? From the ferry?" Emma asked.

The man was holding the hand of his young daughter, but Emma didn't see the son or his wife nearby.

"No flying baseball caps today," the man acknowledged to confirm his identity. "Can I return the favor?"

"Oh gosh, yes please! That would be great!" Emma said with relief, and she blurted out her request again.

"My grandmother asked me to re-create an old family photo by taking a picture here," indicating the plaque embedded in the

Fort wall. "And then I'm supposed to email it to her, but I don't have my phone with me right now."

The man gave a little laugh, "Yes, that would be pretty hard to do without a phone."

She grimaced and gave an eye roll, acknowledging the absurdity of her situation. "I know. It's complicated."

Emma thought about trying to explain the cell phone detox thing but that would take too long, and she wanted this horrifying exercise to be over as soon as possible.

To her great relief, Baseball Cap Man flashed a bright smile and shrugged, "Sure, no problem." The couple who was posing for a photo under the plaque earlier now stepped aside. He said, "The coast is clear, move on up."

Emma promptly climbed the stairs to take her spot, right where she had been in the photo taken nearly two decades before. "At least this chore is almost done," she consoled herself.

The man's daughter stood by his side, shifting her weight back and forth from one leg to another while Emma positioned herself on the steps for the picture. "If you can get the plaque right here and the sign for the Fort over there in the shot too, that would be perfect," she requested, indicating the key landmarks from the original photo. He centered the shot and said, "OK, I've got it lined up. On three…"

He began the count and his daughter chimed in, "Say 'spaghetti!'"

Emma's mother also used to say "spaghetti" instead of the usual "cheese" before photos. It wasn't something she heard often outside of her family and now hearing someone else say it was a surprise, a little pop-up lilac that made Emma laugh, giving her an authentic happy expression as the stranger captured the photo.

"You have a great smile!" Baseball Cap Man said.

Emma blushed and mumbled a thank you. Before she could climb down from where she stood, the man's daughter raced up the stairs, "Daddy, I want a picture with her too!"

Emma stopped halfway down the stairs. Why on earth did the girl want a photo with her? What should she do? Play along? Should she go back to where she was standing? Was that too forward? She looked back at the girl's father for guidance.

A bald man wearing a Hawaiian print shirt placed his hand on Baseball Cap Man's shoulder and said, "How about one with all of you?" and held out his other hand for the phone.

Before she knew what was happening, Emma took her place beside the plaque again, Baseball Cap Man joined her on the steps, along with the little girl and her brother who mysteriously materialized from wherever he had been hiding, and she was instantly swept into a family photo with people she didn't even know. At the daughter's command, they all once again said "spaghetti" and the bald man took several shots, "just to be sure."

Emma's exterior smile camouflaged the horror she held inside. This was supposed to be a simple exercise: talk to one stranger, snap a quick photo, and be done. But the way events were unfolding, the task was dragging out much longer and becoming more complicated than she ever anticipated.

Now Emma noticed a woman with perfectly straightened hair and a bit too much eyeliner giving her a withering glare from a few yards away. The man's wife? The one who belonged in the empty seat on the ferry? "Most likely," she thought, considering the intensity of the piercing stare being aimed, laser-like in her direction. The woman stood there with an angry expression and arms folded across her chest. She was clearly uncomfortable with Emma taking a photo with her husband and children.

As they climbed back down the steps, Baseball Cap Man asked, "Now, where do I need to send the picture of you?" Emma quickly spelled out Grandy's email address for him and there was a whoosh as the photo fulfilling her grandmother's challenge left the outbox.

"Thank you so much," she said. "I really appreciate it. I apologize for any inconvenience."

She silently added, "And I'm sorry about the fight you're going to have with your wife about this."

Baseball Cap Man answered her pleasantly. "Sure, no problem, you're welcome. I'm happy to return a good deed."

Emma hoped he'd be able to diffuse his wife's anger and explain the innocent nature of the situation.

With the odd task now completed, Emma wanted nothing more than to run and hide. The woman with the piercing stare started walking toward them, and she did not want to get caught up in some sort of domestic confrontation.

"I'm totally maxed out on humiliation right now," she thought to herself. What Emma didn't know was her embarrassment level was about to get a bit worse.

As she turned to go, Baseball Cap Man stopped her and with a little lift of his chin asked, "Hey, where did you get the ice cream?"

She frowned back at him, puzzled. "Ice cream? How did you know..." her voice trailed off.

He shot her a million-dollar smile, followed by a wink that made her stomach do a flip, and then finished with a good-hearted nudge of his elbow on her arm. Emma reexamined the front of her shirt. Oh yes, there was indeed an ice cream drip, just below her chin. A big blob of melty chocolate had fallen right into the gap between the two sides of her hoodie's zipper, at the top of her t-shirt neckline. During the earlier drip-check when she finished the cone, she hadn't been diligent enough and missed it.

She was completely mortified. Here she was, a grown woman, still with the same chocolate ice cream stains she had as a child. She sighed and a rush of color flooded into her cheeks.

Emma was speechless and had no idea what to say so it was a small mercy that when she looked up, the man, his children, and the glaring woman were gone, blended into the anonymous mass of other tourists along with the bald-headed Hawaiian shirt man, and the Portuguese-Greek-Hungarian ladies.

~ 23 ~

"Unbelievable. This has got to be some sort of cosmic test. I'm going to stay positive through this," Emma resolved. "There must be a lesson here, but I don't know what it is yet. Maybe… Drips happen?'"

She rolled her eyes and pulled up the hoodie's zipper to conceal the chocolate stain as she worked her way around the Fort's history displays until she became too warm in the midday sun and had to lower the zipper again. It occurred to her the blob had been there, front and center, while she'd visited the Nature Center, returned the rental bike, purchased the Fort ticket, and anywhere else she'd been in the past hour. She had paraded around half of the island with a chocolate stain on her shirt.

The embarrassment crushed her like a weight, but then she squeezed out from under it. "Perhaps the drip is my trademark and I'll never outgrow it," she thought. She imagined a conversation, meeting a business contact at some point in the future, with the new acquaintance saying, "Oh yes, you're Emma, the woman who always has the drips on her shirt."

"Maybe I'll have clothing printed up with the drips already on them. Chocolate, strawberry, or Neapolitan swirl. Ha, it will be my brand! I'll own this habit, maybe even cash in on it," she imagined, chuckling to herself. She was pleased she was not letting the awkward moment bring her mood down. The more absurd she made her thoughts about it, the better she felt. Perhaps she was on the right track. After all, Grandy did say during this process she might get a little dirty.

She also considered the way Grandy's assignment accomplished several important tasks. Although Emma initially dreaded the exercise, she now saw it ensured she was not sequestered alone in her hotel room (although it was a lovely room, indeed.) It resurrected some happy memories of her parents and drew her into some slightly clumsy interactions with a few nice strangers. She endured a few uncomfortable moments, but the day was still fun. She was proud of how she was able to laugh about the awkwardness, even the ice cream drip. And speaking of the ice cream cone, it was a nice snack, but a considerable amount of time had passed since then. She consulted a map to find nearby food options and selected the Fort's Tea Room as a quick and convenient spot to grab something more substantial to eat.

A small table was available outdoors on the restaurant's upstairs balcony. The space was light and airy, but still benefitted from the shade of the roof overhead. While Emma waited for her lunch order to arrive, she sipped an iced tea and pulled out her sketchbook again. After considering her options for a moment, this time she selected the set of colored sketching pencils.

From where she sat at her table, she had a beautiful spot to take in the picturesque town. It was a fresh perspective on the route of her ride earlier in the day. She imagined the scene was probably similar to what it would have been a hundred years ago.

Time seemed to stand still or at least move at a turtle's pace on the island. The view from her table highlighted the bright green lawns sloping down from carefully preserved Victorian homes and inns. They bordered the main street which curved in a gradual arc around the sparkling blue bay. The black-capped steeple of St Anne's Church towered over the buildings in the distance before the road turned to head north around the island. Sun glinted off the water where a collection of boats floated in the harbor. Over it all, a handful of cloud streaks made swaths of white in an otherwise clear blue sky.

The day could not have been more beautiful. On her way across town, she picked up an old flyer for the Island's Lilac Festival poster contest and tucked it into her backpack. Maybe, depending on next year's chosen theme, she could use one of her drawings as the foundation of an entry for it.

She leaned back in her chair and assessed her sketch. It was hastily done because she wanted to finish before her food arrived, but like her earlier drawing of Arch Rock, it was a good representation of the subject, and she was pleased with the outcome.

The server reappeared and admired Emma's work. "Well, that's a pretty picture," she said, setting down the plate.

Emma looked up happily and returned the compliment. "Thanks. So is that sandwich!"

Her focus had been on the scenery and her drawing, but now her stomach demanded attention.

Eagerly tackling her turkey wrap and chips, she further contemplated the sketch and her surroundings. She was feeling inspired here, more than she'd been in a long time. She was happy Grandy found a way to flip this creative switch back on. Some of her high school teachers suggested she enroll in Art School after graduation, but Emma was unsure about venturing off in that career direction. When weighing her future options during her senior year, her parents strongly recommended more traditionally practical careers like theirs - business and engineering. Back then, Emma couldn't envision branching out into something unknown and creative, like art or design. It would be unconventional. She worried about what her parents would say, and she didn't want to go against their wishes or disappoint them. In addition, she didn't know anyone in a creative field who could serve as a mentor either. As an artist, how could she support herself? In books and movies, weren't artists the ones who were always poor and starving? That wasn't what she wanted for her future.

In the end, she played it safe, got her bachelor's degree in business and launched herself into the corporate world. Her intelligence and work ethic had made her successful in her fledgling career. But now, without her parents, she realized her primary goal had always been trying to make *them* happy. On her own, she was lost, directionless. "I need a new goal. Something that's meaningful to *me*."

It was time to find a new job, perhaps a completely new career direction. The thought made her stomach twist and she mentally batted away the ball of anxiety threatening to complicate her pleasant but fragile new dreams. Today she was not going to let herself get overwhelmed with thoughts of the future. Things would need to happen one step at a time. And for the present, her focus was on finding lilacs and enjoying this gloriously beautiful weather.

After lunch, Emma parked herself on the grassy slope in front of the Fort near several well-established clumps of lilac bushes that still offered their blooms. It was an ideal spot for more world class people watching. For a while, she left her sketchbook stowed in the backpack but donned her sunglasses and lounged on the hillside. It was less breezy here than on her earlier bike ride, and the warm sun made her feel relaxed.

Stretching out her legs, she pushed off her shoes. Blades of green grass reached up and tickled the bottoms of her feet. She leaned back on her elbows and absorbed the activity bubbling up from the town. Leaves and flags fluttered from a fresh breeze off the lake. There were sparkles on the waves in the bay and the swooping flight of seagulls overhead. She closed her eyes and heard the steady clopping of hooves of draft horses blended with the whir of bicycles and shouts of laughter from inexperienced riders finding their balance on two wheels.

People milled around, disoriented tourists making lazy, lost trajectories – three steps this direction, then a pause or a pivot, and half a dozen more steps before disappearing into a shop. There was a couple running, dodging obstacles as they perhaps tried to catch a departing ferry. Island residents and local employees confident in their directions traveled with more purposeful straight-line paths. Some people wore colonial period costumes from the Fort or other historic sites where they worked or volunteered, but mostly people wore vacation uniforms of t-shirts and shorts, sometimes a sundress or jeans. No neckties here in the afternoon sun. The more formal attire would reappear again later, tonight in the dining room at Grand Hotel. For now, groups of tourists sprawled in a scattered array on the lush lawn of the Fort, enjoying the sun and staring dreamily out at the water.

It reminded her of a crazy mixed-up reboot of the Georges Seurat painting she saw during a school field trip to the museum in Chicago, "A Sunday Afternoon on the Island of La Grande Jatte." This was a new modern version of the landscape, "Wednesday Afternoon on the Island of Mackinac." She began trying to commit the details to memory but decided there were too many things she wanted to remember. She again pulled out the paper and pencils to capture the scene. "That's why I have them."

This trip continued to strike all the right notes. She was shaking up her stale old routine, adding variety, trying new things. First, she was active but then she lounged, casual then dressed up, in familiar surroundings revisiting old memories and then exploring the unknown. She had opened the gate on the fortress of her comfort zone, and now relaxed on its front lawn, embracing the unexpected.

Emma thought about the gifts of the beautiful clothing, shoes, and accessories. She had underestimated the fun of dressing up and eating in the elegant dining room. The value of the whole experience dramatically outweighed the minor drawback of not having someone to share it with in the moment. She could enjoy it herself, though, couldn't she? It was elevating her, changing her in good and positive ways. She was happy to scout out this experience to be able to share it with someone else another time.

A little burst of excitement surged through her when she began thinking about the dining experience the chef and staff were already busy preparing. There were still several hours before dinner, but she decided to start working her way back in the direction of the hotel. She needed to check out the pool! There were a few shops on Main Street she wanted to explore, souvenir t-shirts to buy, and fudge to sample along the way.

~ 24 ~

Emma stared in horror at the reflection in the bathroom mirror. She was back at her room to make a quick clothing change. Her plan was to unload her souvenir purchases, put on a bathing suit, and take a quick dip in the pool. However, that strategy was immediately tossed aside as she dealt with this new development. Her face and neckline were a vivid shade of pink, except for white patches around the eyes where her sunglasses had been. Her upper arms above the elbows were pale where they were covered by the t-shirt and hoodie, but her forearms and hands were rosy from when she pushed up the sleeves during her bike ride, lounged on the Fort lawn, and dawdled in the sun on her long shopping spree down Main Street. Her legs were two toned as well, starkly pale above the knees and reddish below where her capris left them exposed. It was the first time in many months she spent an extended time in the sun and her skin reacted dramatically.

"I put the sunscreen in my backpack but never used it. Duh," she chastised herself. "I look ridiculous. Red and white striped, like a warped candy cane."

For a moment she considered skipping the dining room that night. "All of my dresses are sleeveless. How can I go like this?"

But then, she would have to explain her absence to Grandy, who would not consider vanity a valid excuse.

Emma wanted to start living life by her own rules. She didn't want to simply switch to earning her grandmother's approval instead of her parents'. That would be a big mistake. After all, she made a big commitment to herself the night before. She was an adult, an independent woman, and was supposed to be making her own decisions. There was no reason why she couldn't order room service if she wanted to!

But, something inside of her insisted that missing out on a fabulous dinner, with live music, in the elegant atmosphere of the dining room because of something as silly as a mild sunburn was not a wise decision. Maybe that was the important thing.

In wondering what Grandy would think, it wasn't about fulfilling her wishes. It was about examining her grandmother's thought process and learning about her spirit. Did Emma have the option to stay in her room? Certainly. However, she could also choose to get past this minor setback and have a marvelous dinner. She was going to have to own this moment. She would make it work.

Emma went back to her hotel room closet and studied the limited selection of options hanging there. The hot pink sundress was a strong no. She didn't want to hide in her room, but she wasn't trying to light up the Salle à Manger like a neon beacon either. The bright pink color was certain to attract attention, and instead of providing camouflage it would ensure everyone noticed her sunburn. Moving on, she preferred not to re-wear the dress she wore the previous night. That left the second of the two "surprise" dresses Grandy purchased for her.

She held up the garment on its hanger. It was constructed of lilac-colored silk, with gold and silver threads woven through it, slightly ruched in the bodice with pencil thin straps. The skirt floated down gracefully below the fitted waist. It was tea-length, elegant. She frowned at the contrast between the beautiful dress and her awkwardly toasted arms. She needed sleeves.

If she threw on her hoodie, she could pretend she didn't care. It would be a "shabby-chic" vibe. She looked at the garments together. It just looked wrong. It would effectively hide the weird two-tone skin, but it would be an insult to the dress. And there might be more unfortunate ice cream drips she was overlooking.

Thinking of the movie "The Sound of Music," when they made dresses out of draperies, her eyes wandered over to the hotel room window treatment, but she quickly dismissed the idea. That was not the statement she wanted to make and, more importantly, she didn't want to be banned from future visits to the hotel because of damage to the curtains.

Maybe there was a blouse or a sweater she packed but had since forgotten about that could cover her arms instead. Perhaps she overlooked something Grandy pulled from her closet. She went back to the chest of drawers where she stored her unpacked clothes. After rummaging around for several seconds, dismissing one item after another as they clashed horribly with the beautiful dress, she found something she didn't recognize.

"Wait, what is this?" she thought as her hand swept over a piece of unfamiliar material. She held it up to get a better look at the garment. It was the cream colored scarfy shawl thing from Grandy. "Huh," she said as she examined it, tilting her head to one side. Shaking the fabric, the fringe danced a bit. "That's kind of fun." She threw it on over her shoulders. "What do you know? I can totally use this."

She showered, keeping the water as cool as she could stand it, hoping it would calm down the rosiness in her skin. After drying off gently with a fluffy towel, making sure she didn't rub too hard to cause any additional irritation on the red patches, she smoothed some moisturizing lotion on her arms and legs, then started to work on her face.

"Perhaps the temperature of the water helped a little," she thought. The redness didn't seem as bright as it was at first. However, her initial attempt at makeup application made the outline from the sunglasses more conspicuous. She washed it off and started over. This time, she was pleased with how it turned out. She hadn't made the sunglass line completely invisible, but it was now toned down and less obvious. Besides, she told herself, it was a bright summer day, and lots of people had been outdoors. She wouldn't be the only sun-kissed face in the dining room. There was bound to be at least one golfer or poolside lounger who had it worse than she did.

Next, she took on the issue of her hair, and after several frustrating attempts, she was thrilled when she successfully wrangled and pinned it into a glamorous updo. She added the lilac pendant around her neck and the same pretty earrings as the night before.

Finally, she took the fringed scarf and tried draping and knotting it a few different ways. In the end, she created a bolero style shrug. Like the namesake short jacket, it was exotic and stylish in a fun, funky way. The silky material successfully covered the winter white upper part of her arms that clashed awkwardly with the early summer glow of her forearms and hands. The fringe on the edge of the material swayed as she shimmied her shoulders, posed, and twirled in front of the mirror trying to assess the fashion fix. Mission accomplished.

She longed to take a selfie and post it or send it to Grandy. "I could ask someone, I suppose…" thinking about how she asked the Baseball Cap Man to send the photo from the Fort to her grandmother but decided against it. She had gone out on a limb enough today. No stress about a photo, she was just going to savor the moment.

"I crushed this spontaneous wardrobe challenge. I am going to fully enjoy this victory! This calls for a glass of champagne with dinner to celebrate!"

She passed through the parlor, meandering toward the dining room. A group of hotel guests exited to the porch. The open front doors caught her attention, and she was drawn in that direction. The previous night, she amused herself before dinner by wandering casually through the crowd in the parlor. Tonight, she would make a bit of a detour and take a stroll on the porch.

"I haven't been out there yet for more than a second. I only zipped across it on my way going to or from somewhere else."

She stepped through the doors and walked in one direction for a few yards before stopping to look around. The beautiful day had transitioned into an equally lovely evening. Across the front of the porch in each direction, a dotted line of bright red geraniums bloomed along the white geometric patterned railing. The string of flowers was interrupted periodically by massive pillars, reaching up to the soft blue-green ceiling high above. Between the towering pillars, long flag poles stretched out from the railing toward the street to proudly display fluttering American flags. On the opposite side of the porch from the geraniums, a long, neat row of white wooden lounge chairs sat next to the front wall of the hotel.

"This porch is huge. There must be dozens, or maybe even a hundred chairs," Emma thought. Here and there, hotel guests were seated on some of them, a few enjoying pre-dinner cocktails, others reading or taking in the view of a beautiful summer evening. She decided she would walk all the way down one side of the porch, where she would pivot and reverse direction to stroll all the way to the opposite end, allowing her to claim the accomplishment of saying she covered the full distance, and then head in for dinner. When she reached the west end, she lingered a few moments to take in the picturesque view.

An empty taxi carriage passed by on the road below. The driver smiled and waved at her, and she returned the greeting. She gazed out over the lake, at the bridge. It had been a long day, a good day, full of happy old memories and new positive experiences.

"I found a few lilacs today," she thought proudly and scrolled through a mental list of what she had seen and done since she woke up that morning.

Through the reverie of her thoughts, she hazily heard someone say, "Excuse me, Miss?"

Emma ignored the voice and didn't respond. She didn't know anyone here. Why would someone be talking to her? But then perhaps she was in someone's way or inadvertently blocking somebody's view. She casually peeked over her shoulder, just to check. There was only one person there - a man with a hotel ID badge and a professional looking camera.

"Me?" she asked tentatively. He nodded. He definitely was talking to her.

"You look lovely this evening, and there's a great background here," he said. "Would you like a photograph?"

"Me?" Emma asked again, pointing at herself, still hesitant to believe the question was directed at her. She again checked for other people around her to see if she was mistaken.

"Yes, you and anyone else in your party."

"Well, my party this evening consists of me, myself, and I, and I think we're all here," Emma joked. She normally wouldn't have sought out an official photographer for a picture of just herself, but she remembered how she wanted to take a selfie earlier and decided she could send it to Grandy after the trip as a gift.

She continued, "A photograph would be a great idea. Where should I stand?"

The photographer positioned her at the edge of the porch, in front of a row of vibrant red geraniums making a striking contrast with the color of her dress and one of the tall white pillars. With the bridge visible in the background, it was going to be a beautiful photo.

Emma faced the photographer. "Do I say, 'cheese'" she asked, and then thinking about the photo at the Fort earlier in the day she laughed and added, "or 'spaghetti,'" wondering if all smile prompts involved food.

"Say whatever you want," the photographer advised. "Whatever makes you smile the most. I always like to say 'Grand.'"

That was perfect. Her mouth curved into a genuine, happy smile as the shutter clicked. This was indeed another Grand moment within a simply Grand day.

He gave Emma instructions on how to pick up the photo later. She took a last admiring glimpse at the lake, and then casually strolled more than 650 feet past the front doors, more chairs, and finally a giant chess board, to the opposite end of the porch. There she enjoyed a lush green inland view to the east, toward the hotel golf course, before heading inside for dinner.

Emma ate a leisurely and elegant meal without an ounce of concern about being a solo diner. She shared a pleasant conversation with a friendly couple at the next table who just arrived for their first trip to the island. By the time she finished a portion of crème brulee for dessert, she was ready for a walk to burn off some of the delicious decadence.

She hadn't missed the sunset because of the generous length of the summer days in northern Michigan. This time, instead of winding her way past the pool and through the wooded paths down to the shore, she decided to take in the scenic view from a different vantage point. She exited the hotel and headed up the sidewalk along West Bluff Road. The stately homes she admired from afar the day before lined the way, some with turrets, spacious porches, and romantic vintage gardens.

A few other people were out strolling the bluff. A full taxi carriage driven by the driver who waved to her earlier passed in the opposite direction. At the top of the hill the road curved to the right and went deeper into the island. To the left there was a small lookout area with benches. Emma stopped there to get a view over the steep terrain and the lake beyond.

It was a gorgeous twilight moment. The sky was still a pale powdery blue, but the clouds reflected pink and gold from the setting sun, a color combination reminding her of skies painted by the artist Maxfield Parrish. The bridge caught the last rays of daylight and sent them back out again with such startling intensity, it was as if they were somehow magnified. She studied the others who gathered in the overlook area. Were they noticing this spectacular display?

She wanted to yell, to shout, to draw attention to the magnificence of the scene but everyone around her seemed much more subdued. There was a young couple, teenagers maybe, leaning on the white wooden railing, kissing, more interested in each other than the clouds or colors in the sky. There was also a group of older people calmly conversing and occasionally glancing at the view, and one couple gazing out over the water, holding hands. Her parents were big proponents of handholding.

She felt the familiar ache of loss and wished her mother and father were there by her side, giving her someone with whom she could share her enthusiasm. But she also considered that maybe her parents could have, at some earlier point in their lives, stood right in this very spot too.

Perhaps it was on one of those evenings when she was too young to stay up late, and she remained with Grandy in the motel room back in Mackinaw City. Maybe her parents snuck away to this overlook and admired a sunset like this one, then ran breathlessly hand in hand down the avenue to catch the last ferry off the island. Maybe in some mystical way, across time and space, she was sharing this with them. And Grandy too, for all the times she had been to the island and Grand Hotel, her grandmother must know this spot well.

Emma reached up and gently squeezed the lilac pendant on the necklace. They would all be happy she was seeing this view now. How many beautiful sunsets did she miss while she was holed up in her dark apartment? Some days she hadn't even bothered to open her drapes. Her grief and the subsequent emotional storm isolated her and cut her off from the world. But now, she was ready to be a part of it once more. It was time to allow beauty and happiness and hope into her life again. She took a long look at the spectacular sunset view and let it connect with her soul. Emma wanted to remember this feeling forever, the supernatural vibrance of this moment, this desire for a new beginning and appreciation for life. She prayed it would transform her.

What had changed in her over the past few days? She had only done a small number of things, but those things worked true magic. Pushing aside her fears, she was taking action. She was escaping from the dungeon. She was breaking the spell. With Grandy's encouragement, she challenged her doubts, made a few small adjustments, and created momentum. There had been a handful of difficulties and several awkward mistakes, but the benefits of her positive steps outweighed the drawbacks. A seed had taken root, and it was now growing into something much larger.

She spun around, the fringe from her shawl spreading out around her, and walked briskly back down the West Bluff sidewalk. After the previous day's sunset, she had wanted to disappear, to escape and hide. But now, she needed to launch herself into her future.

In a run, she bounded up the stairs, across the porch, and back into the hotel, feeling energized, as if the brilliant, silvery light reflected from the bridge recharged something deep inside of her.

The orchestra was on the stage in the Terrace Room, and big band music drifted out into the parlor. She thought about the wedding she attended the previous summer – how she felt abandoned and alone at the reception when she was the only one not on the dance floor. She remembered the way she bolted, crying, escaping into the bathroom and then how she slunk ashamed and secretive out the backdoor of the banquet center. "What in the world was that?" she thought. Being single wasn't some horrible catastrophe. Her parents were gone, but she was still alive. Alive!

Chip had been a jerk to her, and rudely dumped her at the worst point of her life. That, in retrospect, was such a relief! The more she thought about it, he did her a huge favor by revealing his true colors early in their relationship. Over the past year she picked up on little unsavory bits of information about him, things that a year ago she didn't know. In addition to his unwillingness to stand by her during her most difficult of times, she was shocked to learn he exaggerated most of his so-called accomplishments. He did not graduate at the top of his class, and he was let go from the law firm where he once worked because of ethics issues. She was better off without him.

Her mother always told her, "There are worse things than being alone." She was finally beginning to see the wisdom in that statement. Life is full of challenges, and if she was going to be with someone, she wanted it to be someone who would be by her side in moments of turbulence, not run away when the going got rough.

Emma spied the doorway at the far end of the parlor. That opening led to her hotel room, her own beautiful little space of solitude and sanctuary, and then she looked back at the open double doors of the Terrace Room. Last night she was tired and went to bed early, but tonight, the orchestra was calling to her. She allowed herself to be pulled by an unseen force toward the upbeat melody. Perhaps she would sit at a table and enjoy a cocktail or maybe she would dance. She wasn't sure, and it didn't matter. Emma simply wanted to be surrounded by live music and interesting people and a desire to celebrate life in spite of hardship.

Taking a quick glance around the room, she checked out her seating options. There was a small open table off to the side of the musicians.

"That will be a great place to do some people watching and absorb the atmosphere."

And after a little while, the lovely young woman in the lilac-colored dress found herself on the dance floor, and she began the process of making up for so much of what she missed over the past year.

$$\sim 25 \sim$$

"Are you checking your bag, Miss?" the porter at the ferry dock asked expectantly. Emma firmly grasped her suitcase handle. Was she ready to leave?

She could have set out her luggage for transport back to the dock the night before. However, when she got back to her room after the evening full of dancing, she decided she was not in the frame of mind to think about leaving or going home. With the music of the orchestra still circulating in her veins, she didn't feel like coming back to reality. She was not ready to break the magic spell and deal with the decisions of packing her bags.

She was supposed to divide her belongings. Half would go in the bag the porter would take away for transit to the dock. The other half was what she would need for the next morning. Instead, she dodged the task, saying she would take her bags to the ferry herself. She curled up in the comfy bed for one last night, staring through the darkness at the shadowy flowers on the wallpaper, occasionally humming, and thinking about the sunset and the dancing and the evening's conversations.

The final envelope from Grandy still sat on the dresser. Emma considered opening it but decided to leave one last surprise for the morning.

Right after she was seated for breakfast, she unsealed the envelope. There were only four words on the sheet of paper,

Do something impulsive today!

Impulsive?

Had she ever done anything that fit that description? Not wanting to complicate her morning and over analyze the instruction, she did the first thing she could think of. She requested both bacon and sausage with her mixed berry pancakes. There. Mission accomplished.

But the challenge still smoldered in her mind and by the time she repacked the last of her clothes into her suitcase and zipped it up, she was certain a double meat breakfast was not what Grandy intended.

It should be something bigger.

Something unexpected, even frivolous.

Emma sat on the edge of the bed. This envelope should have been fun. Why was she making it so hard? Like a lightbulb being turned on by a dimmer switch, a new realization was starting to glow in her mind.

"I've always followed a checklist, haven't I?" she asked herself. "My life has been one set of instructions after another. It's comfortable for me. And safe. Now, with my parents gone and my career on hold, there is no official 'approved' checklist to follow and no way to know if I'm doing things right."

This observation led to another. Even her grandmother's carefully prepared envelopes were just a different form of checklist. This insight made her uncomfortable. Had Grandy known this and intentionally made the last one an open-ended task? Was she gently nudging Emma to be more independent and think for herself?

Without a checklist, the world was overwhelming. There were too many options and Emma felt obligated to make the right choice, every time. It was exhausting. What if she made a mistake? How would she be able to recover? And what would people say? The world, especially on social media, had become such a sharp and judgmental place. Perhaps that's why she spent the past six months shut up in her apartment, trying to stay safe.

Emma fidgeted as she sat on the edge of the mattress, then stood up and walked across the room to sit in the brightly colored upholstered armchair instead.

She recognized the movement as a subtle fight or flight reflex. Part of her wanted to run away from these difficult thoughts, but this time she forced herself to face them directly. For the first time in her life, she was going to take control of her own ship.

"I've been hiding behind my grief," she admitted. "Grandy's right. I need to fight. I need to make my own decisions, try new things, bold things, and deal with the outcomes. And not always worry about what others think. Even if I mess up."

When she returned her key to the front desk at checkout, she longed to ask if she could stay another night but couldn't make the words come out of her mouth. She stewed in frustration all the way to town in the carriage. Implementing this courageous new strategy might be harder than she thought.

And now, here she was at the dock already. She wanted to make better, more independent decisions, but things seemed to be happening so fast. Trapped in some invisible force of momentum, carried along by the rushing current of life, there was no time to analyze each new situation to figure out what to do. Her familiar old habits were eagerly elbowing their way past her desire to do things differently.

"Your bag, Miss?" the man repeated.

Emma heard herself say, "No thank you," and then she turned and walked down the sidewalk a bit, to get away from the busy ferry dock area, giving herself time and space to think.

"What am I doing?" her brain inquired. "Apparently, I am staying," her heart answered.

Emma looked up and down at the busy street. She could always go back to Grand Hotel for one more night, but there were plenty of other nice hotels and inns here in town as well, and she thought it might be fun to stay in another area of the island. Surely one of them would have an open room, wouldn't they?

If she had been on a business trip for work, she would have pulled out her phone and checked a reservation app, but the device was still buried deep in one of her bags. And, if she was being honest with herself, she wasn't ready to end the novelty of being without the internet yet. She enjoyed the challenge. It was kind of liberating. She realized even with her occasional cravings to photograph, or post, or check a news feed, she was getting along quite well without it.

Spying a hotel ahead on Main Street, she walked a few paces closer. "No Vacancy," proclaimed a sign in the window.

"Well, there are tons more," she thought.

Crossing the street, she walked in the other direction. The first hotel on that side, had the same sign in the window declaring all rooms were spoken for. She walked to the next hotel and found another No Vacancy placard.

"Darn," thought Emma, "this might be harder than I expected."

Still determined to find something, she walked to the corner and peered up the side street running perpendicular to the main thoroughfare. "Maybe something not on the busiest road," she reasoned. There was a small boutique hotel on the side street, but like the others, it demurely announced its fully booked status.

The sidewalk climbed gently, and Emma walked along with her suitcase bumping along behind her, considering her options. The street led her one block up to the next road running the length of town. "I'll go around the block. If nothing's available, maybe find a tourist information booth."

Ahead at the intersection, there stood a stately inn with a terraced garden. "How beautiful, I'd love to stay there!" Emma wished, and her heart sank in disappointment when she saw the beautifully crafted wooden sign in the front yard also read "No Vacancy." But then, while she was still a short distance away, a tall man walked purposefully down the inn's sidewalk toward the sign. He reached a long arm across a flower bed and removed the "No" portion. Now it read, "Vacancy," and he turned to go back into the inn.

Emma was elated. She raised one of her arms, waved it and started to run up the hill with suitcase in tow as if trying to hail a taxi in a big city. "Hello! Hello! Excuse me, Sir!" she yelled, completely free from any timidity or shyness. She wanted, *needed* that room! The tall man stopped in his tracks and looked in her direction.

Slightly out of breath, Emma reached the front yard of the inn. "I saw you changed the sign," she panted. "Do you have a room available for tonight?" and silently prayed "please, please, please" while she waited for his response.

"We had a last-minute cancellation," he said. "It's for one room, just one night though."

"That's perfect!" Emma said without hesitation. "I'll take it!"

The man chuckled and held up the little wooden "No" portion of the sign. "I guess I'll just put this back on now.

Thanks for saving me another trip!" He replaced it, then offered to help Emma with her bag, and she followed him inside.

The inn smelled delicious, like cinnamon and vanilla. Emma wondered if the aroma lingered from breakfast, foretold afternoon tea snacks in the oven, or emanated from a bowl of world class potpourri.

She provided the innkeeper with the required information to finalize her stay. After handing over Grandy's credit card to cover the charges, Emma requested that the confirmation be sent to her grandmother's email address with the comment, "Impulsive! Staying one more night on the island."

The room wasn't ready for her yet, but they would keep her luggage safely stored until later in the afternoon, when she would be able to get settled in.

Emma buzzed with excitement. This little detour was exhilarating. "So, this is what spontaneity feels like!"

She had no idea what she was going to do with her hastily redesigned day; she hadn't put any thought into it at all.

"I am making up this adventure as I go along!" A string of recreational and cultural possibilities ran through her mind, all the thoughts she accumulated the previous day and stored on the "maybe next time" shelf in her head. A carriage tour of the island? A hike along a scenic coastal bluff? Horseback riding in the state park? Explore the art museum? Or find a sunny spot and sketch?

The chatter of young voices interrupted her thoughts. Two children tumbled playfully into the room followed by an adult. Emma turned to gather her things and move away from the reception desk, creating space in case the incoming group had to speak to the innkeeper.

A little girl's voice said, "It's her, Daddy. It's the picture lady from the Fort!" Surprised, Emma glanced over at the threesome standing in the middle of the room. It was indeed Baseball Cap Man and his two children. With a feeling of relief, she noted the frowny-faced woman with the piercing stare was nowhere in sight. Not yet, at least.

"Well, hello again," he said. We keep running into each other."

Emma laughed and adjusted her backpack on her shoulder. "Yes, it feels a bit like that, doesn't it?"

"I didn't know you were staying at the inn too, he said. We haven't seen you here."

"I just checked in. It's kind of a spur of the moment thing."

"We're going to the butterfly house today," the girl announced.

"Oh, that sounds so fun!" Emma answered her. She remembered seeing the sign on her bike ride. It was another item on her "future things to do" list.

"If you don't have plans, you're welcome to join us," Baseball Cap Man said, pleasantly extending an invitation.

The little girl emitted a "yay" and did a quick wiggly dance of excitement. Her brother joined in with a short sequence of improvised martial arts moves, a tiny disco-ninja.

Emma couldn't help but smile. She was enjoying her solo adventures, but the thought of spending at least a little bit of her "impulsive" time with this entertaining family was more appealing right now, as long as the frowny-faced woman wasn't involved. And if she showed up, Emma could try to befriend her. If the woman was still hostile, she could always leave. It would be nice to enjoy some spontaneous fun and take a break from the deep thoughts that had consumed her for far too long.

"You don't mind?" Emma asked hesitantly.

He shook his head with a laughing "no". Leaning toward her, he shielded his mouth from the view of the children and added "I'd be grateful for some grown up conversation."

"Sounds great then," Emma said, happily.

"This is Sophie," Baseball Cap Man said, laying his hand on the top of his daughter's head. "And that creature over there is Liam."

"I'm a dinosaur," the boy declared, and proceeded to bend his arms and hands to resemble the short limbs and menacing claws of a T-Rex while he stomped around the room, roaring.

"And I'm Todd" he said extending his hand, introducing himself.

"I'm Emma. Nice to see you all, again," she said, meeting his grasp with a professional handshake.

She wanted to ask him about the woman with him at the Fort, the one whose steely glare conveyed a "back off, he's mine" vibe, but just like earlier in the morning when she wanted to ask about staying an extra day at Grand Hotel, she couldn't make the words come out of her mouth.

Between seeing the vacant seat on the ferry and the woman's possessive demeanor while they took the photos, Emma convinced herself the woman and Todd were together as a couple. But now since he said he looked forward to "grown up conversation" and invited her along on their outing, she questioned whether her initial assessment was accurate. "I need to find a way to casually bring it up, as soon as possible, but when the children aren't around," Emma thought.

She wasn't looking to create any waves in someone else's relationship.

$$\sim 26 \sim$$

"Alright, Troops!" announced Todd. "Let's head out!"

Sophie started marching toward the front door, and her brother fell into a slightly unsynchronized step behind her. They paraded down the porch steps and onto the inn's front walkway.

"They're pretending to be soldiers, like at the Fort yesterday," Todd explained to Emma.

"Turn left at the sidewalk," he directed his daughter. When she headed the opposite way, he corrected her. "Your other left!" She stopped, and with hands on hips, shot him a puzzled look while her brother crashed into her.

"Whaaaat?" she called out, not understanding her father's instructions. Todd pointed in the direction they needed to go.

"The other way," he said.   Sophie smoothly executed a pivot with the grace of a ballerina and continued down the sidewalk in a skipping-marching-dancing hybrid movement with her dino-brother in tow.

"Stop and wait for us before you cross the street, please," Todd called out to the children ahead. Then he added to Emma, "No cars here, but those bikes can get crazy."

"And there's the whole horse thing too!" she added.

"Did you ever get your phone issue resolved?" he questioned.

"OK, first I need to say thanks for your help with that," Emma said cheerfully as they walked along. She continued in an animated fashion, "I feel like I need to explain what that was. I've had a bit of a rough year, and my grandmother thought I needed a break from my routine, including a 'technology detox,'" she said, making air quotes around the words. "So, she booked me two nights at Grand Hotel, asked me to put my phone away, and sent me on a bit of a scavenger hunt to find happy memories of my parents."

She hesitated. Her voice cracked at the word "parents," and now she felt obligated to explain the significance. She cleared her throat before lowering her voice so the children couldn't hear, "They were both killed in a car accident last year."

As soon as the words left her mouth, Emma regretted saying them. Even though the usual flood of awkward tears stayed away, she knew she had thrown a wet blanket over a fun and lighthearted discussion. She wished she could retract it, reel it back in like a fishing lure poorly cast into the stream of conversation. She wanted to switch it out, replace it with something sunnier. But she couldn't. It was out there. Floating in the silence.

Todd stopped walking. "Oh no, Emma, I'm so sorry," he said. His tone was solemn. Serious. She took a deep breath and let it out.

"Thanks."

Horrified, she wanted to dissolve through the sidewalk. She envisioned reaching the next corner where he would conveniently remember he already made other plans, or realize he forgot something back at the inn (like maybe his wife) or provide some other invented excuse to distance himself from the sad girl with the dark cloud around her.

Emma glanced over, checking for the subtle cues she learned to recognize over the past year, signs he was preparing to escape from the conversation.

Instead, he nodded his head and started walking down the street again. "Yeah, you really would need a break after something as difficult as that," he said sympathetically. Then he made a subtle course correction in the tone of the discussion, "How is the scavenger hunt going? Were you able to find some happy memories?"

Emma breathed a sigh of relief. He was continuing the conversation and guiding it toward a more lighthearted subject. He handed her a way to save the moment.

"Yes, I have been finding them," she replied, resolving to sound as cheerful as possible. "I found some on a bike ride around the island, and some in unexpected places like during a song the hotel orchestra played at dinner, and of course I was supposed to find the spot at the Fort where we had a family photo taken when I was little. You already know about that one."

"Happy to help," he added.

Emma continued. "I'm supposed to be doing this little game my family used to play. We called it 'Finding Lilacs.' Because of my mom's work schedule, we never made it to the official Lilac Festival for the peak of the blooming season. However, when we did visit later in June there were usually a few late season ones still flowering here and there around the island. We made it into a game to try and find as many as we could. It was what my grandmother had in mind when she sent me here. She wanted me to find not only actual lilacs like we used to but also to search for happy memories of my parents. And she wanted me to turn my phone off, so I wasn't tempted to stay in my hotel room and fall down the social media rabbit hole."

"That's a clever idea," Todd said, nodding. "So, is your grandmother here on the island with you?"

"Nope," Emma said casually. "She insisted this was something I had to do on my own. It's supposed to get me to step out of my comfort zone. I was somewhat hesitant about it, but now I think she was right."

"She sounds like a wise woman."

"Yes. She's so incredible. I've always loved her but the more I learn about her, the more I understand how special she is."

They arrived at the intersection where Sophie and Liam were waiting for them. Todd reached down and grasped one hand of each child. Liam looked expectantly up at Emma and automatically grabbed one of her hands too. They all crossed the street together as a connected group.

With each step, Emma felt the warm, pudgy little boy hand in hers. Her heart melted a little, and it made her smile. When they safely reached the opposite side, the grownups released the children's hands, and they could once again run ahead.

"Stop at the next corner please," their father ordered.

"Okayyyyy," came the unified response.

"If you were originally at Grand Hotel, how did you end up over at the inn?" Todd asked.

"Impulse and a bit of luck, I guess?" Emma said, tilting her head sideways and raising her eyebrows. "I was already at the dock this morning and was about to get on the ferry, but at the last second, I decided I didn't want to leave the island yet. I kept my suitcase and tried to find a hotel or inn that had a room available. Without a phone, it became a bit of a challenge. The first few places I saw were full, and I happened to catch the innkeeper right as he was taking down the no vacancy sign. And voila!"

"You did have some luck with that. They're usually fully booked. I think you'll enjoy staying there," he said. "We really like it."

Emma flagged the "We" in his response. It was something that couples said. Children don't write Yelp reviews about inns.

They continued down the street, repeating the hand holding exercise with the children at each intersection. Sometimes she would hold Liam's hand and other times it would be Sophie's.

She tried to find a tactful way to ask Todd about the woman at the Fort, or ask where his wife was, or if there even was a wife or girlfriend, but every time she was going to bring up the subject, she hesitated and then he started a conversation about something else or one of the children would appear. Emma knew not to ask potentially awkward relationship-oriented questions in the presence of children, but she would need to find out a way to ask though, and soon.

She was keeping a respectful distance, operating under the assumption he was in some sort of relationship with the dagger-eyed woman, who might be running late that morning due to the additional time needed for perfect hair and extra eye makeup. A few times though, it seemed like he looked at Emma a heartbeat longer than casual acquaintances usually did. He showed some sort of interest that increased in intensity with each encounter: from their initial interaction on the ferry, to the Fort, and finally this morning at the inn.

Why was it so hard for her to say the words, "are you married?" or "was that your girlfriend?"

Was it because she was secretly starting to like him?

Was she beginning to admit how much she enjoyed being on the receiving end of the electric jolt that could be delivered with the flash of his smile or the right glance?

And if he was already taken, perhaps she just didn't want to know the truth yet.

$$\sim 27 \sim$$

"I can't believe I have butterflies about seeing butterflies."

Emma was squeamish when they arrived at their destination. This was the first time she would be visiting a butterfly house, and until that moment she hadn't considered the specifics of what was involved.

She found most butterflies and even some moths (like the mysterious luna moth) to be beautiful, but in general she was not a fan of bugs. Until this little adventure, she always thought in a place like this, where people could go in and walk around, the butterflies would be caged or be behind some sort of screen or barrier. However, after listening to Todd and the children, she was shocked to learn if you sat or stood quietly in the viewing area, you could end up with one or more of them landing on you.

She wasn't exactly "afraid" of the insects (that might be too strong of a word), but a not-so-tiny part of her was concerned she would instinctively swat at one of the delicate creatures and harm it. It was, after all, a bug – a multi-legged worm with wings that could drop from the air and land on her, at any time! She shared this thought with Todd.

"No swatting!" he laughed and then joked with an expression of mock concern, "You're not going to get us kicked out of here, are you?"

Emma shook her head. "Not intentionally, anyway."

Todd reassured her, "They're pretty good about keeping the place free of anything harmful. If something lands on you, let it be."

"Got it," she said, slightly more confident. Taking in a deep breath, she blew it out, then shook the tension out of her arms, as if preparing for some sort of strenuous athletic competition.

They paid their admission fees and received a quick introductory lecture. As she listened, Emma debated if the presentation was targeted at her or the children. They were more comfortable in this environment than she was, and from little snippets of their conversations, it was clear to her it was not their first time with this type of adventure.

Their group approached the viewing area, and Emma envisioned a butterfly aerial stampede as the door opened. She pictured a delicate but organized jailbreak, but then saw the multiple sets of doors and curtains providing security to keep the insects contained, gentle checkpoints to ensure the winged residents were not fluttering with reckless abandon out into the lobby.

Passing through the innermost curtain, Emma entered a small tropical wonderland. The air was filled with exotic smells, some floral and others more earthy. There were tranquil pools and small fountains adding moisture to the air and providing the constant sound of falling water. Here and there, colorful butterflies flitted around. A woman was seated on a bench with her arm outstretched. Two orange, black, and white butterflies were perched on her hand, one on her index finger and one on her pinkie, as if she wore winged rings.

Emma scanned the air around her. So far, she was more comfortable in the garden than she expected. Nothing was aggressively buzzing around her, and she didn't feel threatened.

She reminded herself, "stay calm, no sudden moves, no swatting." Here and there, pairs of wings alighted on someone's arm or shoulder and a few people would gather to catch a closer view. Butterflies rested on various flat surfaces surrounding the pools and planters containing the lush tropical greenery. She watched her step and checked carefully before she took a seat on a bench. Next to her, a yellow and black swallowtail alighted on a bright pink hibiscus flower and then beat its wings in a rhythmic display. There was an amazing diversity of sizes, colors, and patterns. Some species were recognizable, resembling monarchs or painted ladies she had seen in her mother's lovingly tended flower garden, but then there were others more exotic or mysterious, like the large gray ones with eerie spots resembling eyes emblazoned on their wings.

Todd came over and took a seat next to her. "Are you doing OK? Not too creepy for you?" he asked.

"This is amazing," she said, her eyes wide.

He nodded in agreement. "It's a great place to visit, especially on a rainy day. It always cheers me right up."

Emma added, "There are so many different varieties, like this guy over here," and she leaned in toward one resting on a small water dish suspended among the plants behind the bench. "Look at the pattern. It's like it's wood grained."

"My favorite is that one over there," Todd pointed to a butterfly decorated with shades of orange and brown. "I like it because of the name: Great Spangled Fritillary. It sounds like it should be an exclamation, like 'Great Caesar's Ghost!'"

They both chuckled.

Liam started acting dinosaurish again and was stomping quietly through the aviary, which made an ideal Jurassic rainforest with the butterflies standing in as surrogate pterodactyls. Sophie came closer and stood next to her father at the opposite end of the bench from Emma. The young girl had one thin arm outstretched, hoping she could attract a butterfly. Suddenly, Sophie's voice cried out, "Mommy!"

Emma's eyes searched the room while her stomach crunched into a knot.

"Sophie's *mother* is here?" she thought, quickly sliding as far away from Todd as she could on the bench. "So, he is married after all," she decided. "Where is she?" Was it the frowny faced woman from the Fort, with the perfect hair and piercing glare? Would Emma have to explain what she was doing here, sitting that close to someone else's husband? Sitting next to the same man with whom she had been in a photo the previous day.

She was about to excuse herself and make a hasty exit from the butterfly house when Sophie's spoke again, this time in a whisper, as a stunning blue butterfly landed on the young girl's arm.

"It's Mommy."

Liam came over and echoed his sister in a small voice. "It's Mommy."

Both children were patient as the butterfly gave a few gentle beats of its delicate wings, displaying the contrast between its brilliant blue topside and the dull protective camouflage underneath. He carefully put his hand on his sister's arm and the butterfly took a few steps and crawled onto his small fingers. It was obvious this was not the first time these children had done this. "It tickles!" Liam whispered. The giant blue butterfly stayed there for a few moments and then took wing.

Emma exhaled, realizing she was holding her breath. "Blue morpho," said Todd quietly.

Sophie looked over her shoulder at her father and stated matter-of-factly, "Or Mommy," and then skipped off followed by her brother who seamlessly transitioned back into his dinosaur persona.

When the children were out of earshot, Emma turned to Todd and asked in a low voice, "Mommy?"

"Their mother passed away a couple of years ago. Cancer," explained Todd in a quiet voice.

Emma gasped, "Oh! Oh my gosh, I'm so sorry." That was not what she expected to hear.

Todd heaved a deep sigh and folded his arms over his chest. "Thank you. When it happened, someone gave us a children's book that used the metaphor of a caterpillar turning into a butterfly as a way to have a conversation about death with your kids. They both know the butterfly isn't really their mother, but if it helps them feel more connected to her," he made a sweeping gesture of release with his hand, "I let them have the moment."

After a second, he added, "They like the blue ones; it was her favorite color. And, for some reason those are the butterflies that always are attracted to my kids."

"The lilacs for me are like the butterflies are for your children. A physical reminder of someone we loved and lost."

Todd nodded. They both sat there silently, letting the solemnity of the conversation dissipate into the tropical atmosphere, replaced by the sound of the waterfalls and a muffled peal of a child's distant laughter.

Todd carefully posed a question. "I noticed when Sophie said 'Mommy' you kind of scooted away. Did you think I was married?"

Emma bit her lower lip and looked guiltily down at the large gap of empty space between them on the bench before glancing back at him. The heat she felt in her face indicated her cheeks were flushed pink in embarrassment. She was still awkwardly wedged against the arm at the extreme far end of the bench.

"Um, maybe? I wasn't completely sure," she said uncomfortably, then continued with a rambling attempt at an explanation.

"I was trying to figure it out and keep a respectful distance in case you were involved with someone because I don't want any problems or anything. You're not wearing a ring but there might be a bit of a tan line there on your finger, and I didn't remember seeing a woman with you on the ferry, but there was an empty seat, and you know, she could have been inside on the lower deck or something? But then there was this woman at the Fort who was super intense and kind of staring at you and scowling at me when we were taking the picture there."

"Oh my gosh! You saw her too?" Todd said with excitement. "I have no idea who she was. She started moving in on us back when we were standing in line to get tickets. When we were taking the pictures, I saw her lurking around again. I grabbed the kids and took off into the Fort. That's why we disappeared like we did. Maybe she was just trying to be friendly with us or something, but she had a weird vibe, especially when I saw the way she glared at people. I wanted to get the kids away from her."

He snickered a bit, "You thought I might be married to *her*?"

When Emma nodded, his laughter rang out and filled the space of the conservatory. It was so warm and good natured, joyous even, that the awkwardness of the moment vanished.

He waited a few seconds and then addressed her again. "But more importantly, you just admitted you were looking to see if I was wearing a ring."

He winked at her as he stood up from the bench and went off to find his children. That wink again, like when he pointed out the ice cream drip the day before. Emma's stomach flipped and all the embarrassment that had gone away came back in a flood.

They worked their way through the aviary's displays and just before the exit, an orange butterfly landed on the back of Todd's shoulder. "Wait, don't leave yet," Emma said. "You have one on you."

"Don't swat it!" he warned with exaggerated concern, and Emma responded with amused annoyance. He leaned slowly toward Emma, so as not to disturb the butterfly, "Here, you need to hold one. Carefully put your hand up here next to it, and it might walk onto you." Emma reached out and gently placed her hand on Todd's shoulder, feeling the warmth of his body through the fabric of his shirt. As he predicted, the butterfly moved forward and crept onto her fingers.

Todd took a step back and Emma said, "Well, look at that. I'm holding a bug."

"That wasn't so hard now, was it?" Todd replied as his eyes locked on hers in a sustained gaze.

Between the tone of his voice and the way he held eye contact, Emma wondered if he was referring to the way she had allowed the butterfly to climb onto her hand or the way he covertly managed to get her to touch him.

Before there was time to decide, a second butterfly joined the first on the back of her hand, and she was now holding two of them. She gave a small exclamation, "Oh, look!" and held her breath. She studied the delicate creatures, memorizing the moment to sketch it later. Three words came to mind: bright, beautiful, and fragile.

In a flash of memory, she recalled those same words had been used to describe her parents lives at their memorial service. "Hi, Mom and Dad," she whispered, and both butterflies flew away.

~ 28 ~

Hello, it's Sophie again. I need to tell you something. I know my mommy isn't really at a Girls weekend right now. It's a story I tell myself when I'm missing her a lot because if I think about the truth, that she died and isn't ever coming back, it can make me very sad. Sometimes I pretend she's just gone for a few days and that makes it easier.

My mommy had cancer. The doctors didn't know what it was at first. She used to be super healthy and did triathlon races. They thought she had something wrong with her stomach and she kept getting sicker. I didn't like it when I saw mommy and daddy crying. The doctor finally figured out what it was and then she died anyway.

I still don't know what cancer is. I know it's a disease but some of those can be fixed so why can't they fix cancer? It makes me mad when grownups won't explain it to me, even when I ask them about it. I think they think I'm too young to understand, but I got straight A's in school last year and I'm good at science so I wish they would tell me, but no one ever does. I wonder if grownups don't even know what cancer is. They do a lot of whispering around me. Duh, I can totally see them, and I know they are talking about things they don't want me to hear. Sometimes grownups aren't very smart.

I don't understand cancer yet, but I do understand dying. Mommy's body was very sick so her heart stopped beating and she stopped breathing, and her soul couldn't stay there anymore so she went to heaven to be with God and Jesus and the angels forever. I know she's not coming back. I am happy she doesn't hurt anymore. She's waiting for us in heaven now, and I totally miss her and want to see her again, but I don't want to die until I'm really, really old. I don't want my daddy or my brother to die either. Now I hate it when my daddy gets sick, even if he has like a little cold. It makes me really, really scared.

I like butterflies. They used to be caterpillars, but then they changed so they are different and can fly around. It reminds me of what happened to my mommy, except I don't think the caterpillars have cancer. It's just what caterpillars do. And my mommy is more like an angel than a butterfly.

When I grow up, I want to be a butterfly scientist and a doctor too so I can explain cancer to people better than they explained it to me. And I would make cancer totally go away.

$$\sim 29 \sim$$

The sun was high overhead by the time they exited the butterfly house. "Would you be up for some lunch?" Todd asked Emma while they ambled back down the sidewalk toward town.

"Sure!" she said without hesitation.

The day was flowing along. There was no need to interrupt its easy rhythm and she had no other plans. After all, she was being impulsive! And it would be nice to have some company at lunch for a change instead of another solo meal. The children once again skipped ahead, and the two adults followed behind.

Todd and Emma reviewed the different ways they spent their time on the island. In addition to their known encounters, they discovered their daily paths crossed or came surprisingly close several other times, including on her bike ride the previous day and on their first night at the shore for the sunset.

She didn't volunteer the details of her emotional disintegration that first night. He didn't need to know how she had almost caused an accident with the peloton of bikers. Maybe at some point she'd reveal that, but not yet. She was learning restraint. Aside from the day she had recently spent with Grandy, this was turning out to be the longest conversation she'd had with anyone in a long time. It was quite enjoyable, and she wanted to keep the positive vibe going.

"I'm still impressed by your 'phone detox.' Todd said, inserting air quotes like Emma did earlier. "That takes some good self-control, but you seem like you're doing OK without it."

"To be honest I was pretty angry about giving it up at the beginning," Emma confessed. "I am rarely mad at my grandmother. In fact, that might be the first time in my whole life," she added. "But after I thought about it for like a second, I decided to trust her. And in retrospect she was right."

She threw her hands in the air and whirled around once as they walked, directing Todd's attention to their surroundings. "I mean just look at this place! We're on this beautiful, unique island and I can't believe how many people I see with their noses glued to a tiny screen. And what's crazy about it is I could easily have been like that too!"

Todd nodded in agreement. "They're handy little contraptions but they can easily become an addiction. We're not a stone age family. We do have a few devices, but I limit usage time, and I'd rather have my kids pick up a book or a ball instead of a screen when they want something to do."

"One thing I do miss, though, is taking photos," Emma said. Not necessarily for social media, although I am guilty of that too," she admitted. "It's just nice to have the visual reminder, a record. In some ways I tend to use my camera roll as a daily journal. But of course, my grandmother thought of that too, and she gave me a sketch pad and pencils to use instead."

"Ahh, does that mean you're some sort of an artist?" Todd asked.

Emma hesitated before answering. She wasn't sure how to respond. "Mm, I wouldn't exactly call myself that," she said modestly, "but I do have an aptitude for drawing, I guess. I kind of put it on the shelf in recent years. I forgot how much I enjoyed it. For the past few days, though, I've been having fun with it again. I did a sketch of Arch Rock from along the shore on my bike ride, and a few views of town from different parts of the Fort yesterday."

They were closer to the busier part of Main Street now. This time when they crossed the road, Todd and Emma kept a firm grasp on the children when they reached the other side so no one got separated from them as the current of tourist traffic grew stronger.

They paused in front of a doorway and Todd said, "Whaddya say, gang? Should we stop here for a burger?"

This proposal was met with a chorus of unanimous consent, and they went inside.

The restaurant's candy pink décor, accented by depictions of dancing cartoon horses on the walls provided a lighthearted atmosphere. They passed through the lively bar area and were seated on the back deck, under a shady umbrella. The harbor stretched out in front of them, with sailboats and fishermen and ferries going about their business.

"This is a dangerous spot," Todd remarked as he settled into his chair.

"Oh?" said Emma, glancing first at the deck railing with concern and then at the two children. She expected him to say something about the risk of the kids being so close to the water. The railing looked solid. Maybe the kids couldn't swim? They seemed well behaved, but was he worried they would spontaneously tumble off the deck? Was the bay prone to sudden tsunami waves? Her first impression of the table was that it was a perfect spot for a fun lunch, and now she was rethinking that. Was she so out of practice being around children that she could no longer accurately judge a safe space for them?

She nervously anticipated Todd flagging down a staff member to ask if they could be reseated elsewhere, but then it occurred to her that wouldn't make sense, because he had just helped his children into their chairs, and he was unbelievably relaxed as he stretched out his legs and tipped his head back to let the sun shine on his handsome face.

"What makes it dangerous?" Emma asked with an element of concern in her voice.

"I could become permanently rooted here. The kids might need to carry me back to the inn," he quipped.

Judging from their reactions, the children had heard this dad joke before. Sophie rolled her eyes, embarrassed. "Oh, puh-lease, not again."

Shaking off her initial concern Emma now shifted gears to play along. She leaned in toward the children and added, "I hear there's one of those little red wagons in the basement we can use if we have to haul him out of here."

Liam's eyes grew wide, as his brain worked to discern if he was truly expected to lug his father home. Everyone laughed.

Emma realized she still had some lightening up to do. Yes, children required vigilance to keep them safe, but every situation was not a tragedy waiting to happen.

Over lunch, Emma learned Todd double majored in math and finance in college. He spent several years as an investment banker, a career he enjoyed until the hours became too demanding in his role as a single parent. He then made the decision to channel his love of carpentry into a new career, a change that allowed more flexibility in his schedule to be with his children.

"I made a few good investment decisions when I was young that made the switch possible. The salary's a bit different," he said with a nervous laugh, "but I set my own hours now. Sometimes it's a bit crazy, but we make it work."

"A math major, really? Are you one of those people who like to curl up with a good calculus book in front of the fireplace on a cold wintery night?"

"How did you know that? Did they tell you?" He asked, humorously pointing one finger at each of his children. "It's supposed to be a secret!"

"Super Top Secret," said Liam.

"Dad, you're a dork. It's obvious," stated Sophie.

Todd's mouth fell open incredulously, "Me?" he asked. "A dork?"

"Yes!" came the emphatic response in unison from the two children. The whole table burst out laughing.

"And there you have it. The board of directors has spoken," he said humbly with a gesture of open arms.

Emma smiled. "I had a math teacher in high school who used to say that, about reading math books in his spare time. He said he preferred that over watching TV, which I never understood. I always tried to figure out if he was kidding to try to get us to study more or if it was actually a thing for people who love math."

"Oh, it is true. A good mathematical equation can be quite beautiful. At times it's like poetry. And it all comes in handy for me now. I do a lot of historic restoration work on old homes and let me tell you, the angles in my woodworking are pure perfection," as he rested his elbows on the table and formed a peak with the fingertips of each hand.

Sophie rolled her eyes and did a face palm in exaggerated embarrassment.

At his reference to equations and poetry, Emma imagined this man's Valentine cards containing mathematical formulas.

Love² > XOXO

They finished their lunch and enjoyed small bowls of ice cream for dessert as they watched several ferries arrive and depart. Todd was right about the table and its prime location. With hunger satisfied and access to a steady supply of cold beverages, it would be easy to sit there all afternoon. However, even the well-behaved children began to get restless and fidgety once they were done eating. Todd announced, "It's time to move on. Maybe do some shopping."

"Fudge!" both children exclaimed together.

"More sugar?" Emma asked sarcastically, eyeballing the children with a frown of exaggerated concern.

"Oh yes," Todd said. "I have a plan," and then followed with a laugh of a cartoon evil scientist.

They left the restaurant with Todd under his own power, not pulled in a wagon by the children, much to their relief. The group visited two different fudge shops, each child choosing the store they wanted and selecting their favorite flavor from it. Liam made a strong case to add a bag of gummy bears to his order. His sister supported the suggestion, so those were also included in the tab.

Emma followed along, thoughtfully selecting a small portion of a different flavor of fudge from each establishment. Todd read the uncomfortable expression on her face at the second stop.

"You're looking a little guilty. You don't cut loose very often, do you?"

"This sugar splurge feels so decadent. I can't believe I'm buying more," Emma confessed. "I already got some yesterday, but it all just looks and smells incredible!"

"Pro tip: it freezes well. We will not be busting into most of this anytime soon," he assured her, holding up the bag.

"Hey, I'm not judging," she laughed, but she liked his idea and made a plan to save and freeze a portion of hers too.

"If you put gummy bears in the freezer, then they're polar bears," Liam announced.

They browsed their way down the street, stopping at various shops, including some she had overlooked the day before. At one boutique, there was a festive display of Christmas decorations. Flexing her newfound impulsiveness, Emma bought two. One was a hand-painted wooden ornament featuring a plume of lilacs and the other was a small glittery butterfly hanging on a thin golden string. Last year, she skipped the holidays, but if she put up a Christmas tree this year, she wanted a few of the ornaments on it to remind her of this trip and this special day.

They continued exploring the shops and the town area until on the far end, they stopped in the Island's library for a quick visit. Todd showed Emma the small deck at the back of the building. "I didn't know this was here!" she said in surprise, admiring the postcard-perfect view of the Straits. "We always walked or rode our bikes right past it and never stopped."

"The island is full of special places, little secret nooks most of the daily visitors pass right by, without even knowing they're here. Everyone is always in such a hurry," Todd commented.

Liam and Sophie made themselves comfortable in the set of white wooden Adirondack chairs available on the deck. They lounged like miniature experts in the activity, their small bodies fully relaxed with eyes closed and feet dangling, as if a day with a butterfly safari, a dockside lunch, and souvenir shopping had been a grueling marathon. "Uh, yeah, I don't know where they got that skill from," their father noted with humor.

"Knowing how to de-stress is an actual superpower," Emma admired. Without missing a beat, Sophie kept her eyes closed, but flexed her wiry arms as if to show muscular biceps.

"I am Super Soph," she announced confidently.

"Hey guys, don't get too comfortable, we still have one more stop to make. We need to put some of these souvenirs to use." The kids scrambled into action, as if fully recharged by solar power during their brief lounging session, and they disappeared around the corner of the library building.

"Such sweet children," Emma thought. As she turned to go, she inhaled the pleasant scent of a lilac blooming somewhere nearby.

~ 30 ~

Todd rested his tanned forearms on the worn picnic table at Windermere Point. From where he sat, he could keep an eye on his children. Emma sat diagonally across from him, feet up on the bench, her arms hugging her knees. During their meandering journey through town, they stopped at the toy store, and she purchased a few small items for the children as thank you gifts for inviting her to join them. Sophie now played with a kite on the grassy area and Liam set about constructing a fort of smooth stones from which his new dinosaur action figures could reign over the beach. With the children out of earshot, Todd asked Emma for more details about her life in the aftermath of her parents' accident.

Taking a deep breath she began, resolving to pause if the tears welled up. She wanted to share her story articulately and rationally, to see if she could do it without losing composure and crumbling into a soggy mess. This time, as she pieced together the events, it wasn't sadness that bubbled up. Instead, she picked her way through the rockslide of other feelings, of powerlessness, alienation, and isolation that swept through her life and buried her alive.

"And then all of my friends just kind of disappeared," she shared. "I mean they were there online, on social media, but in person?" She shook her head. "They mostly stopped showing up."

Emma unspooled her frustrations in one long, continuous string, like the thin strand lifting Sophie's kite into the sky.

"When a few of them did call me, they would ask questions that went too far and triggered my emotions, and I would end up crying on the phone and then they cut off the conversation because they didn't want to deal with the tears. And then, they didn't call anymore, and I stopped trying to contact them too. I know I had work to do to pull myself together, but it was like most of them didn't even try to take a minute to understand what I was dealing with."

Emma took another breath and continued. "And the guy I had been seeing ended up being a total jerk."

The wind blew stray strands of hair across her face. She reached up to push them away. The tone of her voice reflected her anger.

"I know no one likes a downer, but oh my gosh, both of my parents just died, and they all act like I'm supposed to carry on and be happy and the same as before, you know?" She stared out across the lakeshore.

"Yeah," Todd said gently. "I actually do know."

Emma's stomach contracted in an involuntary spasm. She buried her face in her knees. She was allowing herself to vent, ridding herself of pent-up anxiety but not thinking about who was hearing it and his own recent loss experiences. Had she been insensitive? Self-absorbed? Rude? Had she done the thing others did to her?

She started to apologize, "Oh my gosh, I'm sorry. I didn't mean...," but he raised a hand and stopped her.

"No need to feel sorry," Todd said. "What I meant was I've gone through a lot of the same emotional challenges as you have, so I might understand things a little differently than some of your friends. I had a similar kind of experience as you, in a way."

Emma slid her feet off the bench, placing them flat on the ground. "I can't imagine going through what you did, and with children too, wow. That must have been very difficult."

"Ironically," he said, "the kids may have helped. It gave me purpose. I had to keep things moving forward for their sakes. Some days, I would paste on a dad face and make it all about them for a while. I'd try to make it as normal as possible, trying to show them life does go on. And I ended up getting some benefit out of that too. They brought me so much comfort, so much joy even."

He gave a nod of his head toward the beach, in the direction of Sophie and Liam, on the rocky shore. "I see a lot of their mother in them. That helps. It's like she's not totally gone. Like it validates what we had, preserves it. It reminds me I didn't imagine it."

In the distance, a ferry horn sounded, and he continued, "That validation is part of who you are for your grandmother now. I'll bet there are times when she watches you and sees your mom when she was your age."

Emma nodded, "Yes. She tells me that." Then she added, "It's a lot of pressure though. Now I feel like I'm the 'legacy'. Like I have to do whatever it is I'm supposed to do with my life but also be this exceptional achiever to honor both of my parents and take care of their unfinished business too."

Todd laughed, "Please tell me that's not your internal dialogue, because that would be an enormous burden." Emma had been watching the waves roll into the shore, but now her head swung back to meet his eyes briefly before she glanced downward.

She nodded and answered uncomfortably, "Um, yeah. It is?"

"Well, then that explains the need for the whole intervention thing. Kudos to your grandmother for successfully getting you out of your apartment."

Emma gave a weak smile.

Todd continued, "No, really. You can't keep doing that to yourself. It's way too much pressure. You don't need to pull off some special achievement to honor your parents. You honor them by just being you. All that any parent wants is for their child to be happy. I swear." He held up his hand in a symbolic gesture of oath.

He nodded in the direction of his children.

"Look at them. Their mother didn't give them some iron clad mandate to complete her unfinished business, and I guarantee your parents wouldn't want that for you either. And if your friends can't be patient enough to get through this with you, to give you time to deal with things or be considerate enough to talk about what makes them uncomfortable instead of ghosting you, then maybe they aren't the right people to be in your inner circle anymore.

"A death is hard on everybody, it's painful for you and awkward for your friends. It takes forgiveness, in both directions. Some of those friendships are worth reconnecting with, and others are better left in the past. You'll know which relationships you want to save, and you'll eventually find other people, new friends to replace the ones you've outgrown, but not if you stay in your apartment all day."

Liam and Sophie continued to be engrossed in their own activities.

"They're handling it pretty well I think, but they still cry sometimes," he said. "We all do."

For a few moments, there was only the sound of the wind.

The intensity of the topic and an assortment of difficult memories made Todd restless. "Hey, I'm going to get a lemonade, can I get you one too?"

Emma nodded. "Sure. Please."

He walked away, tilting his head side to side, then rolling his shoulders to work out the tension as he headed off to the concession stand.

There was a lot to digest from that conversation, uncomfortable truths about the way she'd handled the past year and she needed a few minutes to process things too. "Forgiveness, in both directions," he'd said. That one hit the bullseye. She had some work to do there.

She managed to get through the discussion without crying though. It was a bit of a milestone. A small victory. No, a big one. Emma stood up to stretch. She reseated herself at the picnic table, this time on the side where Todd had been sitting, facing his two children who were playing on the shore of the point. She retrieved her sketch pad and pencils from her backpack.

Liam was now building some sort of pyramid structure out of bits of driftwood and rock, while Sophie expertly wrangled the kite at the edge of the grassy area.

"She's good with that kite," Emma mentioned when Todd returned with the two cold beverages.

"Yes, she is," he said, handing Emma her lemonade. "She has excellent eye-hand coordination and instincts with the wind. One of her friends has this cool little radio-controlled yacht they race on a local pond. They have to trim the sails to catch the wind, like on the real thing. She already informed me she wants to get an actual sailboat when she's old enough. She's saving her allowance for that. Sophie's more goal oriented than her brother. Liam lives in the moment. He's more of a daredevil. He'll try things with zero concern about aftereffects. He dives right in, regardless of risk.

"I want them both to be brave. To try new things. To not be afraid to fail. He's giving me gray hair already though, and he's only five. I try to remember what I was like at that age."

Emma laughed softly as she tried to imagine a five-year-old Todd. He settled himself back in his old spot, now on the same side of the table as Emma and as she sketched, he watched the children play.

After a few minutes, he got up and jogged over to review the progress on Liam's architectural efforts. They consulted on a few features. Todd collected a few larger stones and pieces of driftwood to provide additional construction material for his son and deposited them in a pile near Liam's pyramid. Then he walked over to where Sophie was reeling in the kite. She was skilled at making it swoop and dip but not crash. Todd conferred with her, reminding her not to let the aerobatics of the kite get too close to where others were enjoying the open beach space.

After kissing his daughter on the top of her head, he returned to the picnic table where Emma was finishing her sketch.

"Are you feeling bold enough to show me your work? Or are you more of the reclusive artist type, never sharing your talents with the outside world?" he joked as she signed her name and put the date in the corner.

She put her pencil down and carefully tore the sketch from the book. "For you," she said, handing it to him.

He reached out to accept it and then studied the paper in his hand. "Emma, this is incredible. You just drew this? Here, right now?"

"Mm-hm," Emma acknowledged with a smug nod. Her confidence in her artistic ability was growing. She had sketched a beach scene, with a small boy crouched down building a stone structure and a young girl flying a kite, with one of the lighthouses and a bit of the bridge in the background. It captured the simple beauty of the moment, the likenesses of the two children and the atmosphere of the island.

"I'm totally framing this. This is very special, and much more meaningful than a photograph."

Emma smiled modestly and said, "thank you."

Silently, she agreed with him. Except "meaningful" was an understatement. As she drew the scene, the details of it were simultaneously etched into her memory. Emma perfectly preserved the captivating tilt of Liam's head while he concentrated on his building project and the way the lake breeze lifted Sophie's hair gently off her shoulders as she reeled in her kite. Even without a photograph, she would now remember this afternoon forever.

Finishing the last of her lemonade, Emma glanced down at her watch. Although she was thoroughly enjoying her time with this family, she feared she was in danger of overstaying her welcome. She gathered her sketchbook and pencils, stashed them in her backpack, and stood up.

"Todd, I want to say thank you for letting me spend the day with you and your children. I enjoyed your company, all of you."

He frowned with concern. "You're not leaving now, are you?" he asked.

She nodded.

"Did I say something upsetting?"

"Oh goodness, no!" Emma clarified. "The conversation was great! Really great. But I need to head back to the inn to make sure my room is all settled. My check-in this morning was a last-minute thing and without a reservation, and they can't call me if my phone is off. I want to make sure things are still OK."

"Oh, absolutely," he nodded. "That's a good idea." His brow furrowed slightly as he sorted through the implications of this sudden development.

Then, he spoke again. "Would you like to join us for dinner tonight? We're taking a carriage to the restaurant in the woods." Smiling, he leaned forward for emphasis, "It's really fun." Then added, "We can meet you in the parlor of the inn about ten minutes before 6?"

Another gust of wind from the lake whipped Emma's hair and blew it into her face as she considered the offer. She gathered her hair in a handful off to one side and said, "You don't mind me tagging along?"

"On the contrary," he said, sounding a bit formal, "I'm confident I speak for my children when I say we'd all be delighted if you would join us."

She gently bit her bottom lip while she mulled over her options, but it was an easy decision. "OK, then! That sounds great, see you in the parlor, ten minutes to six," she repeated the time to confirm it in her memory. "See you then!"

Emma lifted her hand in a small wave. She made her way across the lawn to the sidewalk and down the street in the direction of the inn. She walked a short distance before turning to see if she could still see them on the beach.

From where she stood, she could no longer see Todd or Liam, but she caught a glimpse of Sophie's kite, floating and dancing in the sky, just like her heart.

$$\sim 31 \sim$$

Everything was all in order with her room when Emma returned to the inn. She retrieved her key from the desk, then climbed the long set of stairs to the second floor. Unlocking her door, she pushed it open and gave a small gasp of delight. The room was beautiful. There were plenty of windows offering both natural light and fresh air. A gentle breeze made the lace curtains flutter, beckoning her to go inside.

While unpacking a few items from her suitcase, she admired the elegant canopy bed. She ran her hand over the cool marble top on the dresser that reminded her of one at her grandmother's house. Grand Hotel already carved out a permanent place in her heart, and now this inn was rapidly claiming space right alongside it.

There were about two hours before she was to meet Todd and the children in the parlor downstairs. Emma adjusted the bedside alarm clock as a "get ready" reminder and made herself a cushiony nest of pillows against her bed's headboard. She could relax and sketch for a bit. From there, she could be both comfortably nestled into the bedding and see out the windows of the room to catch glimpses of horses and bicycles as they passed by.

Grandy advised her to boldly put the best parts of herself out into the world, and she was once again realizing how much she enjoyed drawing. So far, everyone who caught a glimpse of her sketches gave her an unsolicited positive reaction. Perhaps this was a way she could put some of her grandmother's advice into practice.

Images of the morning's trip to the butterfly house were called forth from her memory. They took shape on the paper while the island's calming music of carriages, muted pedestrian conversations, and harbor noises drifted in through the open windows.

She awoke, not to the alarm, but to the sound of a delivery driver stacking heavy crates of something on a sidewalk outside. He was not being gentle. Slam. Bam. Then a quick shout, and another thud.

"Whoa," Emma thought as she shook the cobwebs of sleep off her brain. "That was a weird dream." She pondered the lingering remnants of it: a chorus line of dancing horses, where some were talking on cell phones and others flung wreaths of lilacs to their admiring audience.

She retrieved the pencil from where it had fallen out of her grasp, closed the sketchbook, and glanced over to see how much time she still had before she needed to get ready for dinner. She stared at the clock face for a few seconds. The time wasn't making sense.

"Wait, what?"

Reaching over, she grabbed the clock, first studying the numbers on its face and then the buttons. She had updated the alarm time, but in her distracted state thinking about Todd and the children and the day, she neglected to turn the alarm function "on".

Her initial plan had been to rest and sketch for thirty minutes allowing plenty of time to pull herself together. But the clock now indicated she already used up far more than that. She was left with just twenty minutes to get ready for dinner.

She leapt out of bed and for a moment stood frozen in the middle of the room, in a strange crouching stance. Was this another fight or flight response? She couldn't figure out if her body was telling her to sprint or spar. It was going to be both. Run to get ready *and* fight the clock. She would not be late!

Emma had a rush of adrenaline as she whirled around the room. Everything was unfamiliar and her thoughts were scattered. Where did she put this item or that thing? She would recall a specific object and then wonder, did she put that in a drawer here or was she remembering a detail from when she was back at Grand Hotel? She forgot what was unpacked and then if it was still stored, was it in the big bag or in her backpack? Her toothbrush – where was that stashed? She wasn't careful to pack in an orderly fashion earlier in the morning when she threw things into her luggage because at that time, she thought she was headed to the ferry and then home. But then, of course, her plans changed.

She jumped into the shower, appreciating the inn's scented bath products because she couldn't find the little travel-size ones she brought. She regretted she didn't have time to linger under the refreshing spray of the showerhead. It was better than the one she had at home. But for now, she only had fourteen minutes left to get ready.

Combing out her hair, she plugged in the blow dryer. Using her fingers and a round brush, she managed to get it reasonably dry and falling into gentle waves. Ten minutes to go.

Deep breath. She examined her face in the mirror. Luckily, most of the previous day's sunburn faded and although there was time spent outdoors today, the sunglass marks were no longer as dramatic. Her morning routine, again based on thinking she'd be on the ferry, then in the car, was mostly sunscreen and lip balm. Was that just this morning? It seemed a lifetime ago. She smoothed on some tinted moisturizer, added a few coats of mascara, and a swipe of berry pink gloss on her lips. Seven minutes left.

Now, clothes. Would everything be hopelessly wrinkled? There was no time to try to iron anything. She let out a muffled outburst of frustration. "Why didn't I figure this out earlier before I fell asleep!" But then she reminded herself she hadn't planned on napping: it was the natural outcome of a dose of fresh air, a dash of physical activity, and a super comfy bed. She wanted to look nice, maybe a little dressed up, but not over the top.

She remembered the pink polka dot dress from Grandy. "Oh yes! That would be perfect for tonight!" But then she feared it would be impossibly wrinkled. It had been crammed in the suitcase all day and it wasn't one of the items she managed to hang up earlier. Extracting it from the pile of clothing, she gave it two good shakes, then held it out at arm's length.

"What is this miraculous fabric?" Emma exclaimed with relief. The dress had been smashed in the suitcase all day, and yet there was not a fold or crease on it that wasn't supposed to be there. Score! She added the lilac crystal necklace and pulled a section of her hair back on one side, fastening it with a barrette. Inhale, exhale, two minutes before she had to be downstairs.

She needed shoes. She rummaged around in her suitcase. Fancy? No. Sandals? Maybe, but in her haste she could only find one. That left her sneakers. That will have to do. She slid them on without even untying them first. Time to go!

She grabbed her wallet, the scarfy-shawl thing (in case it got chilly) and nearly tumbled down the stairway in a mad dash to get to the parlor.

She could hear Sophie and Liam chattering on the other side of the doorway. Emma stopped for a moment to compose herself before entering the room. She didn't want to run into the parlor all flustered. Grasping the railing of the stairway, she took another deep breath and slowly let it out.

"Don't worry," said a familiar voice behind her. "It's just us."

Startled, Emma whirled around. It was Todd. Somehow, he descended the stairs right behind her without making a sound. He caught her in her frantic natural state, while she was attempting to put on a façade of being composed.

"Oh, hi!" she exclaimed awkwardly. "You're here. I thought you were all in there," and she gestured toward the room where Liam and Sophie played.

"The kids were excited and came downstairs early. You look nice."

"Thanks, you do too." It was the first time she had seen him without his baseball cap since the ferry and his freshly washed hair formed a crown of sun-lightened curls around his head. They walked around the corner, into the parlor to collect Sophie and Liam, who both cleaned up quite nicely too.

"I was running around like crazy up there," Emma explained. "I tried to relax for a bit, but I messed up the alarm, and I just woke up a few minutes ago. I couldn't find the sandals I wanted to wear, and I even think my hair still wet." She grasped a handful of her light brown waves and as she let them fall through her fingers, the shampoo's floral scent filled the air.

"We did not take naps." Sophie announced proudly.

"Yeah, and you guys were supposed to," her father said sternly. "And that's not going to be a problem, right, you guys?"

"Right!" Sophie and Liam both responded, but their father raised his eyebrows in skepticism. He mouthed the words "too much fudge" and Emma pressed her lips together to stifle a giggle.

The group left the inn and went down the walkway to where the carriage taxi was scheduled to pick them up, retracing their steps from earlier in the day. When they reached the street, they saw the horse drawn cab approaching in the distance, moving slowly but steadily along.

"The pace of things here cracks me up," Emma said. It's a big reminder of how crazy the so-called 'real world' has gotten."

"That's for sure," said Todd. "I like to come here for a few days to recalibrate."

The taxi carriage pulled up to the loading zone, and they all climbed aboard, with Emma and Todd on the outside spots of the long seat, squeezing the two children into the middle.

"Just to clarify, there will be no falling out of a taxi today," said Todd. Liam responded with a thumbs up, and Sophie nodded, appearing ladylike as she glanced around assessing the view from where she sat.

The driver waited a few more minutes until a young couple climbed aboard into another seat row. "I think that's everyone!" the driver announced, and the carriage gave a little lurch to begin its slow plodding journey to the destination, accompanied by the musical drumbeat of horse hooves.

"It's a bit of a stretch but by any chance were your parents Monty Python fans?" Todd asked.

"Oh my gosh," Emma said. "Coconuts!" And the two of them laughed heartily.

Their route took them in front of Grand Hotel. Since her stay there, it appeared different to Emma. No longer a stranger, it had become a friend. She knew a few of its stories now and even created a few new ones of her own. The taxi continued up the steep hill toward the overlook. "I watched a great sunset from up here a few days ago," and she pointed to the area where she stood to see the magnificent bridge shining brightly in the evening sun.

But then she corrected herself, "Wait! That was last night! It seems like so long ago," she laughed. The carriage stopped. The children sat up taller as if to see what was going on. Emma wondered too.

The driver turned around in his seat and explained. "Steep hill. Giving the team a break."

"See what I mean?" said Todd. "Recalibrate. Horses need a break. And sometimes, after we climb a big hill in life, people do too."

Emma nodded. He was right.

~ 32 ~

Todd leapt effortlessly from the taxi when they reached their destination. If he was the cork of this champagne bottle, then Liam and Sophie were the bubbles as they excitedly tumbled out of the carriage. Emma flowed out in a more reserved fashion, accepting Todd's gentlemanly hand as she gracefully made the step down to the ground.

Nestled back in the trees, the restaurant resembled a European storybook mansion. "This is totally cool!" Emma exclaimed. "I didn't think it would be like this. Ha!" Adding a small laugh at the novelty of it.

Todd smiled smugly, "Yeah, it's pretty neat, isn't it?" A gentle breeze caused the trees around the restaurant to jostle their leaves slightly, as if waving a jazz-hands welcome to the diners.

"I'm hungry," announced Liam.

His father said, "Well then, we won't get anything to eat if we just stand around out here, will we?"

The entryway was decorated in a warm rustic style. They still had a few minutes before their scheduled reservation. After checking in with the host, Todd showed Emma one of the special features of the restaurant. Off to one side of the building, there was a single lane of an old-fashioned duckpin bowling alley, with its short squatty pins and small bowling balls.

"Ahh," said Emma with delight. "One of those secret Island nooks you mentioned earlier."

Todd nodded. "Exactly."

"Oh please, can we play a game?" pleaded Sophie.

Todd granted her a parentally non-committal reply of "We'll see," but before they were able to arrange a few tries of the lane, the host summoned them.

Emma thought she was walking into the setting of a fairy tale as she entered the main dining room. A warm red color on the ceiling and walls was accented by massive timbered arches. Large leaded glass windows, speckled with occasional colored panes, permitted sunlight to enter during the day and lamplight to exit at night. The hungry foursome followed the host across the diamond patterned floor to where their assigned table awaited.

The room's cozy atmosphere was at the same time both elegant and decidedly unfussy. Chandeliers made from antlers added style with a rustic edge. The tables were dressed in white, but instead of an unforgiving layer of starched linen highlighting every crumb or drip, each one was draped with a large sheet of crisp paper. And to be sure the children felt welcome, a selection of crayons was included.

"Crayonnnnns! Can we, Daddy?" asked Sophie as she confidently reached for the container. She may have been denied the opportunity to try out the bowling alley, but she was not going to let this chance slip away.

"Yes, but remember your manners. You both need to share."

"Cray-ons! Cray-ons! Cray-ons!" chanted Liam.

Emma sat across the table from Todd with the children on the other two sides. After helping the younger diners with their menu selections and then deciding on their own, Emma and Todd began working on drawings too. They chatted casually about random topics as they all worked on their masterpieces and shared the art supplies.

"Who's got the green?"

"I need the red crayon."

"Brown, please!"

Todd built a wall around his drawing using his napkin, a candle, and the small vase of flowers.

"Oooh, so secretive," said Emma.

"Super Top Secret," answered Todd.

Emma finished her artwork and covered it with her dinner napkin, then leaned back in her chair. Liam and Sophie were done too, making random scribbles on the side of their main drawings. Finally, Todd set down his crayons.

"Are you guys done yet?"

Sophie answered on behalf of the rest of the table, "We're all waiting for *you*, Dad."

He laughed, "Of course you are. Ready for the big reveal?"

A chorus of yesses circled the table.

"What have you got, Liam?" Todd inquired.

"I have a cannon and a soldier and a kite," the boy announced proudly, "And the cannon is BLASTING the kite out of the sky." He made an explosion noise and threw his arms up for emphasis.

Sophie rolled her eyes. Emma struggled to muffle a snort. Todd laughed and shot Emma a wide-eyed look as he shook his head.

"That's quite dramatic of you, Liam."

"Very original," added Emma. "And what has Sophie made?"

"I have a blue morpho on a hibiscus flower, like we saw this morning at the butterfly house." She displayed her creation and described it with a polished grace far beyond her young age.

"That's lovely, Sophie!" said Emma.

"And you remembered the butterfly's scientific name too! Well done," Todd added. Then he turned to Emma and said, "And what have you drawn, Miss Emma?"

Emma removed her napkin with a theatrical flourish to reveal a depiction of two scoops of ice cream, topped with colorful sprinkles, and a swirl of melting chocolate streaming down the base of the cone. One large drop was placed at the edge of the table as if it was about to drip on her pink polka dot dress.

"Ice cream!" said Liam and Sophie in unison.

"Melting, with a drip," remarked Emma, tilting her head sideways. This time it was her turn to offer Todd a wink across the table.

He burst out laughing. "That's excellent."

"And yours?" Emma wondered aloud, peering over the table, hoping to catch an early glimpse of the final piece of art.

Todd removed the obstructions blocking her view. His drawing was upside down from her perspective. In the candlelight, she could see he had made an attempt to sketch some sort of tree. No, it was more like an oval shaped shrub, with brown trunk and branches, with swirls of green leaves, and random splotches of pink and purple.

"It's supposed to be a lilac," he said.

Her eyes shot to meet his. Their gazes locked on each other. She knew if she tried to speak, her voice would be distorted by emotion. After a second she mouthed the words, "Thank you."

He offered her a smile and a single sincere nod of his head.

Emma was deeply touched. He not only acknowledged an important symbol of her journey, but he also planted a beautiful new memory right in the middle of it. He had given her a lilac.

"Hey, this is some of the best artwork I've seen all day," remarked the server, who arrived with a loaded tray of food. The delicious smelling plates were distributed around the table.

Emma savored the moment, the company, and the atmosphere. "Keep things light and fun," she reminded herself. Things were going well.

Dinner conversation was lively and covered a range of topics: favorite colors, favorite ice cream flavors, and favorite holidays. The color and flavor categories tallied a variety of answers, but Christmas was the unanimous holiday winner.

"If you could be an Olympic athlete, what sport would you compete in?" They first debated the Summer Games, then Winter, and pondered why there aren't Olympic-level competitive snowball fights. Birth places, hobbies, preferred pizza toppings, and the age-old peanut butter debate of crunchy vs smooth were all brought up for review.

The children mentioned their mother several times. It was clear in this family she was frequently discussed and remembered. Honored. Respected. Emma was impressed by the way Todd guided the discussion about his late wife. He held his own composure, and Sophie and Liam did not collapse into a puddle of tears. They all loved and missed her, but their grief was evolved beyond where Emma had gotten stuck with the memory of her own parents. This family, this father and his young children, had achieved the emotional resilience she longed for.

Emma had a flash of Grandy and her pre-trip lecture. Her hand went to the lilac pendant on the chain around her neck.

"They are in that place of strength where Grandy is encouraging me to be." They knew how to find their own lilacs. For the children, it was the bright blue butterflies, and peanut butter sandwiches cut into triangles that reminded them of their mother. They were confident in what their mother loved about them, and they were putting it back out into the world, as best as they could at their young ages. Sophie and Liam had endured a tragedy, but they had also done a lot of emotional work to find their way to this place of acceptance and peace. These children were so young and seemed innocent and fragile, but in this special way they were strong far beyond their years. She admired Todd for how he handled his own loss and for ensuring his children's hearts were protected. They had all experienced deep sorrow, and yet they were still able to laugh and be normal, even exceptional.

"I know I'm not quite there yet," Emma thought, "but now, by learning from Grandy and from Todd and his children, I can picture where I want to go in my own journey of healing and growth."

It was getting dark outside when they left the restaurant. Emma turned to Todd and announced, "Great Spangled Fritillary, that was delicious!"

His laughter rang out. "See, I told you it was fun to say. I tell you, that phrase is going to catch on!"

Sophie and Liam ran up and down the idyllic tree-lined street while they waited for the taxi to arrive. "By all means, use up the energy, please, before we get back to the inn," Todd stated as they sprinted and skipped. "They're like little supercharged engines," he said.

"Powered by fudge?" Emma asked.

"And gummy bears," he added. "And general childhood exuberance. Sometimes I wish I could skim off a little from them and use it myself."

Emma turned and glanced back over her shoulder at the restaurant, the warm glow from inside now spilling outward into the twilight through its windows. "You were right. This place is a special treat. Thank you for inviting me."

"Absolutely. You're welcome. I'm glad you came. The whole day has been great. I'm happy we ran into you this morning."

She nodded, "Me too," and their gazes locked on each other for more than a few heartbeats, as fireflies started to twinkle in the darkness, and the taxi appeared in the distance.

Emma stepped into the carriage first and then gave Sophie a hand. The little girl climbed into the seat next to her, announcing, "I'm going to sit next to Miss Emma."

Liam followed, scrambling up into the same row and squeezing past both of them saying, "I'm going to sit next to Miss Emma too," as he wedged himself in on the other side of her. Emma slid a bit more to the center to avoid squishing him and to keep the whole boy safely inside the carriage.

"Hey, what if *I* want to sit next to Miss Emma?" Todd asked as he stood at the curb, arms raised in exasperation.

The driver laughed, "Sir, I think you're out of luck."

Todd let out a sigh of faux frustration as he slid into the seat behind Emma and his two children. "Now I get this whole giant, huge, comfy seat back here all to myself!" he crowed.

"And we have Miss Emma!" Sophie stated.

"Yeah, we have Miss Emma!" added Liam as he snuggled in next to her.

Emma enjoyed the coziness in the pleasant evening air. She stretched out her arms and wrapped one around each child, holding them securely as they leaned on her, the children using her as a pillow for the leisurely drive home.

Todd leaned forward and gently touched her shoulder. "You OK up there? Do you want me to bring one of them back here?"

"Thanks, we're good," Emma said, turning to display a contented smile and firing off another wink at him.

For Emma, the trip back to the inn passed much too quickly. This had been an incredible day, and she did not want the evening to be over.

She was pleased that when they reached the end of the ride, Todd suggested he and Emma sit in the back garden behind the inn for a bit. "I'll get the kids settled in for the night and then meet you back down there so we can talk a little more. Our room is right above the garden. If they need anything they can give a shout through the open window."

Emma walked down the brick pathway, around the corner to the yard behind the inn. A small grassy area was encircled by tall, green shrubbery. She could tell there was at least one still blooming lilac in the mix, seeing the familiar bunches of flowers and inhaling the scent. It looked like the one that perhaps had been the inspiration for Todd's drawing at dinner. She walked over to it and inspected the blossoms, still soft and fragrant but showing signs of being near the end of its season.

Strings of tiny white lights were strung through the branches of a tree and acted like a handful of stars, shedding a gentle glow over the area. Emma took a seat on an ornate wrought iron bench next to a small pretty fountain. She was becoming fond of these cozy little outdoor seating areas.

A lamp shone in an upstairs window of the inn. Soft voices carried through its screened opening, two lilting in a higher register, one in a deeper, stable tone.

"That must be their room," she thought. The lamp turned off, and then glowed again. "Someone wanted the light left on," she mused. Would it be Liam or Sophie? Or both? After a few moments, footsteps approached down the garden path, and Todd entered the back yard.

"So here we are, full circle, not too far from where we started the day," he said, settling himself next to her on the bench.

"And what a day it's been!" Emma noted. "I have to tell you," she said, keeping her voice low and her tone sincere, "your children are amazing."

Smiling, he glanced up at the window. "Thanks. They are pretty special," he said proudly. "You were great with them today. I know a lot of people wouldn't choose to spend their day wrangling a couple of rowdy kids."

"Honestly, today was kind of perfect. I don't think I'd have changed anything. Well, maybe I would have done a better job of making sure my alarm clock was turned on this afternoon. That's been a problem for me lately."

"Even that turned out OK," he reminded her. He stopped speaking for a moment, letting the sounds of the fountain fill the air.

"My children don't always connect easily with strangers," Todd said. "But over the past few days, they've come out of their shells quite a bit."

"This isn't typical behavior for them? Really?" Emma said, sounding a bit puzzled. "They seemed pretty… outgoing?"

She recalled the times Sophie had been humorous and animated, the way she asked to be in the photo with her, and the ways Liam boldly campaigned for the extra gummy bears and insisted on squeezing in next to her on the carriage seat.

"They haven't been very social the past few years. They withdrew a bit when their mother passed away. They've been extremely reserved around people they don't know well. But after you saved Liam's hat on the way over here, I think they saw that as some sort of ice breaker. A peace offering. Maybe a sign. I don't know if you know this but they both watched you on the ferry after that. And I confess, when I saw them doing that, I watched you a bit too. I wanted to find out who you were. What you were doing here. Who you were traveling with, if anyone. They asked me about you later in the day, wondering if we were going to see you again while we were on the island. It was Liam who spotted you at the Fort and pointed you out. So, I grabbed the opportunity to talk to you again. And then when you were here, in the parlor, this morning. Well, I knew I would regret it if I didn't invite you along.

"I'm glad you did." Emma was amused and humbled. Even from the first day on the ferry, they had all been curious about each other.

A child-sized head was silhouetted just above the sill of the open window. Liam, she guessed. "I think we're being spied on," she whispered. Todd casually looked upward.

"Yes, I see," he whispered back.

A nearby cricket began a brief chirping session and as it ended, Todd spoke again in a low, serious voice.

"I haven't dated anyone since… their mom," he revealed. "I didn't know how to go about introducing someone new to them. How to explain I'm not replacing their mother, but you know, maybe we could see if there's room for a new person in our lives? And then there's the whole risk of… things not working out? They've been through so much already. I can't imagine putting them through another difficult situation. It's complicated with kids. Really complicated."

Emma nodded. What he said was completely logical. It made sense. He needed to be more cautious than anyone she had ever dated in the past. Much more cautious. He was going to protect his family. His serious tone sounded like he was apologetically laying down the groundwork for some sort of boundary. A protective barrier. A rejection. For the first time in months, she foolishly dared to let herself be happy, but now it was going to be snatched away again.

She felt something when they were together though: chemistry, a spark, a lovely and mysterious attraction.

Maybe he picked up on it and was trying to find a way to politely say, "no thank you, too soon."

Maybe this discussion without the children around was a way of explaining why he needed to gently apply the brakes before things went any further.

Maybe he saw she still had work to do in healing her wounds of grief and he wasn't interested in taking a risk on a work-in-progress.

She had the urge to hit a cosmic pause button, to freeze the scene before anything was said that might tarnish the perfect day. She wanted to preserve it, like a scene in one of her sketches or like the tiny lilac flowers captured at peak bloom in her necklace, before anything could make the memory of it fade.

But then he continued. "So today was kind of an unexpected surprise. A very, very good one. We've catapulted past the whole tricky part of introducing you to my kids, if that's where we want to go with this."

Todd and Emma both turned their heads to face each other, smiling for a few moments as some sort of mutual realization took root and began to grow. He *had* felt what she felt. And he wasn't pushing her away. She nodded.

"Daa-aad." A small voice carried through the still evening air like the chime of a bell.

Todd angled his gaze up to the top floor of the inn. "Things OK up there, buddy?" he asked the shadowy figure in the window.

"I can see you." Liam stated.

"Yes, Liam. I can see you too. Now get back in bed and look at your baseball book," the boy's father instructed. Emma and Todd both quietly laughed. The small head momentarily disappeared from the window, but then reappeared and was joined by another.

"Can you see? Are they kissing?" Sophie asked in a loud whisper, followed by commentary from her brother.

"Eeeew, gross."

Emma covered her mouth to stifle a laugh. In the darkness Todd couldn't see the shade of pink spreading across her face in an embarrassed flush.

"They haven't mastered the art of surveillance yet, but I think that's a plus," Todd said.

Then he sighed, coming to terms with the intrusion. "I guess they're still a bit restless though. Perhaps we should call it a night?"

Emma reluctantly agreed. It was a little heartbreaking to think the beautiful day was coming to a close, especially considering the revelation of a few moments prior, but Todd had parental responsibilities to attend to. She understood.

"We'll see you at breakfast in the morning, right?" Todd asked optimistically. "We'll be down there at 8AM. We can exchange our contact information then. Don't forget to bring your phone." With a little nudge of his elbow before he stood up, he added sarcastically, "If you still know where to find it."

She smirked, "Ha ha, very funny. And yes, 8AM breakfast sounds great."

"Good night, Miss Emma."

"Good night, Mr. Todd. See you in the morning."

Emma was relieved this was "good night", a simple pause for a few hours until breakfast. He hadn't told her "Goodbye." She would see them all again tomorrow. It was safe to let herself feel happy. It wouldn't be snatched away tonight.

There was such an intense feeling of warmth in her heart she was sure she must be glowing, emitting some sort of golden light.

Todd jogged a little as he retraced his steps down the garden path. Her gaze went back to the upstairs window. First the two little silhouettes disappeared from the space between the curtains. Then, from the shadows on the wall, she could see when Todd entered the room. He walked to the window and all three of them, father and children, waved at her. She raised her arm in response, and he drew the curtains closed.

Before she went upstairs to her own room, Emma sat for a few more minutes in the cool green garden, enjoying the remaining sprigs of lilacs and the strings of tiny twinkling lights while attempting to engrave into her memory every detail of the magical day that had just taken place.

~ 33 ~

When she returned to her room after the conversation in the garden, filled with the aftereffects of adrenaline, a dash of romance, and a liberal quantity of moonlight, Emma flopped onto the four-poster canopy bed.

Sleep? Ha! No way. She stared at the ceiling, her mind replaying every minute of the nearly flawless day. She examined every decision, every thought, every emotion.

What if she had gotten on the ferry as she originally planned?

What if she had given up and gone home when she saw the first few no vacancy signs?

What if she dawdled five minutes longer before finding the inn? Would that delay have caused her to miss running into Todd and the children entirely?

Or if she walked faster, wouldn't she have bypassed the inn because the innkeeper hadn't been outside yet to change the sign to show there was a room available?

Everything about the day hinged on a handful of decisions made within a few minutes. She was being guided by a guardian angel or even the hand of God.

For the first time in a long time, things were falling into place the right way, instead of falling apart. It was as if the dark cloud parked over her for the past year was dissolving under rays of sunlight, as if some evil spell cast upon her was reversing, unwinding.

Around 1:30AM, still wide awake, Emma began to organize her belongings, staging them for an efficient departure in the morning. She would rather spend the time to do it then, and make sure she was early for breakfast. She didn't want to miss one possible minute with Todd and the children. They would eat together, and afterward they could take the same ferry from the island. They would still get to share some good times today before they went their separate ways.

She located her phone. Emma held it in her hand, looking at the blank screen. It was only a few days since she had used it, but it felt odd to her. It would be easy to power it on and check a few emails. She could see if anyone posted anything interesting or left her any messages. But the more she thought about it, she knew no notification, no tag, no text could compare with the real-life experience of the day she just had. Not once during the previous day was any conversation with Todd interrupted by a ding or a chirp or someone pulling out a device to check something. They connected, in person, without electronic distraction. And it was wonderful. She left the phone powered off and stashed it in the pocket of her backpack where she knew it would be. She could turn it on at breakfast, when she was ready to exchange contact information with Todd.

With everything set and ready to go, she crawled into bed in the wee hours of the morning. Then, because of her recent string of wakeup mishaps, she got out of bed and double and triple checked the clock and the alarm in case she did need it to rouse her.

When it was time to get up, she showered and dressed in a flash because of how organized everything was. That felt right.

She was even a little early. It was how her mornings were supposed to go. She grabbed her phone and stuffed it in her hoodie pocket. Gently closing her room door, she heard muffled voices in other areas of the inn and smelled delicious breakfast aromas wafting up from downstairs. She inhaled deeply. Bacon. There was definitely bacon on the menu this morning.

She considered knocking on Todd's door to see if they were ready and could all go downstairs together, now that she knew which room was theirs, but then she stopped herself from walking down their hallway. Trying to wrangle two young children into getting dressed and packed on a schedule was enough stress. She didn't need to add to the mix.

Making a quick glance around the breakfast room downstairs, she confirmed Todd and the children were not yet seated among the other guests who claimed tables for their morning meal. Instead of selecting one of the smaller spaces for just herself, she chose the largest round table in the middle of the room with six chairs around it. It was extravagant for a party of one, but she knew she soon wouldn't be alone, and the larger table wasn't unreasonable for a group of four.

The hostess brought her juice and coffee and asked for her breakfast choices.

"My friends will be joining me in a little bit. If it's OK I'll wait for them for a few minutes before I order," Emma explained.

She sipped her coffee, enjoying the smooth, strong brew, and restlessly checked the time. It had been five minutes since she claimed her seat in the breakfast room, but each second ticked by at a snail's pace, making it feel much longer. She began to regret her decision to arrive early. The anticipation was giving her flashbacks to another time when she anxiously waited at a large table for people who never arrived.

"Stop with the negativity," she thought, aggravated with her automatic pessimism. "They're just upstairs. There's no traffic accident situation. It takes time to get kids and luggage organized."

She reconsidered her decision to not knock on their door earlier. "Maybe I should have offered to bring Sophie and Liam downstairs so Todd could get their bags packed in peace?"

Several times she heard footsteps on the stairs or voices approaching and she looked optimistically in the direction of the doorway, hoping to see their familiar faces, but it was always other inn guests, not Todd or the children.

She needed a diversion. "I could turn on my phone," she thought, but then decided against it, wanting to save that ceremonial moment for when Todd was there. There was no reason she couldn't get started on her food while she waited for the others to come downstairs. Then, if they were running late, she could help with the kids.

Raising her hand, Emma caught the eye of the hostess when she reentered the room. In a smooth motion, she swung by the beverage station to pick up a fresh pot of coffee on her way to Emma's table.

"Refill, hon?" she asked sweetly, holding the pot above Emma's empty cup.

"Yes, please, and I'd like to place my breakfast order now. My friends seem to be running a bit late."

The hostess topped off the cup and set the pot on an empty table nearby. "No problem. Who are you waiting for? I've been here all morning. I can tell you who's already eaten. You're one of the last ones today.

"I was going to have breakfast with Todd, and his two children Sophie and Liam."

"Oh honey, I wish I had known that earlier," the woman said. "I could have saved you some time. The front desk told me they already checked out and left early this morning to catch the first ferry. Now what will it be for you today, French toast and bacon or the yogurt parfait?"

Emma was numb. Through the open window the departure horn of the 8AM ferry sounded as it pulled away from the dock.

Todd and Sophie and Liam were gone.

~ 34 ~

Emma's mood swung back and forth like the pendulum of the old grandfather clock in the inn's parlor.

They're gone.
They left me.
This always happens.

Calm down.
You'll be fine.
You've only known them for a day.

How could I have screwed this up?

It doesn't matter,
you still had a great time yesterday.

I'm destined to be alone.

You need to get out more.
You misread simple kindness
as romantic interest.

Her head and her heart were playing tennis, smashing the ball of her emotions back and forth between the two sides of the court.

Emma sat there unmoving, staring into space while her French toast and bacon grew cold. After a short while, the hostess graciously brought her a new, hot plate of food from the kitchen. Embarrassed, Emma tried to stop her from removing the uneaten plate. "Oh no! I'm sorry, it's fine. I'll eat it."

But the hostess swapped it out any way. "We had extra this morning, dear. No rush. Take your time." She patted Emma's shoulder in a motherly way before she returned to the kitchen.

"There is extra," Emma thought, "because three of your guests didn't show up for breakfast today."

Her focus shifted to the beautifully presented plate. She was determined to shake off this emotional setback. A good breakfast was comforting. "This plate looks amazing. I need distraction, this will be a delicious opportunity for that."

She took a bite of perfectly crisped bacon, and it instantly began working its smoky, salty magic upon her. She forced all negativity out of her mind as she savored forkfuls of French toast, whipped cream, and plump, juicy strawberries.

By the time she finished the last of the coffee remaining in her cup, Emma was alone in the breakfast room. She arose from the table and pushed her chair in. Gathering her dishes, she delivered them to the small bussing station near the kitchen door.

The hostess peeked around the doorway, "Oh hon, you didn't need to do that."

Emma said, "It's OK. Thank you," in a sincere tone conveying she appreciated not only the food but the woman's patience and understanding as well.

"You're welcome, sweetie," the hostess said and patted Emma's shoulder again as she passed by.

She already finished most of the hard work of packing during the sleepless excitement of the night before. All that remained to do was take one last cursory sweep around her room before she went downstairs to return the key and check out.

Emma fought to stay strong and keep her thoughts positive, but the powerful undertow of disappointment threatened to throw her off balance.

When she lugged her suitcase past the spot on the stairs where Todd surprised her before dinner, she turned and looked over her shoulder wishing he would appear behind her again, but there was no one there.

"I wanted to ask, by chance, did anyone leave a message for me?" she inquired as she handed over her key. The man behind the desk gave a quick scan of the desktop then shook his head. "No, no messages. I hope you enjoyed your stay," he said.

"Thank you. It was lovely. Really lovely," Emma replied and walked out the door, donning her sunglasses to hide the accumulating pools of tears in her eyes.

Before making the short trip to the ferry dock, she left her suitcase on the porch and walked down the path to spend a few final moments in the garden behind the inn. The previous night it had been so romantic and a bit mysterious, like something from an enchanted realm inhabited by wishes and dreams, but now it seemed ordinary. The fountain was turned off for maintenance, and the strings of lights no longer twinkled overhead. Someone, a gardener perhaps, trimmed off the few remaining sprigs of lilacs.

The magic was gone.

~ 35 ~

Emma's timing to catch the ferry was perfect. There were a few people milling around in the dock area when she arrived. She checked her bag and was able to walk straight on board without waiting.

She wanted to keep moving, keep busy, and keep her mind distracted. First, she took a seat downstairs, on the interior of the vessel, not wanting any reminders of when she first saw Todd and the children on the ferry a few days ago. After restlessly moving from one spot to another several times, she decided to sit on the upper deck anyway. She wanted the openness of the fresh air. Groups of people were sprinkled sporadically around the available seats. She chose to sit in a different area of the deck than she had on the first crossing of the straits, but her gaze still wandered over to where she was seated on the previous trip. The row where Todd and Sophie and Liam had been a few days ago stayed empty, unclaimed.

Had she imagined the past 24 hours? Did she misunderstand something? A familiar emotional numbness was eating away at her confidence. Her beautiful new fairy tale had become a desolate landscape and her positive attitude was melting away, like those floppy watches in Salvador Dali's painting "Persistence of Memory." She felt herself backsliding into the familiar gravity of self-pity.

Suddenly, a vision of Grandy appeared in her mind's eye, and Emma recalled something her grandmother said emphatically several days before. "I've earned this, Emma. This spirit. I've worked hard for it. I've had to fight for it," the vision said.

The voice was loud and clear. It was as if Grandy was standing on deck, speaking the words directly to her. She looked around to see if somehow her grandmother boarded the ferry to lecture her in person. She wasn't there, but that did not lessen the impact of the message.

"What am I doing?" Emma thought. "Why am I reverting to 'Sad Girl' mode? I need to stop this," she thought. "Just stop, stop, stop!" repeating the admonition to make the point to herself. She shook her head as if to shake off the fog while coming out of a dream.

"I had a great trip to this amazing island, filled with incredible experiences. I stayed in an historic treasure of a hotel and at a beautiful, charming inn. I ate fantastic food I would never have considered eating before. I had fresh lake breezes and sunshine. And I found lilacs, lovely and beautiful lilacs! I remembered happy things about my family I haven't thought about in years. I rediscovered my love for drawing and art. I came out of my shell, and I met some nice people, and OK fine maybe it wasn't all wrapped up with a pretty bow on it at the end, but the past few days were great.

"I'll probably never know why they left like that. Maybe Sophie or Liam said something, or maybe Todd decided he wasn't ready yet. I may never understand. It doesn't matter! This was still a great experience. I learned things about life, and about myself. Good things happen, and unfortunately bad things will probably happen again too, and life goes on, either way. You shouldn't let, you can't let, the bad things stop you from making even *better* things happen.

"I will be like Grandy – my dear, brave, wonderful Grandy! I will fight this fight and become resilient. I will work at it, every day if I have to. I will cherish the good things from my time here with Todd and Liam and Sophie. Those are new happy memories, a few special little lilacs for me I will always have."

Then she called forth one of those fresh new memories, one of a courageous little girl, lounging on the library deck Adirondack chair with bravely flexed arms. "Super Soph" she thought and smiled.

"I need a superhero persona of my own," she thought. "Something to represent my new perspective. Something like… Adventurous Emma!"

She laughed softly as she pictured herself on a high mountaintop, hair billowing in the wind, victorious, having conquered an arduous climb. "That's about perfect, I think."

The ferry horn gave its jolting blast, and the vessel motored out of the bay toward the mainland. Morning air, cold and damp, invigorating, swept across Emma's face and filled her lungs. The Fort, the buildings of Main Street and Grand Hotel all disappeared behind a curtain of fog that hung over the bay, like the cast of characters at the end of a play saying, "show's over, thank you for coming, you may now exit the theater."

The whole island was like a different place for her than it had been before the trip. She had been transformed too. The ferry carried her, wave by wave, back to the real world, to a hectic place of cars and fast paced traffic and cell phones. Wait, where was her phone? She searched several pockets until she found the familiar rectangular shape of the device. She started to take it out, but then decided not to.

She was going to do things differently now. She would come back to this crazy world one step at a time.

252

~ 36 ~

Emma's apartment door swung open, and she was greeted by the faint lingering aromas of cleaning products, a hybrid blend of springtime fresh and ocean breeze. She wheeled in her suitcase and looked around with a smile. Grandy's idea for a pre-trip cleaning binge had been genius. It would have been a huge disappointment to come home to old dust and the general residue and staleness of the past few months. The seeds of her fresh start had now been planted.

Earlier in the day, after claiming her luggage and her car from the ferry lot, Emma fueled up with a full tank of gas. She felt good about the upcoming drive. It would be easy to find her way home. Stick to the main road, head south. Done. For that she wouldn't need GPS or even a map.

But when she merged onto the highway, a sign reminded her she had another option. She could take the scenic coastal route down the east side of the state. There would be memories there. More lilacs. Some of it would be familiar territory, but different enough to give her a bit of practice in expanding her comfort zone. And although the coastal route took longer, it was essentially a wide loop that would bring her back to join the other highway later in the afternoon.

"I'm doing it," she said and activated her blinker to merge onto the ramp.

There were long, thickly wooded sections of the drive, occasionally broken up by brief bright glimpses of turquoise blue water. "That's like my thought process right now. A dark forest of ideas, and then, wham, a flash of clarity."

She worked through several different possible scenarios for her future, listing the benefits and drawbacks of each, and she reminded herself of how it would take commitment and hard work to make any of these new dreams into a reality. There would be false starts, mistakes, failures. And she would have to deal with each of them. She would focus on learning and growth, not perfection. She drove without music, the silence giving her a peaceful environment in which to think.

Her outlook changed over the past few days, even in the past 24 hours. She mulled over her reluctance to leave the island the day before. That feeling of discomfort with her life, the thing that had been so strong it stopped her in her tracks at the ferry dock, was replaced by a new motivation. She didn't dread going back to her apartment anymore. Now, she *wanted* to get back. There were things she wanted to do, projects to start.

The first part of this trip up north had initially been fueled by uneasiness. Desperation. She was running away from her situation. Hiding from it. Escaping. But at some point during recent events, something significant changed: her mindset. She now believed a few mistakes weren't the end of the world. Instead, they could be useful. That was part of the growth process. She wasn't going to be dodging her life anymore.

Neither was she an inanimate object, at the mercy of some unforgiving flow. Instead, Emma was claiming her strength and courage. She was gaining wisdom and experience. She had options and responsibility and accountability. And she was beginning to allow herself to dream again.

She began to recognize familiar places along the route she hadn't seen in years, like the pretty stone house with a round turret she used to call a castle, a fun vintage tourist attraction with life-sized dinosaur statues, and a miniature golf course where once she had beaten both of her parents in a wickedly challenging game of putt-putt.

She stopped at a small roadside park with a beach and let the refreshing lake water lap at her bare feet and ankles. She stood looking far across the lake, at the clouds on the horizon. There were many vivid memories along this route, lush plumes of lilacs she gathered into the imaginary vase in her mind. Why hadn't she ever been here with her friends? These experiences weren't meant to be kept private. They were meant to be shared.

The gentle push and pull of the waves brought back a memory of something Todd said at Windermere Point. "It takes forgiveness, in both directions."

She had work to do to repair her old friendships. She wished it were as easy as the motion of the waves. Forgiveness flows in, forgiveness flows out. It would take courage and humility and understanding. But if both she and her friends had those qualities, maybe it really could be as natural as the back and forth roll of the water against the shore.

There were a few places along the route that were different. Her childhood favorite spaghetti restaurant was replaced by a new, trendier eatery not open until later. She sat in the parking lot for a few seconds and sulked while her engine idled and her stomach growled. Then, shifting the car into gear, she continued southbound again, with her eyes open to find a new spot to eat, a place she had never been, a new discovery. After a few miles, she found a small family restaurant with a sign proclaiming,

"Home Cookin'" and a friendly vibe that appealed to her. While she waited for her food, she entertained herself by watching the cars on the highway outside and the patrons coming and going through the restaurant parking lot. She admired the vase of freshly picked wildflowers on the windowsill. This was a sweet little restaurant. She liked it. A new feeling of happiness started to take shape somewhere inside of her. She didn't bat it away or hide from it.

After finishing her turkey reuben, she left a generous tip and a small, signed sketch of the vase of flowers for the waitress who consistently made sure her glass of iced tea was topped off. In her drawing, she took artistic license with the selection of blooms and drew a few lilacs in with the daisies.

Right before the scenic route rejoined the main highway she stopped at a bakery. "I want a pie," thought Emma. She remembered how her mother would pick up a freshly baked lemon meringue or a loaf of cinnamon swirl bread from there. After she paid for her bakery purchase, Emma stepped into the neighboring gift shop to look around. She selected a lovely thank you card for Grandy. Amid the souvenir t-shirts and scented candles, she spied a small plaque with a little verse and some lilacs on it. She picked it up to check the price.

"Emma?"

She spun around. "Cassidy!"

The two women connected in a warm embrace.

Cassidy's voice continued excitedly. "Oh my gosh. Jimmy and I are on our way up north for the weekend and we stopped in to get a pie and I thought it was you over here, but I wasn't sure because it's been ages since anybody's seen you, since Samantha's wedding I think?"

Remembering that awkward day, Emma gave a thoughtful nod. "Yes, probably," then preemptively filled in the answer to the unspoken next question. "I went through a big rough patch, but things are getting a little better now."

"That's great news. We've *really* missed you."

Emma knew what to do. There was no hesitation in her voice.

"Cassidy, would you like to get together for dinner sometime next week?"

"Oh *totally* yes, Ems! Listen, Jimmy's out in the car with the pie already and we're late and I need to run but call me later and we'll set it up! Ohmygosh, *so* great to see you, love you!" and with a quick hug and a little squeal of delight, her friend disappeared out the door. Emma watched her go and then handed the card and the plaque to the cashier.

"Did you find what you were looking for?"

Through the shop window she could see Cassidy opening a car door and giving her another energetic wave from the parking lot before jumping inside the vehicle.

Emma smiled. "Yes, I think I did."

~ 37 ~

A few things along the rest of her drive reminded her of Todd and the children: butterflies in a patch of daisies on the roadside, a billboard for a cancer hospital, and highway signs pointing in the direction she supposed they must have gone earlier in the day. Sometimes there was a tug to fall into the familiar rabbit hole of self-pity: oh, poor lonely Emma! But she challenged the negativity with a barrage of optimistic affirmations: "I had a great trip. I met some nice people. I had fun adventures. I'm making a positive future for myself by remembering the good things and moving forward with new experiences instead of dwelling on disappointments."

She would do her best at whatever she chose for her future path, but she didn't have to be perfect. There would always be ice cream drips. And that was OK. She didn't yet know if she wanted to be a graphic designer, an independent artist, or something else that made use of her creative talent, but it was time to find out, and that thought left her with a flip of excitement in her stomach, the good kind, like what she felt when Todd winked at her.

Todd again. She let out a sound of exasperation. Why were all her thoughts always leading back to him? Less than a week ago she hadn't known he existed. They hadn't even spent 24 hours together, and yet her thoughts kept drifting back in his direction. It seemed as if she had known him much longer. Based on his sudden departure though, he must not have felt the same way she did.

Perhaps, given a few hours to think about it, maybe he had second thoughts. He changed his mind. If he wasn't ready for a relationship yet, she would have to accept that. His heart had been through a lot. He was allowed to mourn his wife, the mother of his children, for as long as he felt was necessary. Todd and his wife had years of a relationship they had built up, but what did he have with Emma? A mere handful of hours.

What was the old guideline they used in college? For every month you're with someone, you're allowed one week to get over him? By that rule of thumb, she should have been over this half-day fling (if you could even count it as that) long before the ferry pulled into the dock at Mackinaw City.

And now, here she was. Back in her old familiar apartment. Emma placed the bags of fudge and the pie on the kitchen counter and seated herself with a flop on her couch. She spent many days in here with the curtains closed like this, but now it was annoyingly dark. She leapt up and pulled the curtains back. Then she opened the window, like Grandy did. Like it was in her rooms on the island. She wanted to let go of the old stuffy gloom and replace it with her new happy experiences. She craved sunlight now. And fresh air too. She needed them. No more of this cocoon stuff.

It was time to give Grandy the lowdown on the trip. She sank back down onto her couch more gently, plugging her phone into the end of the charger she kept on the side table. Emma let it sit for a minute before turning it on for the first time in days. She ignored the annoying barrage of alert tones and notifications filling her screen. She was proud of herself. Not only had she fulfilled Grandy's intent to have her phone put away during her time on the island, but she also kept it off on the drive home.

That was another thing that changed while she was on the island: her relationship with her phone. She did fine without social media, and it was time to rethink how she interacted with the little device. It was a tool, and she was in charge of how and when she used it.

She selected Grandy's phone number, hit send, then put the phone on speaker mode. After a few rings, the familiar voice sang out her greeting. It was nice to be met with such enthusiasm.

"Emma, darling! Are you home? How was your trip? I want to hear all about it."

"Hi, Grandy! Yes, I'm back at my apartment," Emma began. She stretched her legs out and put her feet up on the coffee table in front of her.

"First, I want to say thank you from the bottom of my heart. That trip was exactly what I needed. You were right about so many things, about everything really, from Grand Hotel to the clothes, and the lilacs and the envelopes…"

"How wonderful! I'm glad it all worked out."

"I ended up staying an extra day on the island, kind of on a whim, for the "impulsive" envelope. I hope you don't mind."

"Honey, I'm very proud of you for deciding to do that. You made a marvelous choice!"

Emma wanted to tell Grandy about Todd and the children and the special time they'd all had together. But then, there was the awkwardness of their sudden, mysterious departure that she didn't understand or know how to explain. Because of all the future planning and dreaming she did on the drive, she was riding a positive wave at the moment, feeling emotionally strong and she wanted to keep that momentum going. She couldn't deny it though, if she started to talk about Todd, there was a chance her positive wave would collapse into an ugly cry. Maybe it would be best to take a few days to let her emotions about him settle before she brought it up to her grandmother. Perhaps she'd be ready by the time they met for dinner in two weeks.

Grandy interrupted Emma's thoughts. "So, tell me about your new friend."

"My … friend?" Emma asked, tentatively. How did Grandy know? She was puzzled.

"Yes, the nice young man who took your photo at the Fort. He emailed it to me."

Emma's eyes flew wide open, and she gasped as she sat bolt upright, feet flat on the floor.

Of course, that's how she knew. But wasn't it a bit forward of Grandy to start assuming they'd become friends because of one photo he emailed at her request?

Grandy continued. "There are some nice photos. He sent a couple of pictures to me, one with just you and then there was one of all of you with him and his children in it too. He's quite handsome. It's cute, you have that same little ice cream drip on your shirt like you used to get when you were a young girl."

Emma was shocked. Todd sent the group photo to Grandy. Somewhat overwhelmed at this set of revelations, Emma simply said "Oh."

"I emailed them to you," Grandy said casually, then she added, "He sent another note to me this morning. He doesn't have your email, so he sent the message to me and asked me to forward it to you. Have you seen the note yet?"

Emma's mouth went dry, and she was slightly lightheaded. Todd sent her an email, an explanation. Via Grandy!

Whatever happened, whatever was the truth about the situation, Grandy was now more informed than she was. Emma wasn't sure how she felt about finding out why he disappeared this morning -- it might be something perfectly reasonable or it could instead be something to crush her heart one last time, but one thing was for sure – she was mortified Grandy was in the loop on this.

She spoke slowly in a futile attempt to sound nonchalant. "Um, ... no. I ... haven't checked... my... email yet."

"Well, maybe you should hang up and get caught up on that. Call me back later. Love you, dear! Welcome home!" and then the connection clicked off.

Emma stared at her blank phone screen.

What just happened?

Grandy hung up on her.

So Emma could check her email.

To get a note from Todd.

That Grandy had already read.

What sort of madness was this?!

~ 38 ~

Emma opened the email app and a herd of incoming documents stampeded into her inbox. She scrolled through the list, skipping a host of social media notifications which attempted to distract her by letting her know how many ways she was missing out.

"265 connections have posted since you last logged in."

"There are 34 popular stories you may have missed."

"These 3 friends have birthdays today, send them a greeting."

She ignored them all, remaining focused on finding one specific item from Grandy, sent earlier in the day.

Scroll.

Scroll.

Scroll. Wait, now she was into the previous day's email.

Scroll back.

Stop. There it was.

She took a deep breath and blew the air out, then she clicked on it.

Grandy added a message at the top of the forwarded email.

"Sending this note from your friend."

Emma closed her eyes. My "friend." What a loaded word. Yes, it was good to be friends, and yet it was bad to end up in the dreaded "Friend Zone."

But "friend" was the appropriate term for the short time they had known each other, wasn't it?

Her thoughts started to race. Why did she ever let herself imagine it could be something different? Did she want to continue reading Todd's email to know the truth? Could she handle it if she read the words, "not ready for a new relationship" or "not fair to the children"? Shouldn't she at least be happy she made a friend in her turbulent emotional state? Wasn't that enough? What if it had been an empty vacation flirtation for him, one of those ethereal moments that disappeared when the sun rose, and reality took hold? Maybe she should let the beautiful day live forever in her memory in a perfect little time capsule. She couldn't hide from the truth forever though. Grandy already knew what happened, and she was bound to bring it up at some point. Emma had to face the facts. She needed to know.

She reached her conclusion. "Most importantly, I have to stop overthinking things. I guess that part is going to take some practice. We had a great day together, and there's always value in that. Nothing can ever take that experience away from me. I will be strong, no matter what the email says," she whispered. Then she opened her eyes and read the rest of the message.

Todd's original correspondence began with this introduction:

"Dear Grandy,
Two days ago, I sent you the photographs of Emma taken at the Fort. Unfortunately, my children and I had to leave the island unexpectedly early this morning without saying goodbye. Could you please forward this note of apology and explanation to Emma?
Regards, Todd"

Emma's stomach crinkled into a tight knot. She lowered the phone and looked out the window. "He mentioned 'saying goodbye'," she thought. "So, then, this is it, I guess. The end of the road. Fun while it lasted. The official goodbye." She blinked her eyes, willing the tears not to come, steeled her emotions, and read on.

Dear Emma,

I'm very sorry about our sudden disappearance this morning. We were all looking forward to having breakfast with you and riding back to the mainland on the ferry together.

Unfortunately, we had a bit of a medical emergency. Liam woke up early, and while in dinosaur mode, decided to stick gummy bears into his ears. One got stuck deep in his left ear. I was concerned because he has a history of ear infections, and I couldn't get all the candy out. Liam panicked and started crying loudly. I grabbed the children and our luggage, left our key at the front desk, and went to urgent care at the island medical center to see if they could extract it. After a successful "bear-ectomy," I thought it best to go straight to the dock and catch the earliest possible ferry (at this point both Liam and Sophie were restless and needed my full attention).

I sincerely apologize for any inconvenience or concern we caused you. In hindsight, I should have either left you a message at the front desk or called the inn or found some other way to get word to you earlier about what was going on, but my thoughts in the moment were focused on Liam. I feel terrible about leaving you stranded at breakfast. I hope you didn't wait too long for us, and you understand the reason why we left the way we did.

Emma, I've thought a lot about the conversations we had yesterday. I want you to know that all of us, Sophie, Liam, and I, have room for a new person in our lives. We would all be thrilled if you would like to continue what we've started and see where this leads.

Fondly,

Todd

(PS. Sophie and Liam say hi)

At the bottom of the email, Todd included the information for how he could be contacted. Emma set the phone down and took a few deep breaths until her hands stopped trembling. She stood up and paced back and forth a few times. Then, she burst into an energetic dance inspired by Liam's tiny disco-ninja moves from the day before.

She picked the phone back up and clicked on the hyperlinked phone number at the bottom of the email. When the familiar deep, warm voice answered she said, "Hi, it's Emma. I'm home."

~ 39 ~

It happened the following year. Islanders called it a miracle. The media called it "a perfect storm of beauty." An unprecedented combination of winter and spring weather conditions kept all the island lilacs lingering as tight buds well past their usual bloom date. Some speculated this year they might be permanently stunted and wouldn't even bloom at all. But when the long-anticipated warmth finally did arrive, it set the captive blossoms free, all at once. Every lilac on the island burst into glorious bloom within a 24-hour span and released their heady fragrances out into the world upon the warm lake shore breezes.

The island-bound ferry rolled gently on the straits as Emma and Todd snuggled closer together. The captain nudged the engine up to cruising speed, and a puff of wind caught a plume of spray from the waves, blowing it across the top deck. Passengers generated squeals of laughter and delight. "That spray feels good today," Emma said.

Todd pressed a kiss onto her cheek and pulled her close with the arm that rested gently on her shoulders. His other hand reached into his jacket pocket to feel for the small square box, making sure it was still secure.

It was Todd who first noticed it as the boat maneuvered into position in the harbor. He leaned over and whispered into Emma's ear, "Breathe in."

Emma gave him a sideways glance and a quizzical expression as if to say "Really? I already know about the horses." She complied with his request though, and tentatively drew in a shallow breath, expecting the faint aroma indicating the island's equine presence.

But this time it was different. Her eyes grew large, and her jaw dropped in surprise. "Great Spangled Fritillary! You can smell the lilacs from way out here!" She closed her eyes, threw her head back and breathed in deeply.

They hired a dock porter to transport their luggage to the inn, and took a quick walk, arm in arm, down Main Street.

"It doesn't feel right," Emma said, "being here without Sophie and Liam."

Todd laughed, "I wouldn't worry about it. Grandy has so much planned for them they'll never even miss us! It's nice we'll have some quiet time at the inn, and it's only a few days before they'll join us on the island for the rest of our vacation and we'll all be together at Grand Hotel."

When they reached the inn, Todd took Emma by the hand and led her down the familiar path toward the back garden. "Let's see how their lilacs are doing," he said. As they rounded the corner, Emma gasped in amazement. The lush green lawn was almost completely encircled in a pastel wall of pale purple, pink, and white lilac blossoms. The garden's air was awash in their sweet floral perfume. The effect was breathtaking.

Emma stood in the center of the lawn, arms outstretched, rotating as if in a trance while a handful of delicate butterflies flitted from bloom to bloom, enjoying the sweet nectar. "This is absolutely magical. I may never leave this place," she whispered.

When she finally turned to face Todd again, he was on one knee, presenting her with a diamond ring that sparkled in the sun and captured the colors of the lilacs surrounding them.

"You've made our lives beautiful again. As beautiful as this garden. Marry me, Emma," he said. Marry all of us, me and my children."

Emma beamed and nodded. "With all my heart, yes to you and yes to Sophie and Liam. Yes, to all of you!"

Todd slid the ring onto her finger and stood up to embrace her, while a celebratory whoop escaped from an upstairs window of the inn.

Todd and Emma looked toward the sound. Grandy, Sophie and Liam were there, waving, dancing, and cheering.

"Wait, what?" laughed Emma in surprise. How did they get here? I didn't think they were coming to the island until a few more days from now!"

"They didn't want to miss this moment," Todd explained. "It's a special time for all of us."

"This is just perfect," she said, filled with joy.

He glanced around at the abundance of flowers surrounding them. "It won't be hard to find your lilacs this year," Todd noted.

With a smile, Emma kissed him sweetly and replied, "I know. This time, there are lilacs everywhere."

~ The End ~

<u>The Heart of Spring</u>
By C. L. Birk

Find me where the lilacs bloom
When winter's gloom has passed,
Where love and sweetness fill the air
And Hope's arrived, at last.

~ Acknowledgements ~

There are so many things we put off until "someday."
- A stay at that hotel we've always wanted to visit
- A relationship that needs repairing
- A book we've always wanted to write

The events of the past few years should have taught us all that we don't have time to waste. Things can change quickly. Our "someday" is now. Live your life. Fight for your spirit. Put the best parts of yourself out there, boldly, every day.

Thank you to Mackinac Island's Grand Hotel for being such a wonderful inspiration. The inn where Emma stays for the additional night on the island is loosely based on the lovely Cloghaun B&B, with a fond memory or two from the elegant Hotel Iroquois blended in. Emma and Todd's garden behind the inn, however, exists only in our imaginations.

The Woods restaurant, a fabulously real place, was initially recommended to me by a pirate (but that's a different story). Island regulars will easily recognize the Pink Pony, and on some days there just might be a handsome cabinetmaker having lunch there.

There are two butterfly conservatories on the Island. Two! Visit, and don't be afraid. Also, thank you to the Mackinac Island Medical Center for answering my questions. The staff I spoke with was friendly, but I hope you *don't* have to visit them!

Special thanks to Mrs. Gregory, my second-grade teacher, who once upon a time selected me for participation in a young authors conference. I will always be grateful for that experience. It ignited a spark that still lives within me.

Thank you to Dianna from Promote Michigan who organized the Walloon Lake Writers Retreat last March. Thank you to Cristen and Gema, and all the participants at the workshop. You helped me finally see myself as a "real" writer.

Thank you to Terri Savelle Foy for showing me the effective way to do vision boards and affirmations. It worked!

Thank you to Trish Blackwell and her amazing College of Confidence. Your coaching on how to reframe negative thoughts and clear away that pesky log jam of fear and doubt has been life changing.

Thank you to my family, friends, relatives, colleagues, and random kind strangers who encouraged me on this journey.

And finally, loads of thanks to Jill - wonderful friend, reader extraordinaire, and champion dreamer. You deserve the world's biggest and best Key Lime Pie for all your support.

Now, go! Find your lilacs!

CLB
August 2022

Reader's Guide / Discussion Questions

1. Emma has always travelled with other people, so making the journey to northern Michigan alone is a big adjustment for her. Have you ever travelled by yourself? If fear of travelling alone is stopping you from going somewhere you want to visit, what actions could you take to make it less intimidating?

2. Technology can be both a blessing and a curse. Have you ever tried to "unplug" from your cell phone for a day? For a weekend? Or longer? How did it affect you?

3. The pace of transportation on Mackinac Island is slower than what most of us are used to. How would your daily life change if you had to rely on carriages, bicycles, or walking for your mode of travel?

4. Emma's recovery is not a straight line. She makes progress, but then experiences setbacks. Have you tried to make changes in your life? When you encounter obstacles, how can you encourage yourself to keep going to reach your goals?

5. When she travels to Mackinac Island, Emma is revisiting one of her favorite childhood vacation destinations. What are your favorite vacation spots from when you were young? Have you revisited them now that you are older? Did you encounter memories from earlier visits? Did the place change from how you remembered it?

6. Emma frequently thinks about famous works of art. Are you familiar with these paintings? Did you search for any images online to see what they look like? Do you have any favorite works of art?

7. Is there a wish that you've been putting off for "Someday"? What steps could you take to turn this dream into a reality?

8. Emma is surprised to learn that she has more in common with her grandmother than she realized. Have you discovered any surprising ways you are similar to a parent or grandparent?

9. Emma's breakup with Chip was a blessing in disguise. Have you gone through any losses that can be reframed as blessings?

10. Some of Emma's friends are uncomfortable being around her when she is grieving, and she is hurt by their distance. Emma discovers that forgiveness is key to restoring these broken friendships. Are there any relationships in your life that could be aided by a dose of forgiveness, as Todd says, "in both directions"?

11. Emma makes progress in her recovery when she begins to reconnect with others, with nature, and with her talents. In what ways can you create new connections, strengthen existing connections, or restore broken connections in these areas?

Thank you for reading *Finding Lilacs*.

Join the mailing list at
picnicbasketpress.com
to be notified of new releases.